UNDER *the* ALMOND TREE

UNDER *the* ALMOND TREE

LAURA McVEIGH

www.tworoadsbooks.com

First published in Great Britain in 2017 by Two Roads
An imprint of John Murray Press
An Hachette UK company

1

A CIP catalogue record for this title is available from the British Library

Hardback ISBN 978 1 473 640 832
Trade Paperback ISBN 978 1 473 640 849
Ebook ISBN 978 1 473 640 856

Typeset in Hoefler Text by Hewer Text UK Ltd, Edinburgh
Printed and bound by Clays Ltd, St Ives plc

Hodder & Stoughton policy is to use papers that are natural, renewable and recyclable products and made from wood grown in sustainable forests. The logging and manufacturing processes are expected to conform to the environmental regulations of the country of origin.

Hodder & Stoughton Ltd
Carmelite House
50 Victoria Embankment
London EC4Y 0DZ

www.hodder.co.uk

For my family
with love

'There is something in the human spirit that will survive and prevail, there is a tiny and brilliant light burning in the heart of man that will not go out no matter how dark the world becomes.'

Leo Tolstoy

List of Characters

Samar's parents

Dil / Baba – Father

Azita / Madar – Mother

The children

Omar – Samar's eldest brother

Ara – Samar's elder sister

Javad – Samar's elder brother

Samar

Little Arsalan – Samar's younger brother

Sitara – Samar's younger sister

The grandparents

Baba Bozorg – Grandfather (Dil's father)

Maman Bozorg – Grandmother (Dil's mother)

Other family

Amira – Azita's sister

Cousin Aatif – Azita's cousin

In Kabul

Arsalan – Family friend

Mati and Abas – Brothers who befriend Samar

In the village

Amin – Childhood friend of Dil / Baba

Nazarine – Neighbour, widowed mother of three girls

Masha – Daughter of Nazarine, friend to Ara

Naseebah (Nas), Robina – Daughters of Nazarine, twins, Samar's friends

Najib – Teacher

Leaving Afghanistan

Hafizah – Woman who befriends the children

Parwana, Benafsha – friends to Samar and Ara

Abdul-Wahab – Fighter

On the train

Napoleon – the *provodnik*, ticket collector and keeper of the samovar

Part One

There are some journeys we never wish to take. And yet we go. We go because we have to, because it is the only way to survive. This is my journey, the one I never wanted to make. But I have made it. Something has survived. Some things cannot, will not, be forgotten.
They travel with us to the end.

Chapter 1

Omar, my eldest brother, was born on a snowy cliffside off the Kabul–Jalalabad highway, one of the most dangerous roads in the world, on a cold February night. My mother stood with the snow – a heavy snowfall which had caught them unawares – in drifts up round her thighs as she doubled in agony, her screams echoing out across the valley and bouncing off the sides of the Kabul Gorge. The only person there to help her was my father, who had never before seen a child come into this world – much less his own – and he was paralysed with fear watching his beautiful wife, her face contorted with pain, her breathing heavy, her cries guttural and wild.

Of course, you are right to ask what they were doing, outside in the freezing night at such a time, alone in treacherous mountain terrain. Well, they were running. Which was all they had done since the first time they had met, as their union – a love match from the start – was so improbable, so ridiculous, so reckless that my mother had been immediately cut off from her family. She was thrown out of my grandfather's home in disgrace. Disowned by her father, his last words to her were simply, 'Azita, you are no longer my daughter.'

Her mother said nothing.

My father did not have much greater luck. His parents, though gentle mountain folk, nonetheless felt the shame of his temerity and, fearful of retribution, distanced themselves too from the mismatched couple. And so Azita and Dil (Madar and Baba as they are to us) had begun life together as outsiders, and outsiders they remained. When they married, only cousin Aatif and Baba's best friend Arsalan came to the ceremony and for anyone who knows . . . well, this is not how things are ordinarily done.

Not long after the wedding, when my mother fell pregnant with her first child, the threats began. At first it was small things. Being jostled in the marketplace. Returning home to find the door swinging open, the food taken from the larder. One day she found a nightdress that had been hung out to dry ripped in half and smeared with blood. It was then that they decided to run. They would become nomads. They would live off the money my mother's sister had given to her. They would live off the kindness of strangers if their own family had rejected them.

My mother's sister Amira had brought them all that she could. She also handed over a family heirloom of gold jewellery, thinking it would be of some future use to them (this altruistic theft would later cost Madar's sister her place in the family when the truth was finally discovered, and would send her to Russia far from home – but we will come to that by and by). So now the sisters wept and embraced. It would be, though they did not know it then, the last time they would ever see each other. Such were the hard choices love imposed upon my mother and my father – offerings as proof of their determination and resolve.

On the night that my eldest brother Omar made his way into this uncertain world they had been running from a group of mountain bandits who had tried to rob them and take my father's car – a 1972 rust-coloured Lada, a wedding gift from Arsalan and my father's pride and joy. It was the love of his life after my mother and his soon-to-be-born son. On a journey to Kabul, where they hoped to see Arsalan once more and to seek his help, their car was shot at as they nudged their way through sudden falling drifts of hard snow along the hazardous mountain pass.

One shot pierced the side door and the bullet lodged in the carpeted floor of the Lada next to my mother's ankle. It was at this point in proceedings that Omar decided he was ready to see the world, even though, by all calculations, he should have stayed put until the frosts had lifted. And my mother, a woman of strong unperturbed will, decided that the car was no sort of safe place for the birth of her child, and if they were to be shot on the hillside by Mujahideen bandits then so be it, but she would place her trust in Allah. My father knew there was no point in arguing with her, an instinctive wisdom that led them to have six children and an eventually happy marriage despite the challenges faced – and there were many.

He gathered up his *patu* as a warm woollen blanket from the back seat and they both trudged uphill in the deep snow, taking shelter behind boulders.

'Let their bullets pierce that,' my mother spat indignantly in the direction of the for-now silent sharp(ish) shooters who were probably making their way across the looping valley roads to plunder both vehicle and what they may have assumed were the dead or dying passengers – killed either by shots or by the bitter cold winter night. There was a full heavy moon and the air was still so that her screams, for all she tried to muffle them, echoed out wide into the frosted air. Omar had decided to make his way into the world and it was not long before he slipped out into the waiting *patu* held by my father's shaking hands. Immediately he was swaddled, rolled in layer after layer. My mother, having brought her baby into the world, straightened herself up and leaned on my father, all the while staring into the eyes of her adored son. Delirious and triumphant they stumbled back down the cliffside towards the car, leaving a trail of blood seeping dark into the white drifts of snow.

By now two of the sharpshooters had made their way to the car and were waiting patiently for my father to return with the keys. One was smoking hashish. The other stood, rifle tucked under one arm, keeping watch.

My father was shaking from head to foot. He was not a coward nor was he a fool and he could see the danger they as known Communist sympathisers faced. My mother, however, having just created life, was even more commanding than usual, and she walked straight up to the men saying, 'Brothers . . . come see, look, this child, a miracle. All thanks and praise be to Allah. But we must get him to warmth and safety. You brothers must help us.'

And whether bewitched by her beauty, caught off guard by the strange turn of events, high on hashish or cowed by her defiant tone, to the amazement and immense relief of my father the two men fell swiftly into line with her plans, all thoughts of robbery erased when presented with the greater responsibility of ensuring this night was not the infant's last on this earth. And though they were blackguards, and rough and somewhat high, they too were sons and had once been children – and were now barely adult – and they were glad of the warmth of the car and of not having to kill this couple and their newborn son and all was good in the world that night.

This is how my mother tells it, breathless, and each time she tells the story the mountain ruffians become more and more noble. The stars shine brightly in the cold night sky and we can hear Mermon Mehwish singing on the radio in the car and my father, mother and the two Mujahideen singing along as they travel down to the lights of Kabul.

But of course that is not how it happened. My mother has a gift for storytelling – she can reimagine the worst of nightmares into the best of dreams. It is a gift that has kept her and all of us alive over the years. When my mother tells the story my father weeps and grows quiet and we know that however it was that Omar came into this world, it was not through the kindness of strangers.

But why have I started with this story of Omar's birth? I have started here because sometimes you have to go back to go forward. This is what Madar tells us each time that the train reaches its end points on this perpetual Trans-Siberian journey back and forth between Moscow and Vladivostok. The moment in which all six children plead, beg, cry, jump from the train. Of the six of us, I am the fourth child, Samar – before me are Omar, Ara, Javad, and after me Little Arsalan and baby Sitara. It is that heady time on the platform when all we want to do is stop, to be done with this never-ending travelling from Asia to Europe to Asia. One day, when my parents have either figured out what to do next, or have run out of money (and surely that day must come soon), then we will be able to leave this train and begin a new life. Somewhere safe. Somewhere where we do not have to run.

Chapter 2

The train's wheels grind unexpectedly to a halt. We are all jolted forward.

Omar and Javad hang their heads far out of the open window to see what is happening. We are halfway across the Circum-Baikal railway bridge. The drop below is ominous as the train sways gently on the line, then waits. Passengers from the other compartments pop out into the corridor, a few cautiously looking out.

'Maybe it is a problem with the gauge,' Omar and Javad confer.

My brothers are experts on trains now. And bridges. And engineering. Omar says he will become an engineer one day. He has been studying engineering by correspondence course for the last year. He picks up and sends assignments from all along the line, sending the *provodnik* Napoleon, ticket collector and keeper of the samovar, to run into the stations along the way to collect his latest parcel of study notes. The compartment is filled with Omar's sketches and calculations. He thinks the men who built these bridges, who blasted through the granite and crystal all along this rocky shore, the men who dug and excavated and dynamited long tracts of inhospitable Siberian land, building magnificent bridges and tunnels, fending off the threats of floods and landslides, these remarkable men were true adventurers bending the land to their will. To create a world in the image one designs – that is what Omar wants.

'Leave that be, Samar.' I have taken down one of Omar's sketches to look at, the steels criss-crossing back and forth in an intricate pattern.

'You won't understand it,' Omar sighs, smiling at me.

'So explain it,' I say, sitting next to my eldest brother, becoming a part of his new world of beauty and ingenuity.

'For a start you have it upside down.' He laughs, bemused by my interest. I right the sketch.

'That's better. See, look . . .' His fingers trace the outline of the drawing. Omar's eyes shine bright as he explains his workings to me, surprised and pleased to have such an eager audience.

'But how do you know it will work?' I ask him, wondering at the degrees, the angles, the twisting metal structures he is conjuring up with mere pencil and paper.

'You don't,' he says. 'You don't always know if it will work. You just have to try.'

I admire his self-belief, the way he is so certain. Next to Omar I feel safe – like the world is a series of solvable calculations yet tangible and solid underfoot.

'Shush,' calls out Ara. She is studying French in the next compartment – taught by Madar – and we are disturbing her conjugations.

What, you are surprised? Just because we are itinerant does not mean that my parents have overlooked our schooling. Sadly it is quite the opposite. We learn mathematics, geography, science, history (my favourite), philosophy, politics, Russian, English and French. We read (me, I read Tolstoy's *Anna Karenina* and treasure an old battered edition of an encyclopaedia that in truth we all share). My mother wants us to be equipped for life. In the evenings we have music. Baba has a transistor radio and tunes it in to whichever station is local. We listen to classical, folk, rock; even jazz, Russian, Mongolian, Chinese – whatever we can find depending on where we are on the journey.

One evening we gather round to listen to Stravinsky's *The Firebird*, all of us squeezed into compartment no.4, a candle flickering on the reading table. Sitara is on my father's lap, Little Arsalan and I are on the floor; Ara, Javad and Madar are on the bed opposite and Omar is standing in the doorway. The train has stopped to take on more supplies and change over the restaurant car but none of us move, we are so wrapped up in the music and listening to our mother tell us the story of Prince Ivan and the beautiful Firebird.

'Prince Ivan,' Azita says, her voice low and melodious, 'enters the magical kingdom of Koschei the Immortal and in the garden he sees this beautiful Firebird, which he catches. It begs to be set free and promises to help the prince.'

'Then what?' Sitara asks, looking over at Madar. Sitara, who is the baby of the family, is still at the age where she listens to stories each night. We all pretend this story is for her when really we are all drawn into the warmth and the candlelight and the gentle rocking of my mother's voice.

'The prince discovers thirteen princesses, beautiful princesses,' Madar says, 'and he falls deeply in love with one of them so he decides to ask Koschei for her hand in marriage.'

My mother smiles at my father as she tells this part but Baba is far away, looking out of the window.

'Koschei says no and sends his magical creatures to attack the prince, but the Firebird flies in and bewitches them, and puts a spell on Koschei.'

Javad, using the light of the candle, begins to make shadows of the bird behind Baba's head. Sitara shrinks in closer to Baba, frightened by the music and the shadow play.

'Then the Firebird shares the secret of Koschei's immortality with the prince.'

'What is im . . . immor . . . tality, Madar *jan*?' Sitara asks.

'The ability to live forever,' says Baba.

'The dream of fools,' snorts Omar in derision.

'The Firebird tells Prince Ivan that the wicked magician's soul is contained in a gigantic, magic egg,' continues Madar with a straight face. 'So the prince destroys the egg, the spell is broken and Koschei's palace disappears along with Koschei. The princesses and Ivan remain. They are now awake at last.'

The music spirals on and on towards its triumphant end and we listen to the audience clapping with wild applause. I picture the concert hall full of men and women dressed in finery, the dancers on the stage, the orchestra in the pit – all scenes I have learnt from my beloved Tolstoy.

'Baba *jan*, will we ever see such a thing?' Sitara asks.

'One day, one day we will all see such a thing,' he answers, wrapping her up in a warm bear hug.

My sister Ara has a beautiful singing voice and sometimes as dusk falls when we all gather in the restaurant car for supper, she will sing, mainly old Afghan songs or the songs of Farida Mahwash – like us another exile, another nomad. Ara will sing music that melds together Arabic, Persian, Indian influences like the melting pot that is our country. Madar will cry. Sometimes even Baba's eyes will be wet with both joy and sadness. For in the years before we fled our home in Kabul, music was banned. Can you imagine? To not be able to listen to music, to sing, to play an instrument, to even hum a tune. What harm? What harm can it do to sing? So when Ara, trembling, stands in the corner of the restaurant car and forgets her own beauty to share these songs we all feel alive and free. All the passengers in the car applaud. These are some of my favourite moments, when we are all together, when life is beautiful.

Anyway, we are stuck halfway along the Circum-Baikal Bridge, looking out at larch, pines and birch trees on the cliffside and to the other side the vast expanse of the lake. As the train has stopped and we have the windows open, I sit listening to the calls back and forth of the bush warblers that flutter round the lakeside. We know all the birds and most of the animals along the journey now. Javad and I can sit for hours matching sounds and feather colours and markings to images and descriptions in the encyclopaedia, or we ask Napoleon, who is a font of knowledge for all things journey-related. We have little else to do and it helps us pass the time.

'What is the matter? Why have we stopped?' my mother asks Napoleon, who is passing by at that very moment.

'There is a deer, stuck on the bridge; we are waiting for it to move.'

'A deer?'

'Yes. Either it will jump or it will manage to turn itself round and travel back into the forest. If it doesn't move soon, the driver will have to . . . well . . .'

Napoleon casts a furtive glance round at us children. Sitara's eyes nearly pop at the thought of the deer tottering on the line high above the lake (the world's deepest lake, in fact).

'Perhaps I could help,' says Javad. He is the kindest of my brothers, the one least inclined to hair-pulling and name-calling, the one who worries most about everything. Javad dreams of being a vet or a zoologist and living in London or America, or perhaps in a safari park in Africa. We met some South Africans on the train once who told us all about somewhere called the Kruger National Park and now Javad dreams of such places.

'Thanks, but I don't think . . .' Napoleon shakes his head. He is a genial, kind man, given at night time to quiet melancholia, who has grown fond of us all, this strange itinerant family with a seeming passion for constant train travel.

'Let me. Please,' Javad begs.

'Javad . . .' Madar calls after him but he is already ahead

of Napoleon and snaking his way up the carriage into the next and onwards to the front car and beyond to where the driver sits in the locomotive.

My mother sighs but she has learnt by now that you cannot live your children's lives for them, no matter how appealing that may seem, so she shrugs and waits. Five minutes later, Omar, who still has his head stuck out of the window, cries, 'Hey, it's Javad. He's on the bridge, he's with the deer.'

'What is he doing?' asks Baba.

'He's . . . he's talking to it.'

'Watch him try and charm the deer! Precious . . .' mocks Ara, trying not to care, tensely peering over Omar's shoulder.

We all hold our breath, conscious of the stupidity of our brother's actions; a collective intake accompanied by assorted silent prayers, and then, after what feels like an eternity, a cheer goes up from the carriage nearest the front.

'What's happening?' asks Baba.

'He's done it. The deer is . . . he's managed to get it to go back. Hurrah!' cries Omar.

After a few minutes the train starts up again. There is a toot from the driver and everyone is laughing and cheering. Javad bursts back into the carriage, his eyes shining. He is the hero of the hour. But it is not that, I think, that makes him look so happy, nor is it the feeling of having stroked and cajoled the frightened deer as it tottered on the steels of the track. No, he is giddy with fresh air and the touch of his feet on metal and cheating death. I feel a pang of jealousy at how alive he looks at that moment. He is no longer a passenger. Baba breaks out a bag of sugar. Omar races up to the samovar with the teapot and then we all sip warm sugary tea to toast Javad's safe return.

'To Javad,' says Omar, thumping his younger brother on the back.

'To Javad.' A smile flickers on Ara's lips as she lifts her glass to cheer Javad's success.

It is good to see Omar and Javad laughing together. Lately they have often taken to arguing – we all have. Omar, Little Arsalan and I tend to side with each other in these battles; Ara and Javad join forces more often than not, though allegiances can change overnight depending on the topic and the stakes involved. Ara and Javad are by nature fiercer, given over more easily to emotion, confrontation and affront. Omar and I try to cajole, to play peacemakers – him as the eldest, me as the middle child.

'What did it feel like?' Little Arsalan asks, watching Javad with renewed interest and respect. Javad shrugs his shoulders.

'Did you touch the deer?' asks Sitara, wide-eyed and amazed. 'Did it talk to you?' Javad nods. She leans in closer. He gestures to her as if sharing a secret.

'It said . . .' He whispers in her ear and we cannot hear. Sitara's mouth opens wide.

'Don't tease her,' says Omar, quick to come to Sitara's help.

'I'm not,' says Javad, cooler now, turning to Baba, who looks at him so proudly as he tells him all over again the story of how he coaxed the deer back along the bridge and off the track to safety.

I take my old copy of *Anna Karenina* – I am reading it slowly in Russian – and I move down to the restaurant car where I can sit undisturbed by the window and read and just for a short while escape, escape into another world, another skin than my own. I hide behind my hair and turn my body towards the window. I am so small, slight – a shadow girl – that I imagine other passengers do not even notice me there.

I have taken to reading on the train. Firstly, it passes the time. Secondly, it partly mollifies my mother, who sees it as a sign that I am gaining an education and an awareness of the world about me (though if she realised the content of my beloved *Anna Karenina* I venture she would greatly disapprove). Thirdly, and most important of all, it shields me from the prying voices of strangers and their incessant questioning. Worst of all is the question: 'Where are you going?' Some days I lie and pick out a stop along the route – Irkutsk, or Ulan-Ude; sometimes even Moscow – and say, 'That is where we are going.' And if they ask, 'And what will you do there?' I say, 'Live, just live.' Have a bed in a room that does not move at night; have a space of my own, a space in which to be still and think and write. A garden to play in. A place to grow things. I want no more than that. Except for happiness. Why do we crave to be happy?

I take solace from Tolstoy's Anna, from her misery and sadness, and recognise the same clawing need for peace in myself; and so I bury deep into this fictional world, oblivious to the *taiga*, the wilderness of the forest that we hurtle past. Further along the carriage, American and English tourists take dozens of pictures of blurred landscapes. The Americans are loud in their appreciation. Others are quieter, soaking in the rolling views.

For me the world is that of Anna and Vronsky, at least for an hour or so – I imagine myself ice skating in St Petersburg, dancing at balls, falling in love with someone unsuitable and handsome and witty.

There are two Russias in my mind – this, the swirling, romantic, epic Russia of Tolstoy; and the other Russia, the Russia that invaded then abandoned my homeland. That Russia I cannot love, without really knowing why.

Chapter 3

I was five years old when we left Kabul for good. It is a terrible thing to run from your home in the middle of the night, to see the fear in your parents' eyes and to know that you are never coming back. It is a terrible thing to no longer belong. But when you can no longer read, learn, sing, even walk alone in the sun, you cannot live. You cannot remain. So the memories I can cling to, good and bad, I tend like a garden, for they are what hold me to the Afghan soil.

My earliest memories were of the house we were living in in Kabul at the time – the only home I had known then. It was a large, modern, imposing two-storey building painted pale yellow with a flat roof, far grander than the low mud-coloured homes that clustered in the shadow of the mountains making up most of the city. Instead, protected from the incessant dust, set back in its own walled gardens behind Shahr-e-Naw sitting up from the park, the front of the house was flanked with tall conifers, while pine and larch clustered round the sides. Rhododendrons spilled around the front door next to rose bushes and honeysuckle so that when you walked into the house the scent would waft in with you.

The courtyard in the middle of the *kala*, or compound, was where I spent most of my time. It was full of flowers and fruit trees – walnut, wild peach, juniper – and in the middle was a beautiful almond tree where I would sit in the shade of the green leaves, or in springtime under the blossom, playing with Javad and Ara when they returned from school or with the neighbours' children who were closer in age to me.

The house was on what had been a tree-lined street only a couple of years earlier. This was before the Soviets started cutting down the trees (to better see the Mujahideen snipers, they would say). Outside the courtyard and compound walls the city was being destroyed, though I did not realise that then as Madar and Baba sought to shield us from the chaos that was heading our way.

From the roof of the house you could see out across the city ringed by the white-capped mountains of the Hindu Kush. I remember once sneaking up with Javad to sit and watch hundreds of brightly coloured paper kites flutter, sweep and climb in the evening sky. You will not see those kites in Kabul now – like all things of beauty the Taliban have banned them. They are afraid of beauty, afraid of what is in the people's hearts.

Sometimes in the restaurant car in the evenings Madar and Baba tell us about how the city used to be.

'The Paris of Asia,' Madar sighs. 'There were shops, cinemas, restaurants . . .'

'And record stores,' adds Baba. 'You could go and hear music from all around the world. Duke Ellington – Duke Ellington came to Kabul, you know. Jazz came to Kabul. 1963. Ghazi Stadium. Five thousand people. Imagine that.'

It was hard to try to place this city of colours and music and freedom in the one we had left behind but we would all nod, lost in imagination, soaking up their nostalgia for a city long disappeared.

'Faiz Khairzada did that,' Madar says, thoughtful. 'And the ballet – the Joffrey Ballet came too, and Eisenhower – when I was a child. It was a different time.' She looks sad.

It is almost impossible for me to imagine Baba and Madar like this – young, hopeful, in a world full of possibility that then just disappeared. It seems too cruel.

The yellow house belonged to Arsalan, who had taken us in. Though he was my father's best friend, he was my mother's friend too. They had all studied together at the Kabul University, Baba introducing Madar to Arsalan not long after they met at that first fateful Communist meeting, long before the Soviets came and things began to change. Madar and Baba often speak of this night when they met – up in the caves behind the city, in amongst a group of students curious to hear about new ideas, new ways of living; all feeling reckless and revolutionary, the candlelight flattering, the stolen glances between Madar and Baba the start of a true romance that blossomed at the university. It is a story of adventure and intrigue we all love to hear told over and over.

Madar was training to be a doctor – she has always had a gift for healing people, making things better even when the pain is unbearable. My father was to become a lawyer, then move into politics. That was what he wanted to happen, at least, and what his father wanted for him too, once the opportunity arose – a life far different to his own: one full of possibility.

'In those days you could do anything, be anything, imagine anything,' Madar tells us, smiling and nodding.

I, for one, find this hard to believe. But I listen to her. Her voice draws me in.

As a young boy, while up on the mountains of Baghlan tending the sheep and goats with my grandfather, Baba had one day seen a mudslide coursing down the valley towards the opposite gully and he had shouted to some walkers below, alerting them, giving them time to run in the other direction and thereby saving their lives. It turned out that those walkers were Arsalan, then a young boy like my father, and his father, visitors to the Hindu Kush that spring. And so Baba and Arsalan played together in my grandparents' mountain village and became firm friends, with Arsalan forever indebted to my father. Arsalan's family were wealthy and political like my mother's family and it was they who looked after my father from then on, who helped with his education, who later gave him somewhere to live in Kabul, who encouraged him to become a lawyer because that was what Arsalan wanted, because Baba had saved his life. At least that is how Baba tells the story.

And now what Arsalan wanted was to continue to look after my father and my father's growing family.

Arsalan was unmarried and he treated my father as his brother, my mother as his sister and us as kindly as if we were his own. Those earliest of years in the yellow house were happy. But one day, when I was five, things changed as if overnight and the happiness, the lightness, suddenly evaporated and the air became sullen and dark. I never really knew what caused it but when anything bad happened from then on we would blame it on the Soviets, on the fighting, later on the Taliban, on the anger of men – anything but look to our own hearts.

If I think back hard enough I remember images, sounds, sensations. I was so small then it is a wonder I remember anything at all. But now, as we drift from country to country, never settling, I find these memories become all the more important to me. I remember flashes – my mother and Arsalan arguing in the doorway to the courtyard at the yellow house, her holding me in her arms, her heart pounding, him calling her Zita. I remember his smell as he leant in towards us, his hand raised over my mother's shoulder against the doorframe and his eyes intent, locked on her. He was talking about my older sister Ara and about Omar. Madar was crying. I remember trying to wipe away her salty tears with my chubby little fingers.

The image stayed with me because she did not often cry and so it shocked me. Madar took me by the hand to the almond tree in the courtyard and, kneeling down so that she could look into my eyes, she told me to play quietly and that she would not be long. I remember watching her walk away as she retreated indoors with Arsalan. Soon I was so busy playing happily in the dirt of the yard that I was slow to realise the arguing had stopped. After a while he came out into the courtyard again and swung me up in the air, round and round, before leaving. My mother's eyes were red from crying and I could tell something was different.

After that time Madar was pregnant and she spent most of the days in bed in the dark, sobbing and staring at the walls. She no longer fussed over us. She didn't even bother to scold us when we tried to provoke her. It was as if the light that usually danced in her eyes had dimmed and all of her fierceness had ebbed away. Baba said we should not disturb her and that she was depressed. How I hated that word; without understanding it, I knew it was responsible for taking Madar away from me. From that time I was no longer at the centre of her world as I had been before but left to play on my own in the shade of the almond tree while my brothers and sister were at school.

Arsalan would return to the house more and more often during the mornings after Baba had left and my mother would grow paler and quieter each time. She no longer looked happy to see him arrive.

On the day that my younger brother was born there was a terrible argument in the house between Baba, Arsalan and Madar. Arsalan had come the night before, bringing a doctor with him. He seemed nervous. Usually he was so big and loud, raucous, someone who filled up the space and air around him. He slept on a chair by the foot of my mother's bed and my father too paced up and down all night in the room, then passed to the courtyard, then back to the room again. It was a drawn-out and painful labour with my mother screaming long into the night.

My sister Ara came down, dragging me from bed. She told me to stop up my ears and we all sat in a row, glum and uncertain, wrapped in blankets on the flat roof looking at the night sky over Kabul, listening to the shelling in the distance, blocking out as best we could the shouting downstairs, banished until the affairs of adults were resolved.

Little Arsalan (as the baby was then named by my parents in honour of their friend) was born with the dawn and was a loud, raucous baby from the first seconds. Strong lungs and tiny fists balled up tight. Shortly after he came into the world, his namesake, having held him and wished him good fortune, left. It was the last time we saw my father's friend alive.

The next time we saw Arsalan was a week later. Omar found him hanging from the almond tree in the courtyard, all the life and laughter gone out of his strong body, his eyes glazed, his limbs limp.

On seeing him there, my mother almost dropped the baby, and her screams pierced the Kabul air. She became hysterical. Baba in comparison remained calm and, taking Arsalan's knife from its ledge above the kitchen door, went over to the tree and cut down his friend, whose corpse dropped with a thud into the dust. Baba did not cry or scream or pull at his hair. He did not seem in the least surprised that Arsalan, his lifelong friend, should have met such a sorry death. Instead he turned and, gesturing to all of us to be quiet, said, 'This is what happens when the winds change. They will come for us too soon enough. We need to leave. This is no longer our home.'

Madar did not hear him, however, for she had collapsed on the ground, still cradling in her arms the baby, who was screaming at the top of his one-week-old lungs.

On that same cold February day the last of the Soviet troops left the country. At the time of course I knew nothing about this, nothing of the politics that surrounded us. I had no idea what this change would mean.

Much as we did when he used the word 'depressed', when Baba talked of Soviets or Russians or Communism we would all nod politely and look knowledgeable but of course we did not know, did not understand beyond the fact that the Soviets had been the enduring disappointment of my father's life. He who had taken up with Marxism and Leninism, with ideals of common, shared brotherhood and equality, he who had listened so earnestly at those earlier clandestine hillside meetings, had found it all in the end a betrayal.

Things grew strange in the household. Madar and Baba, who before had always been the best of friends, so warm and kind with each other, seemed cold and stiff in each other's presence. They would talk quietly late into the night in muffled tones. Ara and Omar would hover by the door trying to make out what they were saying and relaying back down to each of us to pass on to the next. In the dust bowl of Kabul this passed as both entertainment and as essential information gathering.

'I think they will take us to the mountains,' Omar said.

'Why?' asked Javad.

'Because Baba is disgusted by Gorbachev, says he's a weak fool . . . that the Mujahideen have it right after all.'

'Not likely.' Javad shook his head.

'Perhaps we will go to Madar's parents,' said Ara. She yearned to finally get to meet our maternal grandparents, who seemed so remote, so like royalty from the grand, awestruck presentation of her familial upbringing that my mother was wont to share by the fireside late in the evenings.

We did not know what would happen, but one thing that had become dishearteningly clear to us all was that Madar and Baba, who had always been a team against adversity, were splitting in opposite directions.

I know now, having read Tolstoy, that romantic relationships face these challenges from time to time and that such problems can be overcome. But then I just remembered the sense of doom and panic we all shared, the sense of being on the edge of a world we did not understand.

One thing that they argued about before we left the yellow house for good was money: Madar's money, Baba's lack of money. Baba wanted them to take Arsalan's money as well as that which Amira had given Madar. Arsalan had, it turned out, been a very wealthy man. Late at night we could hear our parents talking.

'Take it, Azita . . . he would have wanted you to.' Baba was almost shouting at her.

'No, it's blood money.' Madar was crying. 'We'd never be able to wash our hands clean of it. It would poison everything, bring bad luck,' she sobbed.

'Azita, be practical. Think of the children – their future.'

We heard Madar run outside to the garden, slamming the kitchen door behind her.

We did not know where Arsalan's money had come from; we did not know what he did, how he'd filled his days or nights.

'Business,' was all he would say when asked. 'Business is good,' or sometimes, with a furrowed brow, 'Ach, business is slow.' This was before they killed him.

It is probably Arsalan and his dirty money we have to thank now for keeping us in transit east to west, west to east. It is probably Arsalan's money that saved our lives and got us out of Afghanistan. And it is Arsalan's money my mother seems intent on spending by taking this journey over and over, she and Baba arguing all the while over where will be safe to call home. We can only guess at this, from snatches of angry conversation between our parents. We have escaped. We are alive. Should we be unhappy about this too?

Sometimes the conversations in the restaurant car turn political, but the meaning of these is not clear to us either – Baba seems to both love and loathe the Soviets. Madar is quieter; she does not say what she thinks, what she believes to be right, to be best for our country. Here, too, something between them is broken and buried.

'This is what happens,' my mother says, 'when men fight over ideas.' Countries are destroyed, lives are damaged, and you realise that nothing is forever. This is one of Madar's favourite sayings: 'Nothing is forever.' I hope she is right, for as much as I enjoy Napoleon's stories and the beauty of some of the journey and the curiosities of our fellow travellers, and as much as I cherish the all-too-brief stops along the way, I am ready to find a new home. I am ready for this not to be forever.

'Look at cousin Aatif,' Madar cries.

We all shrink round the table, fearful of the long shadow of beloved cousin Aatif.

'He could have been anything, anything at all,' she says, shaking her head in sorrow and confusion.

He was ready to find a new home too.

I remember him visiting us at the yellow house. He was gentle and kind and interested in talking to me, enjoying my constant stream of questions, my five-year-old curiosity about the world around me. His laughter was warm and deep and Madar was always happy to have him visit – to hear news of home from him.

At first when he went to Iran and no one heard from him we all blamed the post, the telephone systems, the distance, the being in a strange land. But when the silence continued we all began to fear that something terrible had happened to Aatif. He was not the kind of person to go off and cut all ties with his family. He was not proud like my grandfather. Madar and Baba spoke to everyone they knew to try to find out what had happened. We could not bear not knowing. We could not bear the silence. Months passed, then years, and it became another sadness we would carry with us; a wound that would never quite heal.

Stories came back, from others who had travelled there; stories that frightened us. And when, fearful for our own lives, we finally fled, we did not go towards Iran. We did not wish to disappear as he had.

Ara has shifted away from us; when my mother weeps, Ara becomes uncomfortable. Ara was older when Aatif disappeared. She was always his favourite. Starved of a large extended family, we were all greedy for this cousin who dared to befriend us, who came to the house to eat with us, to play in the courtyard, to sit and talk politics with my father, to talk about family with my mother, relaying news she would otherwise have had no way of knowing.

'He didn't deserve to disappear,' Omar says. Madar looks at her eldest son with gratitude – that he can speak with warmth of cousin Aatif, that he has not forgotten his kindness. She seems grateful that he remembers, and that for him Aatif is not yet gone forever.

Ara stands further up the carriage, pressing her cheek to the glass. I wonder what she is thinking about – if she remembers him too or if she is just trying to forget. Madar's hands tremble and she busies herself with fixing Sitara's hair, brushing it until it shines, Sitara fidgeting on her lap.

We grow silent, subdued now, and draw away from Madar, leaving her buried in thoughts of the past. After a while though, when we have forgotten once more about Aatif, when we have remembered how to be cheerful, we begin to play 'What if . . .' It's one of many games we have developed to pass the time on the train – a game in which we imagine other possibilities, other realities, inhabiting lives other than our own. In the end you can only look at the scenery or dwell on what has been for so long before you itch for activity. The rules of the game are simple. It starts with one person saying to the others, 'What if you were . . . [and then we think of a famous name, or find one by flicking through the encyclopaedia] . . . what would you do?' For example, the last time we played this Omar was Rumi, Ara Marilyn Monroe and Javad was Elvis

Presley. I got Albert Einstein. Well, you can imagine the conversation between these four characters.

'Three intellectuals and a heartbreaker.' That was Madar's joke, which I did not understand.

'Hey, Samar,' says Omar, 'why do I have to be Rumi? And you get to be Einstein? Surely it should be the other way around?' I shrug my shoulders and smile. 'This is how it goes,' I say. Omar does not have a poet's soul. He scowls at us all, reluctant at first to play, but gives in in the end, won over by our enthusiasm for the project. We can pass hours this way, the characters becoming more and more outrageous and silly. Ara adopts the voice of Marilyn and waves her arms in dramatic arcs – like an actress, she says – watching her reflection in the window, practising for fame. Javad is giggling. He finds it harder to stay in character.

The other passengers – Australians, Americans, a French couple (all actual tourists) – watch our games, some with irritation, some in amusement. Madar spends a lot of time saying 'Shush,' and sending placatory smiles up the carriage. Javad starts to dance in the aisle, shaking his hips up and down in the most ridiculous manner. He loves an audience. Ara hums 'Blue Suede Shoes' and 'Jailhouse Rock' and claps her hands as he prances up and down the carriage. Omar attempts to quote Rumi's verse and I try to look convincingly like a genius, cogitating. I ruffle my hair and squint. The others laugh, distracted momentarily from Javad's gyrations.

Baba isn't with us and so we feel free to play. He has gone for a walk. This always makes us laugh, the idea of going for a walk on a moving train, but it is something he does every morning. 'My constitutional,' he calls it. He is like a caged animal on the train and we can see the gloom in his eyes. He is not a good traveller. It takes all Madar's energy to smooth over his moods and to soothe him with promises of the train stopping soon, of them reaching agreement on where to stop, where to start over.

Little Arsalan runs up and down the carriageway following the undulating hips of Javad. Little Arsalan is no longer quite so little but the nickname has stuck and he will forever be Little Arsalan to all of us. He is resigned to this. Madar tells him how brave, handsome and fierce Baba's friend was and how he is named in honour of him, and this mollifies him somewhat. Sitara claps in time with Ara as Javad dances, giggling at us all the while. Madar bounces her gently on her lap, watching us all, her brood, her eyes soft as she smiles back at our antics. She is no longer sad, like before. Train travel suits her.

Another way in which we pass the time is by reading the encyclopaedia and testing each other on recall of facts – years, dates, timelines, lists of countries, capitals, details of the lives of famous figures, schools of philosophy, lists of trees, plant life, mathematical terminology. We sit huddled around the book, opening it out on the small table between our seats, flicking from page to page in wonderment at the world to be explored and known.

'How many countries are there?' Omar asks, holding the book open on his lap away from our prying eyes.

'One hundred and twenty,' says Javad.

'Seventy-six,' guesses Little Arsalan, looking up from his sketching.

'Not this again,' sighs Ara. She is becoming reluctant to play with us now, seeing herself as too grown-up, too sophisticated for our childish games. She is watchful of the other travellers, alert to how they perceive her and us. Sometimes I think she is embarrassed by us.

'Samar?' Omar asks me, smiling. The others look up.

'About one hundred and ninety,' I say.

He laughs. 'Good guess – almost right again!'

I feel a quiet happiness that I can make him laugh, that I can know the answers. I find I have a gift for this, and of all of us it is me who spends the most time reading, and playing back facts and astonishing truths to the rest of the family.

Only Javad takes as near an interest in the books as me – but only for the pages about animals and habitats, the things that interest him most.

Baba and Madar try to engage us all in the places we pass through; their history, facts, outstanding features. Napoleon, the *provodnik*, is called upon to give lectures on their history. We talk with him in Russian, this other language that has travelled with us from the beginning, almost as familiar now as our own.

'It is a time of great change for this country,' he tells us as we travel through the *taiga*, his tone portentous (this is one of my newly acquired favourite words – everything is *portentous* at least twenty times a day at the moment. Next week it will be something else).

He says, 'We are witness to a important moment in history.'

Feeling that everything so far that has led to us being here has been one big moment in history after another – a series of eventful happenings – so what, I think, that these people live with turmoil too? I feel a swell of quiet anger.

But Ara and Omar are interested in this – this new freedom that is sweeping the Soviet states.

'You know what this means, Samar?' Omar asks me.

'No.' I pretend not to care.

'It means more rock and roll. More Elvis Presley.'

'Elvis is dead,' I say. 'Hamburgers.'

Our train creaks along, travelling the line back and forth over the years, its engine kept running more by the skill of the driver and the engineers than anything else. We creep along this stretch at 35 miles an hour, inching our way from Asia to Europe and back as the train has been doing for years, even before things changed. But yes, things are changing.

'Communism is dead,' Baba says with what we take to be a wistful glance towards Madar. Things are opening up. This is what we hear all the time. But what does this mean to us? Only Madar and Baba remember Afghanistan as it was. Our memories are of war, destruction, uprooting and loss. All the more reason to welcome these new freedoms in Russia, argues Omar. But I can't. I envy them their newfound happiness, their excitement faced with the possibility of a new world. I wish that for my own country. I wish that I did not have to flee and begin again somewhere else.

'Freedom comes at a price.' This is what Madar says and while I do not understand exactly what she means, I agree that to gain something you lose something. Always.

Napoleon shakes his head at me.

'Come, Samar, why so glum?'

Everyone is happy. Further up the carriage the Russians are chatting with some Scandinavian travellers, everyone joking. There is the clink of glasses as loud laughter spills down the train. I feel so sad.

Sensing this, Napoleon gives me a pat on the shoulder as if to say, it's all going to be okay.

He sees me in a way that the others cannot. Sometimes I feel that Napoleon knows me better than I know myself. Who I am, what I feel about all that has happened, it keeps shifting, changing inside me. It is in those moments that Napoleon pulls me back. I feel his hand resting on my shoulder.

'Einstein's thinking, look,' laughs Omar, his voice shaking me out of my reverie.

'Come,' calls Madar. Baba has returned from his constitutional and it is time for the restaurant car. We leave our game and, hungry now, go in search of supper.

Ara has slipped away. I watch her in the corridor near the next carriage, standing by the open window and rocking back and forth on her heels, self-aware and beautiful. I am in awe of her at times. She seems so otherworldly, so grown-up. I hear her laughing and then realise she is talking to someone. I can't see who. Whoever it is is sitting in the compartment opposite where she leans in the passageway. I have not heard Ara laugh like this before, or talk so animatedly to a stranger. At the table Little Arsalan and Sitara are fighting over the salt shaker, Baba and Madar trying to coax them apart, to find a peaceful resolution. I slip off the seat and wander through the car in the direction of my sister, who, seeing me approaching, turns to stare out of the open window as if she had not just been deep in conversation with a stranger. As I pass her by I glance into the compartment, and there is a young man, blond and tanned, with a wide white-toothed smile.

I stop by Ara, feeling protective towards her now, and tug at her hand.

'Ach . . . leave be, Samar,' she says, her eyes flashing dark.

'Samar? What a pretty name. Hello there,' he says, staring at me, his voice all American – smooth and confident, and at ease in the world. I blush and put my hands to my cheeks to hide my embarrassment.

'Don't talk to her,' Ara snaps back and pushes me away from the door, back up along the restaurant car, needling her long nails into the back of my neck.

'Say nothing, nothing,' she orders and I can tell her eyes are darkened with anger at me. When we return to the table peace has been restored and everyone is so busy eating from bowls piled high with steaming stew that they barely notice us slipping on to the edges of the seats to join them. Later that evening Ara will sing once more to everyone in the carriage but now I realise she sings not for us, but for the stranger who stands at the door to the restaurant car, watching her the whole time.

The train travels through long tracts of inhospitable terrain. Sometimes all you see for days are the steppes and the plains. I have always enjoyed this part of the journey the most – the passing through places where one would never wish to stay but that hold a strange, eerie beauty all of their own. There, with the heavens open wide above, streaked with silent stars and constellations, so vast and beautiful, then I would feel that our journey was not purposeless after all. If I could only clear my mind of thoughts long enough and listen to the night sky I would hear what it was the universe wanted to tell me.

My brother Javad says I have a baroque sensibility. I had to look that up.

Baroque: an exaggerated artistic style to produce drama, tension, exuberance and grandeur.

I don't think you can exaggerate the grandeur of the night sky, the immensity of it, so I disagree with Javad, but then we disagree often. When you spend so much time so close to each other, cooped up on a never-ending train journey, even the most benevolent of comments can irk. We can spend days, weeks even, not speaking to each other. Instead we communicate through other siblings, parents or even Napoleon, if there are no family members present.

Tolstoy has it right about unhappy families. Are we unhappy? Sometimes. And yet sometimes, when we are all gathered together I feel that we are the happiest family there could ever be.

It is just this train journey. It is getting to me, to all of us now. I just want it to stop. I feel like we have always been running. Baba and Madar try to make it feel like an adventure, to be enjoyed rather than endured. We talk about our dreams for the future. Omar will be an engineer and build bridges to rival the Circum-Baikal. Ara says she will be a lawyer like Baba but I know she dreams of being a famous singer. I catch her practising in the reflection of the windows at night. Javad, he dreams of being a vet or working in a safari park – he has a gift for kindness and is afraid of nothing. Little Arsalan is too young to know but Madar says he will be an artist. Certainly he has covered the inside of the compartment with enough crayoned pictures to fill a gallery. Madar has told us all about galleries, famous painters, people who spend their days creating works of beauty or provocation. This appeals to me too though Omar says I will end up a teacher.

'Yes,' says Baba, 'a head full of facts, a talent for learning.'

I wonder about this. I am not sure I would make a very good teacher – for one I am not very patient and anyway, who would I teach? I could not teach in Afghanistan, that is an impossible dream. Though that is what is needed. No, I think, I will write. I have started to write our journey each day, to capture our conversations, our arguments. I write down what happens with the other travellers we share this train with. I sit watching, noticing. I try to describe the mountains, the grasslands we pass through, to note the colours of the sky and the temperature of the carriage (persistently warm). I write down my conversations with Napoleon, the parts of his story he shares with me, now that he has come to know us well, this homeless wandering family.

A highlight of the day is when the train stops – sometimes for ten or fifteen minutes, sometimes longer – and we disembark and stretch our legs on the platform, seeking out the sunshine on our faces. It is always a strange sensation when the driver stops the train. The carriage empties quickly and we all stand, unsure at first, getting used to the sensation of no longer moving. Omar and Javad are usually quick to run as far as Napoleon will let us go.

'Stay where you can hear me,' he says. A couple of minutes before we are due to leave he calls out and blows on a whistle, gathering up all his travellers. He tells me proudly that in thirty-two years he has never lost one.

This, of course, was before the day we lost Little Arsalan – though this turned out to be a temporary separation.

We had stopped by Lake Baikal at Mysovaya and Little Arsalan had wandered off in the direction of the water. For some reason – perhaps because Sitara was crying and Madar was occupied, perhaps due to some other cause – Little Arsalan disappeared. Napoleon made his usual call and we all traipsed back to the train. It was only when we were all sitting in the carriage that we realised he was missing.

'Stop!' Madar screamed.

'Madam?' said Napoleon, unaccustomed to having my elegant mother shout at him.

'The child is missing,' she said, pushing Baba off the train. 'My son, Little Arsalan. Help us. Please.'

Napoleon, seeing the gravity of the situation, rushed out to the side of the train to signal the driver. The train waited as Napoleon and Baba scrambled back down the bank, calling for our brother. Their voices echoed out, over and over. We could sense the impatience of the driver to be off. Our fellow passengers, worried now for the fate of the little boy, also climbed back down off the train and started shouting. Soon the din was so loud that it would have been impossible to hear Little Arsalan should he have attempted to call out. Ara wanted to go and look as well. Madar refused. She would not lose anyone else. Eventually, just as we were about to give up hope, Napoleon returned triumphant with Little Arsalan perched on his shoulders.

He passed the child to Madar, who didn't know whether to shout in anger or cry with happiness. She clasped my little brother to her chest while boxing his ears gently.

'He almost went swimming,' said Napoleon, a look of intense relief on his face. Lake Baikal is the deepest in the world, one of the largest in the world. None of us can swim. We knew then that Napoleon had saved Little Arsalan from certain death. That evening Baba toasted Napoleon and we all celebrated the safe return of the little explorer. It was the last time Madar let him out alone when the train stopped.

Most of the time we are just in this state of perpetual movement but with no sense of a destination or even of getting any closer to an end point. Madar and Baba argue in the passageway at night. We catch snatches of conversation. Arsalan's name is repeated often. There is something unresolved there. I crane my neck against the flimsy door to the compartment left ajar by Madar and try to eavesdrop. But it is no use. They share what they want to share with us, no more than that. They think this keeps us safe.

I dream at night about Afghanistan, about the yellow house. Nothing can keep us safe.

During the interminable days we coax Napoleon into sharing the chess set with us, or teaching us chequers. Javad is best at these games and whoops in victory each time Napoleon lets him win. At other times Madar spends long hours telling us stories of her childhood, her student years, meeting Baba, the hopes and dreams they share for their family, for all of us. She paints a picture of childhood in an Afghanistan where women work as much as men, where a Marks & Spencer clothing store opens in Kabul selling mini-skirts and causing queues round the block.

'Yes, short skirts,' Madar says, 'can you imagine?' We shake our heads in disbelief. Women, should they choose, do not wear burkas in these stories and they are free to go about their business. Our eyes widen as she speaks. She tells us about the zoo and how as a young girl she used to go to see the animals and cry to see them unable to roam free.

'It seemed so cruel,' she says.

Madar tells us how she would listen to Radio Kabul and how she and her sister Amira would dance to the latest songs and how this was never really frowned upon.

When we ask her about her parents, the grandparents we have never known, she grows quiet. 'There is nothing to say,' she tells us. 'In the end they would not help us.'

Baba snorts. 'And in the beginning,' he says. We know not to ask anything more. Not about this.

'Tell the story of you and Baba *jan* again,' Ara says. Recently she has become interested in romance.

Madar smiles and tells us once more about how she was a student at the university in Kabul studying medicine.

'Your mother,' says Baba, 'would have made a fine doctor.' She flinches at this.

'Anyway,' she says, 'we were always studying so hard. Always working on the books. Then there were a lot of protests, almost every day.'

'Who by? What over?' Omar asks.

'Oh, all sorts,' says Baba. 'Socialists, Poets, Communists. It was a different kind of city. Live and let live,' he sighs. 'At least it was for a while, before the fighting started again.'

'Yes, well,' continues Madar, 'so there were a lot of protests and rallies . . . the young were always out shouting about something or other. It was . . . infectious. It swept us up – this feeling that we could make the country as we wanted it, that what we felt counted. That is when the meetings in the mountains started happening. Small groups of us would drive up at night. It was ridiculous. I mean, why not meet at the university instead, or the cafés . . .'

'Danger,' says Baba, 'we knew it was dangerous. We knew there would be disapproval. We wanted it to be like a secret club, I guess.' He laughs.

'It was like a secret,' Madar says, smiling at him.

'Anyway, we met and that was that.'

'Then things changed. Soon it was a different kind of danger. So after that we just began to concentrate on the books instead,' says Baba, his eyes searching for Madar's agreement. She nods, as if pleased with his account.

I try to picture them both meeting this way in a world where young women and men are not forbidden to mix. What that freedom must have felt like.

And yet there is something missing. I look at them both, their heads bowed close together as they sit with Sitara on Madar's lap. I find myself thinking back to the yellow house. Memories of Arsalan standing with his arm over Madar's shoulder, the look on her face. I recall the sense of something unspoken between them. So I cannot believe in this perfect fairy tale of young Communist love between Madar and Baba. But it is the only version they will share with us. All love has its secrets. I am beginning to learn this.

I leave the boys' compartment that they share with Baba and follow Ara next door to ours.

Out of the window of our four-person berth, I watch the edges of the steppes race by – vast, empty, peaceful in the falling dusk. The outlines of the mountains are silhouetted black, receding in the distance. There in the near darkness are Buryat nomads sitting by fires near their yurts, their camels settled down on their haunches after a long day's trek. It is comforting to think of other people who journey ceaselessly from place to place as if it were normal.

There is nothing normal about our journey.

We have these two compartments in the *kupe* carriage, more comfortable than the cramped third-class *platskartny* berths further along the train. Our compartments are next to one another and in this one we girls sleep. Madar will join us later and keep a watchful eye.

The boys and Baba will sleep next door. When we first joined the train, we were always fearful, taking great care to double lock the door and developing an elaborate system of coded knocks. As time passed we became more confident, more at ease – this was after all home now. We would wander unperturbed late at night up to the end of the wagon to the samovar to get boiling water for late-night tea, or we would hang out of the open windows of the carriage taking in the surroundings, watching the sky, and wondering where we would eventually call home. It is funny what can become home after a while; how you forget. I don't want to forget.

I remember small things, sounds, smells. Laughter mixed with the sound of distant shelling. Then Baba and Arsalan arguing in the courtyard, quiet so that they cannot be overheard but so much anger between them . . . With their voices lowered and in between the constant noise of the traffic and the shouts of passing street sellers beyond the courtyard walls, I cannot hear what they are saying. Something about Baba threatening to leave . . . Arsalan talking him down.

Arsalan saying, 'It's just business, treat it like business.' Then giving Baba money for something. Baba crying. I see Ara running into the courtyard, crying out, 'Baba, Baba,' and both men turning at the same time. Baba wiping his eyes with his sleeve, hiding the money, lifting up Ara who clung to him.

'Look, Baba.' She shows him something. Arsalan just watches them both. This moment comes back and it unsettles me.

I can also see us all in the garden, lying on the grass, Ara reading a book of stories in Russian out loud, her voice faltering over unknown words, Madar coaxing her on. There was a fine layer of dust coating the leaves of the plants, the scent of summer in the air, the city a tinderbox and us oblivious, believing ourselves immune, protected by the walls of the compound. Something else, too . . . some men coming one day and knocking on the door, shouting for Arsalan. Madar swearing she didn't know where he was, that this was our home now, that no, he hadn't been in a long time and why, why would she lie? I remember the men pushing past her at the door and into the *kala*. One of them standing over me, tall, placing me in shade. Looking at me for a long while. Madar crying and saying Baba will chase them and how dare they and to get out, get out, get out. I remember this.

Then there was the time Javad cut his head on the stone by the door to the courtyard, just bounced off it, a deep gash appearing. Arsalan was there that day and he grabbed Javad, just scooped him up and rushed him to the Soviet hospital, even though Madar pleaded with him not to go out.

And Madar, on her knees before we left, digging in the dirt under the almond tree until her hands bled. These thoughts wind their way through my daydreams, fragments of a life now abandoned, and I try to make sense of it all as I get ready in our compartment to settle down for sleep for the night. Ara is with me.

'Samar?'

Ara is sitting on the bunk bed above my head. Sitara and Madar are still in the boys' compartment as Madar helps Baba settle them for the night. We all struggle with sleep now, with letting in the darkness.

'What?' I ask her.

'Do you believe in happiness?'

I stare at the frayed edges of the sheet hanging down from the bunk above my head. The train is rocking gently as we pass through the vast, empty plains of Siberia.

'Well, do you?'

Ara is a strong-willed character. Like my mother, she is very beautiful, with dark flashing eyes and long glossy black hair. She twists her head down over the side of the bunk bed so that she is upside down, her hair reaching almost to the floor of the carriage.

'Ara! You'll fall.'

She rights herself and then climbs in beside me.

'If I tell you something – a secret – can you keep it?' she asks. Her eyes shine bright with excitement.

I shrug. Generally I try to steer clear of Ara's dramas. She and Madar are prone to arguing about anything and everything, with Madar strangely always giving in to Ara in the end. This is unusual because it is Madar that we think of as always being fierce, like a lioness with her cubs.

'Samar? Promise me.'

The desire to be part of a secret club wins me over and I lean in towards my elder sister.

'What is it?'

Ara squeals. 'You can't tell anyone.'

'Okay, okay. I get it. It's a secret.' I wait.

She starts to brush my hair.

'You are almost pretty now, Samar,' she says lightly. It is meant as a compliment but stings me to the core. I realise I do not have my sister's fine bones and easy beauty, and that Sitara, in her own soft, gentle way is also considered more beautiful than me. I am the bookish one, the one with ideas – that is what Baba always says proudly, not realising that all girls have feelings and vanity.

'Don't . . .' I push her away.

'Oh . . . Samar . . . I . . .'

We sit in silence, the girlish intimacy broken. She tries once more, turning to me. She mouths quietly: 'I am in love.'

And there it is, whispered, passed like a parcel to me to unwrap. Ara is in love.

'The American?' I ask her. I feel my cheeks burn once more as I remember his smile and the way his eyes teased me.

She nods.

'Tom, yes.'

A stupid name, I think, for a stupid boy. And he is an American. How could she? This is all I can think.

'And does he love you?'

'Yes.'

I can feel the distance between us growing vast. Ara is no longer just my sister, she is a grown woman capable of being in love and of being loved. Suddenly I see her as others must see her and I grow fearful.

'You cannot love the American,' I say, uncertain.

'Ach . . . what can you understand? You are too young to know what love feels like.'

She dismisses me out of hand and stands up, looking down at me.

'I can and I do love him,' she says.

'Baba will not allow it,' I counter.

'You can't tell Baba. You can't tell anyone. It is a secret. You have promised.'

I close my eyes as the train rocks slowly. This is a secret I do not want to hold on to. I don't know what to do with it and it sits in my mind like a grenade waiting to go off.

'He will leave,' I say. 'Sooner or later.' I remember how he looked at me and I cannot believe he will truly love Ara, and Ara alone.

'I am going to Paris. *We* are going to Paris.' She says this defiantly and then raises her hand to her mouth as if she has said too much.

'Ara, you can't. You just can't. We . . .'

I am stunned. Who is this new 'we'? How can she think of leaving us? After everything we have been through, we don't leave each other. We don't. I feel panic well up in my throat.

Ara laughs, a nervous unhappy laugh. She strokes my hair.

'One day you will understand,' she says. 'You'll see, when it happens to you.'

Ara pulls herself up onto the top bunk once more and I watch the night stars pulse through the window, until at last the rocking of the train sends me into a heavy sleep, pushing thoughts of Ara and her complicated love life far from me as I dream.

All too soon it is morning and light streams into the compartment.

The train has stopped. I wake, slow and reluctant, still angry with Ara.

'Samar? Where is Ara?' Javad asks, suspicious, sticking his head round the open compartment door. We both look up at the bunk above my head. It is empty.

'I don't know,' I yawn back through bleary early-morning eyes. Travellers are milling about outside, jumping from foot to foot to keep warm on the platform. Everyone stays close to the doors of their respective carriages, anxious not to be left abandoned in the remote Mongolian wilds.

I shrug my shoulders in Javad's direction and turn, pulling the flimsy blanket over my head to shut out the early light. He shakes me, frantic and anxious.

'Samar, we must find her.'

'Have you looked in the restaurant car? In the bathroom? Outside?' I ask, hopeful of being left in peace. Javad shakes his head repeatedly, his eyes shining like a crazy person's as he pulls the blanket off me.

'Come, Samar, we have to find her.'

My sister Ara is almost a grown woman, opinionated and strong-willed like my mother. If she does not want to be found by Javad she won't be, I reason. Not in a hurry, anyway. I do not take her talk about Paris seriously. We are a long way from Paris. I guess where Ara has gone but I will say nothing.

Besides, she is in love. She has told me so and sworn me to secrecy.

Ara has told me I do not understand love. She dismisses me as unknowing, uninitiated. It is true I know only what I have observed, what I have read – how in Tolstoy, Anna's heart beats faster when she senses Vronsky nearby; how the world falls away for them both, how the beloved becomes the world. Becomes everything.

I have seen these feelings burn in Ara's eyes now and know the American has captured her heart. I am not jealous, I tell myself. It is good, after all, that it has happened, that she is happy – is loved and loves in return. In the end that is what we all wish for, isn't it?

Further down the carriage a drunken woman is singing in French.

' "Un An d'Amour", an old Nico Ferrer song,' Madar says. I do not understand all the words, and the woman's singing style doesn't make comprehension easy, but I can guess. She slurs her words and leans over the table, winking at the Russian men opposite. I wonder about all the songs written about love and heartbreak. These songs would not exist were it not for broken hearts and yet the person singing has survived this terrible tragedy, and they go on. They sing new songs – they create something out of their sadness.

There is a commotion outside. The sound of the whistle warning of departure – the shouts in Russian, English, French, calling everyone back onto the train. The carriage fills up once more. The windows have misted with condensation from the cold outside and the heat inside. I trace my breath on the glass. There is still no sign of Ara. Omar and Baba are talking to Napoleon, pleading with him, but there is nothing to be done. He shrugs his shoulders and turns away, apologetic. She has disappeared but the train cannot wait for her. This will be one passenger he loses.

I realise I will have to tell them about the American. This fills me with dread – I am frozen between the fear of Ara being lost to us forever and the fear of revealing her secret. Baba's gestures are more and more animated. His voice is louder. Javad is crying. I trace a heart with an arrow through it on the frosted early-morning glass.

Madar is rocking Sitara back and forth in her arms. Ever since we fled Afghanistan the slightest atmosphere of tension or undercurrent of anxiety can set Sitara off into a deluge of tears and wailing. The only way to soothe her is a constant gentle rocking back and forth – like the movement of the train itself. Is she crying because Ara is missing or is it just that the train is no longer moving? I cannot tell. She is frightened of stillness, of lack of movement, for it is abnormal to her. All she has known, all she can remember of life is running, constant movement, and now this train trundling across Asia with its inevitable back and forth. And we are no longer moving. Sitara screams, her face red and crumpled. Madar rocks her a little faster and sings to her quietly under her breath.

Omar looks at me. I see his face coming closer. My cheeks burn with shame. I apologise to Ara silently in my mind over and over for what I am about to do. I am going to betray her. I am going to share her secret. Faced with no choice at all – for I cannot remain silent any longer on this – I cave in.

'She is in love.'

'What?' Baba shouts and comes barrelling down the carriage towards me. I shrink back.

'Ara, she is with the American boy.' I point down the carriage by way of explanation, all the while saying nothing about Paris. I cannot mention Paris as that would show the madness that has fully taken hold of Ara and that I am in on things more deeply than I care to admit. Besides, Ara may be in love but I reason she is not stupid and she would have to be really stupid to get off the train in the middle of the Siberian steppes that are nowhere near Paris. Not without a plan. She is not stupid. I cannot vouch for the American, however. Or for the madness of love.

Baba's face turns dark. For an instant I shrink back even further, readying myself for his hand to fall on my head. He has never once hit me, nor do I think he is capable of it. I know I am his favourite daughter and yet, after all I have seen, I am ready for any horror, for the last bonds of trust to split apart. I know fear, I have seen what it can do to men and so I pull away just in case. He notices and pain flickers across his face – he has not meant to frighten me.

'Where is she?' he asks, pushing me in front of him and Omar. I take them down the carriage. We are followed by Napoleon with his worried expression (he does not welcome scandal in his carriage). He also holds on to a look of hope (for he too is a little in love with Ara – we all are, in a way).

Madar glances at me as we pass by – I cannot read her expression. She keeps on rocking Sitara whose cries are muted now. Little Arsalan plays cards at her feet. Madar seems neither surprised nor angry and I wonder, did she know? Did she know about the American boy? Does she not care any more? I feel our family falling away from me, away from each other.

I knock on the door to the American's compartment. Baba hammers on it. Omar pushes it open. There is no one inside. I feel dread seeping through my pores as I slide down by the door and start to shake. I was so certain we would find her here. But she has gone. Baba and Omar pull up the seats in an attempt to will her there – to find some sort of sign. But no, there is nothing left. No belongings. The Americans have gone and they have taken Ara. My world shrinks around me.

Napoleon edges away. He is uncomfortable with witnessing so much loss. He cannot look at us and hurries along the train. It will be a long time before he comes back. When he does she will still be missing. Ara is never coming back.

I realise this now and it hits me with such force that I cannot breathe.

She is gone.

Everything is tearing apart. I try to hold on to it all, the happiness and love, the squabbling and petty arguments. Blackness swirls around me. My head hurts. The carriage is too warm. I try to breathe but the panic rises in my chest. There is nothing I can do.

You cannot undo the mistakes of the past. You just live with them, you bury them deep in the hope that they will be lost to you forever but of course they are always there. Sooner or later they rise again to the surface. I think of this as I think of Ara.

I close my eyes and I picture her. She is walking towards me in the garden of the yellow house above Shahr-E-Naw, the sun on her face, smiling. She is holding out her hands to catch me should I fall as I swing holding onto the lower branches of the almond tree, my bare feet kicking in the air. She is laughing and singing. She is beautiful. I remember everything.

I do not want to let go of her, to face the truth. I am not ready for that. My mind will not let me.

So instead I write. In this empty train carriage I sit filling notebook after notebook. I write about my beautiful family and our crazy train journey. I describe mishaps and dramas, arguments, tears and shared laughter. I write about everything we will do when we finally stop travelling. When we begin to live again.

I hold on to hope. I cling to what is no longer there.

I think about Ara and Omar and Javad, about Little Arsalan and Sitara, Baba and Madar. I think about all that was left behind, all that was lost. I see it flickering by, as if through a window – watching someone else's life, not my own.

I cannot let go. Not yet.

Imagine what is possible, Madar used to say to us. Anything is possible. I need to believe that is true.

Part Two

All our journeys, no matter how far
they take us, lead us home.

Chapter 4

After Arsalan died we became nomads. Baba said it was no longer safe to stay at the yellow house. For a week we were lost, purposeless, while Baba and Madar decided what to do next. I had nightmares in which Arsalan's face would float into view, laughing, the rope caught round his neck. Ara would settle me back to sleep then. Madar was also lost to us during that time. She would rock back and forth, staring at the sky, staring at the tree in the courtyard, her lips pursed tight in anger, unhappiness, fear or guilt. It was impossible to tell which.

The gunfire and shelling in the city below became more sporadic, less purposeful. Those who had remained in the city through it all sensed the coming change. The Mujahideen were chasing out the last of the Soviets, shooting down their helicopters with American missiles. And now the Soviets were leaving. The Mujahideen were closing in, taking over. Fighting amongst themselves, each group wanting to be the victor. The Taliban was yet to come. Kabul was changing hands once more. By then we were used to war. And this was just a different war. At least that is what we thought. At first.

Our country has been at the crossroads of war for centuries. Madar has schooled us all over the years in the history: the three Anglo-Afghan wars, the Soviets, the Mujahideen and then later the Taliban. We are experts in war, in fighting, in destroying all that is precious. I am not suggesting we are the world experts in war. I am sure there are other countries, nations, peoples that could take that prize. When you stop to think about it most nations seem to ebb and flow through fighting and battles, inside borders, outside borders, a constant seeking. Is it not enough to be happy? Clearly not. I have no time for war or warriors, for those who destroy all that is good, all that is right. I say this, yet I would fight to the death to protect those I love. Perhaps it is not so different.

Baba would talk about the fighting, especially with Omar and Javad. I would eavesdrop from behind the door, listening to him tell of the cost of war, of ideas, of man's stupidity. How ideas are to blame. If we could all just share the same ideas . . . But that will not happen. I know this from my brothers and sisters. We are all as close as any group of people can be and yet we seldom agree on the simplest of ideas.

We fled the yellow house later that week. I remember Madar, her face pale, her eyes sad and swollen from crying. She, more than any of us, had loved the yellow house. She had tended to the flowers and the plants. She had made it 'home'.

We took few possessions with us: a scarf here, a dress there, some new boots not yet worn in by Omar; his old ones, too small now, were abandoned in the corner of the room. He packed his worn *patu* for warmth in the cold winter nights. We took a *pakol* Javad was fond of wearing, sandals, warm jumpers, trousers, shawls, Baba's *patu* still stained with patches of blood that had never quite washed out, along with Little Arsalan's blankets, some rugs, cushions, kitchen pots, the transistor radio, things we thought we would need. Random belongings of varying sizes and ownerships were jumbled together in a couple of large suitcases and a leather trunk. Madar wept constantly. In the end it fell to Baba to organise us all. With Ara as his deputy he tried to gather the things we wanted and the things we would miss if they were left behind.

Javad became sullen. Ara was distracted, forced into the role of helper as she watched Madar weeping in the corner, then dashing around throwing odd pieces of our life into the still open but rapidly swelling suitcases. There were whispered conversations between Omar and Baba. Then Omar was gone, taking some message or other with him. None of us asked where he had gone. We were all too busy trying to stay out of the storm that swept through the yellow house in the wake of Arsalan's death.

Baba told us how in the dusty streets below, the last of the Soviet tanks and trucks had rolled out of Kabul to head back across the Oxus. The soldiers had left their stations and the old Soviet grip on the Afghan throat loosened as a new wave of men with weapons and the desire for power swept into the city. Others were leaving too – ambassadors, foreign workers, 'anyone with common sense,' Madar muttered through her tears.

There was no time to mourn Arsalan. He had been buried on the day we had found him hanging from the tree. Baba and three men, who came to the house and who we did not recognise, took away his body. When I think now of Arsalan I remember this big, gruff warm person who wanted to protect us all, to make us family, and yet saddened my mother so much, and I am confused as to what I should feel towards him. I cannot ask my parents.

After Arsalan's death they spent the first few days arguing over his money – money he had wanted my mother to have. Whatever decision they made after those initial fitful arguments, for which my mother clearly had neither the strength nor the appetite, it was as if they had pledged never to mention Arsalan again.

Madar planted saffron around the base of the almond tree. I watched her from the window upstairs one night before we left. The others slept but I stood there watching, unnoticed, as she worked long into the dusk digging deep in the dirt, breaking the earth with her fingers until they bled. She went into the house and came back with a box full of leaves. She planted them up around the base of the tree, smoothed over the earth and then wrapped her arms around the trunk where she stayed for the longest time. When I woke up in the dawn light I went to the window once more, curious. Madar was still there, sitting on the ground now, resting against the tree, asleep. It was, I suspect, her way of saying goodbye; then he was wiped clean from our family discussions, banished to our memories. We began again. Running once more.

That morning Omar returned to the yellow house bringing with him a large covered truck, its tarpaulin riven with holes, driven by one of the men who had helped Baba to bury his friend. We spent the day finishing our packing – taking things out, putting things in, taking things out again. It is hard to choose what stays and what goes when you are leaving behind your old life and all you have known. It is difficult to know what will be of most use to you when you do not understand where you are going or why. So the packing took longer than might reasonably have been expected. In the end the cases, trunk and bags were closed up. There was no more time to change our minds. Omar had wanted to take his old bicycle; Baba said no. There would not be room. Omar sulked. We were to take warm, simple clothes, practical belongings only. A pile of books lined the bottom of the trunk: well-thumbed Russian travel guides, grammar books in French, an old encyclopaedia, Madar's university books, books of poetry – one with many pictures of flowers much loved by Madar – all dropped into the trunk destined to travel with us. Then the cases, bags, the heavy leather trunk, all of us children and Madar were bundled into the back of the waiting truck as dusk fell. Baba slid into the front seat next to the driver and we waited a while, silent, each buried in our own thoughts, until night settled over the city and then we left.

We told no one we were leaving. Baba just wanted us all to disappear. 'It is better we do not tell anyone,' he said, warning Omar, Ara and Javad to keep silent.

'Why, Baba?' Ara asked, plaintive. He said nothing and left them sitting solemn and angry at being unable to say goodbye to their school friends. Arsalan's death had unsettled us all and we knew Baba was right, that he understood this in a way we could not. The house no longer felt like home.

Stars blinked overhead as we peered through rips in the canvas sides, one last look at the yellow house, shrouded in darkness now, and the lights of Kabul below. Madar gathered us all to her like a litter of cubs and we tried to fall asleep to the rocking of the truck as it climbed up out of the valley high into the cool night air of the Hindu Kush.

The truck was dusty and dirty, smeared with oil. Ironically enough, it was an old Soviet model, abandoned in the retreating forces rush to leave. This fact, Omar had proudly declared, was how he had managed to strike such a good bargain.

'Ach,' said Ara, rolling her eyes, 'that's because only a fool wants to be in a Soviet truck these days. You may as well draw a target on the roof and be done with it.'

We all shuffled together, uncomfortable, agreeing that there was sense in what she was saying. As the truck bumped along the road winding up into the mountains, Javad had turned quite pale and was trying hard not to be sick everywhere. Little Arsalan didn't much care what type of vehicle he was in and slept happily swaddled to Madar's chest. I leant on her shoulder and tried to sleep but the strange sounds, smells and movement of the truck kept me awake, and so it was that Madar and I were the only ones in the back of the truck not sleeping when we began to slow down as an unofficial Mujahideen checkpoint appeared ahead. It was manned by two young men with rifles on their shoulders, flagging the truck down. They stood by the burnt-out shell of a Soviet tank abandoned and left to rust on the roadside. It was the first of many such signs of retreat we would pass as we left the city behind.

'Fighters,' hissed Baba. Madar feigned sleep.

We had been warned to be quiet in case this should happen. Baba would speak to them. We were to say nothing. Especially about Arsalan. We were never to mention Arsalan again. I peeped out through a tear in the tarpaulin and listened to the crunch of footsteps passing alongside the truck. The men were talking to Baba and the driver. I heard laughter and then one of the men stepped back from the truck, holding a stack of notes in his hands and smiling at Baba before waving us on. We had no more trouble for the rest of the journey and after several long hours of bone-rattling travel through the night, with the driver then breaking our journey to sleep and rest, by early morning we reached Baghlan Province, passing in the darkness first towns then a couple of sleeping villages until we arrived at the narrow mountain road leading to the village of my grandparents, Baba's mother and father, these people we had never met and yet we felt we knew already from all the stories shared by Baba.

The driver stopped again on the roadside and lifted out a small mat from the back of the truck for prayers in the dawn light. We pulled back the tarpaulin to look at the valley and the mountains on either side. I had never before left behind the noise and chaos of Kabul, having only ever known the city, so the space and the silence in the valley overwhelmed me. I sat quiet, waiting, as Javad and Ara squabbled. Baba was awake now in the front, having dozed for an hour or two. After a short while we were off again, bumping along the narrow mountain track. As the truck climbed once more, away from the plains and higher into the mountains, Baba became happier, his mood lighter, smiling and joking with the driver, a thin-faced Tajik called Majeed.

High up in the village someone must have been watching the truck wind its way up the bumpy track. Assuming we were Soviets with a poor sense of direction, a lone warning shot rang out in the valley, bouncing off rocks next to the truck's wheels.

'*Bismillah*,' Baba cried out as a second shot whistled past. Instead of ducking down or ordering the driver to reverse, Baba leant out of the window and shouted up into the village with a special ululating cry that echoed in the mountains. The shots stopped as suddenly as they had begun.

As we rounded the final bends of the mountain path, each bend caused a collective intake of breath as the truck hung perilously close to the edge, its wheels catching on chipped, loose stones and we children hanging out of the side, marvelling at the deep drop into the valley below. Madar, on the other hand, was praying silently. Sensing her fear, Majeed called out, 'It's not the drop into the valley we need to worry about, it's the mines they left everywhere. A parting gift!' He laughed in a crazy way, his eyes searching the road ahead for signs of trouble.

'May Allah protect us,' Madar cried, holding tight on to Little Arsalan and to me as the truck strained on the bends. Eventually it drew to a halt in a dusty square near a shady grove of poplar trees. Above the square the village was carved into the mountainside; a series of winding steps climbed up the hillside, the houses built into caves in the rock. I could see doors and windows for a few dozen houses cut into the rock face. The village seemed so small after Kabul. Majeed wiped the sweat from his brow as we heard the shouts of villagers rushing down the steps to meet us. At the head of the impromptu welcome party stood Amin, a childhood friend of my father, who was holding an old shotgun aloft.

'This is how you greet us, Amin!' Baba laughed as they embraced. Amin looked sheepish and disbelieving that here in front of him was his old friend Dil.

Behind Amin came running Baba Bozorg, my grandfather. Madar was frantically flattening down our hair, straightening our clothes and sending us spilling out of the back of the truck before, a few seconds later, she stepped down gracefully, her head carefully covered, holding tight to the still-sleeping Little Arsalan in her arms.

My grandfather was crying with what I took to be shock and happiness to see us all clambering out of this unlikely vehicle – unscathed, fortunately, no thanks to Amin. My grandfather wrapped his arms around Baba's shoulders as if checking he were not some sort of illusion or otherworldly *jinn*, but really, truly, his son. Other villagers who had come out to see what all the commotion was about watched us, curious. As for me, used to city life and city kids, these mountain children seemed so wild and free with their dusty bare feet and their skin turned brown from the sun and the mud of the hillsides. It was a cold day, with snow on the mountain-tops, but the sky arched blue and cloudless overhead already. The air seemed so clean and clear that we breathed it in in huge, hungry gulps.

Grandfather lifted each of us children, hugging us, twirling us round in the air.

'And who is this?' he asked me. 'And you?' This to Javad. We smiled and told him our names. 'Again,' he cried, 'tell me again.'

His eyes smiled and he laughed with a deep throaty laughter that infected us all so that we began to giggle too – no longer on our best behaviour. After the panic and chaos of the last week at the yellow house, this warm welcome felt like a homecoming. Grandfather led the way to his house, climbing the steps cut into the hillside, talking all the while with Baba, while Madar and we children all followed behind.

'Keep up, Javad,' Madar chided as Javad held back, staring at everyone. Then came the villagers who had gathered round, the village children darting in and out between us, curious, pulling on our city clothes, drinking in our strangeness in their midst. The driver came too, tired and stiff after the long drive up the mountain roads. He eyed Amin warily as Baba's friend toted the warm gun on his shoulder. A couple of older boys from the village carried the suitcases and dragged the heavy leather trunk along, bumping it all the way up the stone steps to the house.

There on the doorstep our grandmother, Maman Bozorg, her face lined from the sun, welcomed us all with a flood of tears and with glasses of warm chai poured from a kettle that sat over a fire outside the house. Although I had never seen my grandparents before, I felt as if I already knew them well and they knew me, and we all fell quickly into an easy warmth and closeness. At least, I did. Javad did too. Even Omar did, though he was trying hard to seem more grown-up and aloof. Ara, however, did not. She looked utterly miserable surrounded by the flickering light in the dark cave house and withdrew into herself, quiet and thoughtful.

My grandparents' house was built back into the rock face of the mountainside. The whole village was made up of a series of earthen and stone cave houses like this, nestled into the side of the hills. Inside the walls were whitewashed, curved and domed overhead. From high above it would have been hard to tell there was a village there were it not for the women darting from house to house, the early-morning plumes of smoke from the fires, or the men working the land down towards the valley and the village children gathered in the dusty makeshift square below the brown cliffs. Further up above the village the goats and sheep grazed freely on the scrubby hillside under the peaks of the snow-dusted mountains and a view that took in towering crags and beyond that, other lands on the edge of Afghanistan.

Other worlds. It was so unlike Kabul and I stood there, taking it all in.

In the house Maman Bozorg and my mother were fussing over the baby, Maman Bozorg holding him in her arms and tickling him under the chin as Little Arsalan gurgled obligingly.

Baba and Grandfather were clearing space and organising shelter for us. To one side they had a food store with potatoes, bags of flour and rice. The stove was by the door and a pile of cushions and mats furnished the small space. The kerosene-lamp flickered, lighting up the dark corners of the back of the cave house. It was not what we were used to and Madar grimaced.

'You are to stay with us, there is plenty of space and this is how family should be,' Grandfather insisted, gesturing to the meagre chambers towards the back of the main cave. Madar thanked him and Maman Bozorg and it was agreed – this was to be our new home.

Silent, her shoulders shaking, Ara started to cry and stood by the doorway looking down into the valley so that my grandparents could not see her tears. Overhead an eagle, its brown and white wings outstretched, soared. Ara watched it hover, circle and then, sensing its prey below, dive out of the blue. Ara's shoulders shook all the more. I went to her and, without knowing why, I placed my hand in hers and we stood there together, searching for the eagle that had dropped out of sight.

Behind me Madar looked lost, uncertain, and though she smiled and laughed with Maman Bozorg as if they were old friends, it was clear she too missed the yellow house and the life we had fled.

Later we all gathered round a fire to share a supper of *kofta* and *pulao*. The rice tasted sweet and sticky, a meal made with love. The villagers were all excited and fussing over our arrival, everyone pleased to see Baba once more and scared somewhat by his beautiful, grand wife. After the meal at our grandparents' house, with the women eating inside and the men outside, there was singing and dancing and the flames of the fire spat joyfully at us. I realised that for the first night in as long as I could remember I could not hear gunfire. The night up there in the mountains was so much darker, colder and quieter than in Kabul. We all stood together outside the cave house, looking up at the night sky and out across the country. Our country. A star shot across the heavens. On seeing it, Madar cried out, 'Arsalan!' and then, startled by her own behaviour, she went to the baby who was asleep inside.

That night we all slept in a way we had never done in the yellow house, all jumbled together. We slept the sleep of the dead in the cool mountain air with only the occasional howl of a village dog to disturb the peace that settled over us all. Even Ara and Madar, unsettled by our new living arrangements, slept and this, as Baba Bozorg had said, was how it should be.

This was now, after all, home.

Chapter 5

Home.

Baba Bozorg's voice comes back to me now as I sit in the carriage watching the light fade from the day.

Leaning by the window, alone, with my legs crossed on the seat, I rock back and forth.

I look at the reflections as the landscape blurs past. Sometimes it is as if I am there, as if I am that girl trapped in the glass.

She moves, leans forward, pulls back her hair from her face. There is the shadow of a bruise to the side of her eye.

For a second I think it is Ara.

My mind wanders now more and more. It keeps trying to bring me . . . take me . . . Where? What is it I should hear?

I press my fingers to the glass. The train's wheels click and drum.

I close my eyes and hear Ara's voice telling me, 'Be safe, Samar.'

The girl in the window looks back at me. Her lips move.

She is saying something over and over. I lean closer to hear her.

One word.

Home.

Chapter 6

The mountains, the cave house, living with Baba Bozorg and Maman Bozorg – this became our new home.

And as we settled into village life, conversation on the mountainside seemed to gravitate towards two key topics – the health and wellbeing of the sheep and goats, first and foremost, and then later, whispered in the square, at the well, rumours circulating from house to house of the angry young men who wanted to bring a new order to the country. People said the Mujahideen were going too far, the country was becoming corrupt. Now the Soviets had gone they needed someone else to blame. Whispers and rumours came of new ideas, young men studying in the *madrasas* in Pakistan and all along the border, bringing back new thinking, new ways to restore peace and security.

Opinion was divided in the village between those who welcomed the change and those who sensed it could only bring further unhappiness.

Whenever Baba mentioned these young men, the so-called Taliban, and their ideas, Madar would roll her eyes. 'What do they know, a bunch of illiterate schoolboys with Kalashnikovs?' she would say. At first she laughed, but then as time passed she became more careful, as if sensing loose tongues all about. Madar and Baba no longer spoke of the Soviets or their young Communist love. All that had been abandoned at the yellow house, their hopes left behind to rust like the upturned shells of Soviet trucks and tanks that lined the mountain passes. Here in the valley the Soviets had had more support, less resistance, it seemed, than elsewhere. This I gathered from the talk of the men in the square who wondered what change the Taliban would bring. Still, it was best to say nothing, to pretend these matters could not touch our lives.

I did not really care much about any of this at first. I was too young for it to register as something that would change my life. And why should I care when there was so much fun to be had chasing the goats, watching them hurl themselves, bleating, down the stony mountainside, anxious to put distance between me and them? I spent hours just lying on the grasses watching the clouds make patterns overhead. I would play with the girls of my age from the village and we would run up and down the hill-side gullies shouting to each other, letting our voices echo out in the mountain valley. I was too young to miss Kabul the way that Ara did.

'Come, play . . .' I called out to Ara before running off. She just stood rubbing her cheek, watching me turn into a distant speck on the hillside. 'Can't you see I'm busy, Samar?' she called after me. It was true. I could see she was busy with unhappiness and so I let her be. She remained a lost, solitary figure much of the time in those early days, reluctant initially to seek out friendships, unwilling to admit that this was now home, that she could not remain in isolation, sitting alone thinking about her old school friends and her old way of life.

'Why is your sister so proud?' One of the girls, taller than the rest, with a cruel glint in her eyes asked me one day. I did not know what to say. Surely pride was a sin. I shrugged my shoulders and the girl smiled at me, triumphant. In saying nothing I had permitted it to be true. Ara – whose beauty startled the boys and men of the village and caused envy in the hearts of the girls – was left to look after Little Arsalan and banished from our games on the hillside.

A routine settled over all of us. It was so peaceful to sleep up in the village after the constant shelling and gunfire surrounding Kabul. Here the only night noises on the mountainside were animals. Javad tried to frighten me with stories of wolves, snow leopards and hungry bears but I could no longer hear the fighting and I did not believe Javad's tall tales, so I began to feel safe once more. I ignored the heated discussions between my parents or between Baba and Baba Bozorg. It was easy to tune out the rumours that came back from the market square. Instead I let myself be happy.

The winter snows melted. The hillsides danced with wildflowers and the song of orioles filled the sky as they made their way northward. Baba Bozorg would take Javad and me up the mountain paths to point out the many birds and flowers, and he would teach us about the plants and the seasons and share stories of the hardship of farming on land that was hard and dry since the droughts grew longer each year. 'Yet all is good,' he would say on seeing our eyes widen. 'We are still here, after all.'

But that peaceful untroubled time would not last long.

In the months ahead news would reach the village of heavier fighting between the Mujahideen and these new fighters, news of parts of the country in the south falling under Taliban rule with new laws and edicts in place, news of the ways in which the Taliban were already changing people's lives. They were well armed, trained, focused. They knew what they wanted to achieve, how they would wrest control of the country and bring order once more.

Looking back it seemed to happen overnight, this change, but of course it was happening all the while around us and we were too busy or blind to see, or we pretended it was not happening for we had had enough. Baba and Omar would talk, quietly, and turn away from us, as Javad and I would leave with Baba Bozorg on the bright summer mornings to watch the sheep. Madar, too, was watchful, waiting. Ara occupied herself with caring for Little Arsalan and helping Maman Bozorg, preferring the darkness of the cave house to the staring eyes of the villagers.

'Who are these Taliban?' Javad asked Baba Bozorg one day as we sat on boulders high in the mountains. We were watching the sheep as they wandered over the hillside searching for food on the dry stony ground. Baba Bozorg tapped the earth with a willow branch he carried to guide the sheep back down.

'It doesn't concern you,' he said, his eyes fixed on Javad. 'They have nothing, so they want to take everything. Your path is not theirs, Javad. Look . . .' He stretched out his arms over the valley. 'You have everything. Everything right here.' Baba Bozorg touched his hand to his heart. Javad said nothing and was quiet for the rest of the morning.

But Baba Bozorg was wrong and soon it would concern us all.

At first it had seemed like a few young men, discontented, seeking change; just the zealous thinking of boys on the brink of adulthood. Most people thought it would peter out. But it didn't. Their number grew and with that came a new wave of fighting, and with this fighting came new horrific punishments: the cutting off of limbs, executions, public shaming. Men were to start growing beards; women were to start covering up from head to toe, sky-blue burkas dotting the landscape. As the new laws took hold, panic grew and eventually spread until all over Afghanistan, men, women and children – families like ours – began running to get away from the fighting, from what was coming. Hope had turned to fear and fear to dread.

Many people were so desperate to escape that they preferred to live a precarious existence in one of the refugee camps on the borders, leaving all their belongings and their homes behind, fleeing these young men and their wrath. Baba and Baba Bozorg spoke of this to each other, of how an exodus had begun, adding to all those who had run from the Soviets. People were leaving once more. We heard about this at night, too, when we listened to Baba's transistor radio and foreign voices, crackling through the air, would tell us what was happening in our country. Madar would translate and we would sit by the flickering light of the kerosene-lamp and wonder at our good fortune, to be so far from the fighting, to be safe here in the mountains at the top of the world.

I was glad that was not our life. We were together, even if we had had to come to the mountains to be far away from the main towns and fighting, even if it meant living in the caves, at least we were free and safe.

'Why don't we fight them?' Omar would ask.

The men would shrug and shift away uneasily. By this time Omar had joined all the village men at their daily gathering in the home of one of the village elders. Omar would come back full of ideas and fiery talk. Baba looked on him proudly, his warrior son.

'What do you do when you are under attack? You either submit or defend. We must defend. We cannot outrun the problem. We cannot hide from it, we cannot hide from them.' Omar would argue his point and Baba would nod his head in agreement and then gesture with an arm outstretched to all of us.

'And you cannot endanger.'

That was all he would say to Omar's protests and the two drew apart. Omar began to spend more and more time away from the house talking with the men, his newfound friends. He no longer had as much time to sit and play or talk with me, with any of us. Before, we would have sat together looking at the books Madar and Baba had brought from the city. There was one about flowers and plants I liked. Omar was more interested in one about Russia.

'Look, Samar.' He showed me pictures of a train crossing a high bridge over a lake.

'Imagine building something like this!'

He was intrigued by bridges and engineering – how to make the world work as he wanted. 'One day I'll take you on this journey – we'll all go, travel the Trans-Siberian Railway together.'

His eyes shone as he laughed and I had smiled, thinking what a dreamer my brother was, to imagine us all so far from home. His fingers would trace the drawing of the train route and he would ask Ara – who read Russian more easily than the rest of us – what the names were of the stops along the way. Ulan-Ude, Irkutsk, Krasnoyarsk, Novosibirsk, Yekaterinburg. We marvelled at these places. Omar was making plans for a new world. One that he wanted us all to share.

But now, as talk of fighting grew, he became busy with new plans and dreams – only these were ones he chose not to share with us.

On market day he would stand in the square smoking, when Baba wasn't watching. He would feel bitter at the injustice of the world. He and Javad bickered more than usual and Madar decided it was time we all went to school.

'Hold still, Samar.' She pulled at my clothes and tied back my hair from my face. 'Now pay attention to the teacher. Do not listen to the boys if they tease you. Learn, Samar.' She gave me a stern look. On the first day of class I kissed her goodbye before wandering down to the square. When I looked back she was still standing there on the mountainside, watching me go.

Our days took on a new shape. Instead of playing in the courtyard of the yellow house all day, here I was now expected to join the older children at school. It was in fact little more than a gathering of the village children, those who were not working in the valley below or on the hillside, more boys than girls, but all craning to watch the teacher – Najib, a young pleasant man in his white salwar kameez – write on a dusty chalkboard for a few hours each day. We would sit on mats, the youngest and shortest at the front, the older children at the back. He would teach us reading and writing, mathematics, history and languages. He had studied at Kabul University like Baba and Madar and he knew many things. Najib had a joy of teaching, of imparting knowledge, and he watched us all learn, taking pride in his work. He did not believe that just because we lived in the mountains, far from city life, we should go without education. New worlds were opening up for me and I would delight in tracing newly learnt script with a stick in the dust, following round the curves of the shapes as if entranced. At least until Javad or one of the village boys would come and kick over the dirt, erasing the words I had painstakingly drafted on the ground. Then I would begin all over again, eager for learning. Once more the boys would kick away the markings, laughing at me pulling the heavy stick in the earth. One pushed me over into the dirt as he ran past.

'Leave her alone!' I looked up from the dust cloud. One of the girls, newly arrived to the village and who now lived next door to us was standing there, her arms crossed, staring at the boys. 'Go on!' she shouted, chasing them away and the boys ran off laughing at this fierce young girl with dark eyes. 'Naseebah,' she said, pulling me up from the ground.

I wiped the dust off my clothes. 'Samar,' I said back.

'This is my sister, Robina.' A pretty girl stood smiling behind her. 'We lived down there,' Naseebah pointed down towards the valley, 'but this is my mother's childhood village and now we live here.' I did not think to ask why.

And so I made new friends – Naseebah and Robina, twins, the same age as me, who now lived in the cave dwelling next to Maman Bozorg's house that before had sat empty. Naseebah had dark hair and eyes, and brown skin – like us, for we were all turning darker in the clear-sky days of the mountains. Her sister Robina was strangely paler, a green-eyed girl with wispy blondish hair. They took me into their care, taking it upon themselves to teach me mountain ways. Nas was the serious one; Robina was happier and louder. I somehow helped to balance them out. They had one older sister, Masha, a very beautiful girl who was the same age as Ara. So while I befriended the twins, Ara became close to Masha, who was to be her only friend. Too old to play in the dirt, not yet old enough to be shut away indoors, Ara struck a lonely figure, bereft of her sophisticated Kabuli friends.

Ara and Madar, too, spent long hours in conversation, each clinging to the other for support. Madar, though she wore a tired smile constantly, was struggling with the rough mountain living so far from all she had been used to. What had seemed charming and full of intrigue and had held a kind of glamour and freedom when she had been a university student was now simply a hard life, one of survival against the seasons. At first the village women had tried to engage her in their chat and their work, encouraged in this endeavour by Maman Bozorg, but they all realised soon enough that Madar's mind and heart were elsewhere. Here she and Baba could not argue – they had neither the space nor the privacy – and so often they would go for days without saying much to each other. They feigned commonplaces, enough to pretend that everything was good between them when it wasn't, when it seemed it could never be after what had happened at the yellow house. They had buried their happiness with Arsalan. We children shrugged off this atmosphere of despair – we were too used to it by now to consider it anything other than normal.

Javad, like me, took quickly to the fresh mountain air, to the new freedoms, the space, the vast open skies, to running barefoot after Baba Bozorg's herd of goats and sheep. Here the Soviets had been unable to come with their tanks and their mines. Generally the local people had, it seemed, helped them, all the while also helping the Mujahideen, and so there was not the danger of mines that littered the floor of the valley below. Here the houses had not been destroyed; the people had been left in peace, too far for the soldiers to care about. Here, near the clouds, protected by Allah, we felt safe. And Javad, like all the boys, ran free.

Popular with the village children, with his infectious laughter and constant jokes, Javad settled into living on the mountainside as if it had always been his home. He had no time for Omar's complaining about the Taliban. Quite the opposite in fact. Javad felt that since the Soviets had left he had the Taliban to thank for this new, happier life. He could not see beyond that notion and so my brothers fought often and sulked at each other until Omar would head off up into the mountains – often for hours at a time. We would never ask him where he went or what he did. It was enough that for a few hours there was peace in the family, no arguing. We all craved peace.

My favourite time was market day when Nas and Robina and I would spend the day winding between the various carts laden with oranges, walnuts, rice, melons, grains, sacks of pistachios, pomegranates and trays heavy with bunches of grapes. The village women would bargain and barter, exchanging what food they could with the local farmers selling. People would come up to the village from along the road below. There would be a new energy in the normally sleepy red square.

Taking our haul with us, we would sit in the shade of a small grove of poplar and willow trees just at the edge of the village, planted by an old man the villagers called *malang*. He did not care about war or fighting, working instead each year to plant new orchards or groves – plum, willow, mulberry, poplar or cherry trees, whatever he could find. Digging channels for stream water to reach the roots, caring for the trees for no reason other than the joy of creating small pockets of beauty and shade. We sat there and shared the fruit.

'What will you be when you are older?' I asked Naseebah and Robina.

'A doctor,' said Nas, decided. 'Then I can heal people.' I thought about that. It seemed a fine idea.

'Robina?'

She looked at us both and blushed. 'I would like a good husband and a family.'

'Yes, okay, but what would you do? What would you be?' I asked her once more. She thought for a while.

'Why, I would be a wife and a mother.'

Nas and I shook our heads. The subject was closed. I could not imagine ever wanting to marry one of the boys in the village, or any boy for that matter. But I was lucky. Madar and Baba would let us make our own choices. After all, hadn't they? The villagers had frowned upon this love match but Baba and Madar just tuned out their disapproval. Madar instead wanted us to learn, to study so that we would make something of our lives. But I could not explain this to Robina in a way that would make any sense to her. In that moment I felt how different our lives were even though we lived side by side.

Later, after we had gorged on fruit and handfuls of nuts, I would say goodbye to the twins and gather instead with the other young girls and boys on the corner of the square to play *buzul-bazi*, the sheep knucklebones scattering in the sunlight, the shouts and laughter echoing out round the valley. In the afternoons Javad and Omar would join the other boys in games of volleyball played on a makeshift chalked-up court. Dinner would be *chainaki*, stewed in teapots over the fire, or sometimes *dopiaza* – made from lamb and smothered in onion and tomato sauce. Afterwards we would sit together round the fire listening to the BBC World Service on the transistor radio – one of Baba's finer choices when packing up in haste and leaving the yellow house behind. The radio connected us to the rest of the world, to a sense of possibility. Nas and Robina would sometimes join us.

I would try to reciprocate their kindnesses by telling them about Kabul and the yellow house. I would describe the plants in the garden, the kites in the evening sky, the view from the roof looking out at the snow-tipped circle of mountains that hugged the city. I would share with them stories of the city, stories Madar had stitched into our memories, told over and over, lest we forgot.

'I would wave at the mountains,' I told Nas and Robina. 'I didn't know it then but I was waving at you.' We laughed to imagine each other growing up so far apart in different lives and yet now we were here together, in the same group in class with Najib – and, why, neighbours too! It seemed impossible that this could be true. Nas would hug me close and call me 'sister', while Robina would giggle at us both and call me 'city girl'. I could not decide if that was meant as an insult or a compliment or neither.

Robina followed Javad around like a puppy dog while Nas and I would play, happy to build imaginary worlds and to amuse ourselves with the possibility of what could be. I was learning well at school, quick to take in information and store it away like treasure which I would on occasion show off to Madar and Baba or my grandparents, quoting back facts like glittering jewels held up to the light. Madar, concerned that the village school would be too rudimentary, supplemented our day class teaching us English, Russian, even some French; reading, writing, sharing with us all she herself had learned and knew. She would make us write out everything and would praise our script when it was well executed. Conversations in the house would switch back and forth between the different languages until it became natural to us to do so. 'Learn, Samar,' she would tell me. 'Learn so that you can understand the world.'

This constant learning, of course, put us far ahead of the other children in the class, and Nas and Robina would roll their eyes when I would (correctly) answer yet another unsolvable question posed by Najib. Then I started to come to school with a series of questions of my own for Najib like 'How does electricity work?' and 'How many times would Afghanistan wrap round the world?' (I had recently learnt that the earth was round and spent a long few months trying to calculate its circumference.) Our teacher took these questions well, spinning them back to us all, encouraging us to think for ourselves.

One day Javad sought me out. He pulled me aside and said, 'Make her stop.' I stared at him blankly. 'Her . . . Robina . . . She's . . . impossible.' He spun off on his heels.

Alas, poor Robina was in love but Javad was not ready for romance. Gently, I tried to dissuade her. She pretended it wasn't so and told me it was a ridiculous idea. I shrugged.

I had no experience in guiding young hearts. Besides, it seemed utterly incredible to me that anyone could love Javad. Not in that way. I asked Ara's advice. She mulled it over and said she would talk to Masha and between them they would sort it out. I breathed a sigh of immense relief. Disaster averted, I returned to Javad to report the happy news. He was furious.

'You told Ara?' he shouted at me, his face purple with anger. 'Ara! What were you thinking, Samar? Now she will be forever teasing me . . . Ach.' He sloped off cross and inconsolable. I sat by the well, wondering how I had come to be in the middle of all of this mess and shouldn't he fight his own battles anyway and not involve me in the first place? Nas came to find me. I wiped away the tears before she would notice.

'Robina's mad at you,' she told me.

We sat together in silence. I did not know what to say. Nas gave me a hug and I felt better but determined not to intervene in the romantic entanglements of others again. I never found out what Masha told Robina – but knowing Ara I can only surmise she would have attributed some awful fault to Javad and encouraged her to redirect her emotions elsewhere. In the end, as it turned out, it was good advice, and the childhood love affair floundered before it could really begin.

'You are too young for such nonsense,' Ara chided us all.

Masha and Ara seemed so much more grown-up than us. We looked to them for guidance. Nas and Robina in particular loved to spend time at the house with us all, but especially with Ara and Masha. Their mother, Nazarine, was on her own now, their father having been killed in the fighting. We were not sure whom he had fought for or against, only that she was sad and prone to crying a lot. As a result she was not much use as a mother and Masha tended to her sisters much of the time while her mother stayed indoors sleeping.

'She has a broken heart,' I overheard Masha explain to Ara one day.

'Oh,' replied Ara. 'Is it serious?'

'Deadly,' said Masha.

I had never heard of such an illness before and from then on tended to avoid Nazarine even though, when she was not sleeping or crying, she was a friendly woman with a kind, sad sort of smile. Madar would spend time with her and they would talk.

'Women's business,' Ara would say, as if she knew what she was talking about. We were all growing up and I had become used to this new life in the mountains. It felt like it could go on forever.

Chapter 7

Happiness, however, does not go on forever.

I sit, quiet by Napoleon's box room at the end of the carriage. Outside night is falling and the lamps flicker on. Here I am undisturbed and I pull out my book once more.

Anna Karenina is about to leave her husband, readying herself to flee to Moscow on the evening train, to take her son with her. I am shocked. This woman, who lets her heart lead her, who breaks with what is expected. She must really love this Vronsky character, to take her son from his father. I am both angry with her and yet . . . she is following her heart. She is true to herself.

I struggle with some of the words she writes in her letter to her husband – she talks of *magnanimity*. I do not recognise this word and neither Madar nor Napoleon are on hand to ask. Instead I turn the word over on my tongue. Somehow it is important.

First she leaves this unknown word in her letter. Then she takes it out. It is important twice over. I sound out the word once more. The sounds offer up no clues. And then she sits to write to Vronsky and what – then tears that letter up too. Anna is in pieces, her heart galloping ahead of her.

I am beginning to understand something of the bonds of love, its expectations and demands. I read the passages over and over looking for answers, signs. And then I watch as once it is done, once the letter has been sent and the words have flown from her, she can no longer call them back.

I think of Ara – her singing in the restaurant car. I sing the same words quietly, under my breath, but I cannot conjure her up. Tonight she does not sing for me.

I look at my notebook.

If I can capture the right words, find my way back to Ara, to her singing – if I can journey back – will that dislodge all the other unwanted sounds and images that crowd my mind?

The carriage is stuffy. It is full of the smells of uneaten food, of warm bodies and closed windows. I close my book, my eyes heavy, my mind dull at last, the train rocking me to sleep as my dreams take me back to the mountains. The book drops from my hands but no one is there to see it fall.

Chapter 8

In the April of our fifth year in the village, Omar disappeared. There were rumours he had been taken by the Taliban or the Northern Alliance fighters. Some of the young men, strangers who had come to the village on market day, who had spoken with all of the older boys, were rumoured to be either Massoud's men, freedom fighters or Taliban spies. It was impossible to know which, to know what was the truth. Baba Bozorg was afraid Omar had got lost on the mountain but Baba noticed that some of his clothes and his boots were missing. So we began to believe that the rumours were true and that he had gone off to fight against the Taliban who seemed to be getting closer every day – even here, at the roof of the world, so far from everything. We could not think about the alternative, that they might have taken him as a troublemaker, that he might be languishing in a jail cell somewhere, or beaten, hurt – killed, even. We could not allow any of those possibilities to be the truth.

In the days and weeks following his disappearance we all waited, expecting him to return at any moment. His *patu* lay abandoned on the trunk at the back of the cave house and so I took to wrapping it around me and imagining him returning and shouting at me to put it back.

'He will be back soon, you'll see.' This was Maman Bozorg trying to soothe Ara and me. 'He is a good boy, a sensible boy, he will be back.'

Madar spoke little in those days. If she mourned the sudden loss of her eldest child she did not let it show – in fact it was as if she knew where he had gone but did not want to frighten us by speaking of it. Baba seemed surprised, uncertain whether to feel pride or fear. Baba Bozorg was melancholy. Only Little Arsalan seemed unaffected.

'You should have made him stay.' Javad sulked by the mouth of the cave house. Without the presence of his elder brother he became withdrawn and angry, snapping at us all. 'He will get himself killed, and for what?' No one could answer his question or soothe him.

'Is Omar ever coming back?' I asked Ara this one day as we sat outside, looking out over the valley.

'I don't know.' She squeezed my hand. I could not imagine our life without Omar. Of all my siblings he had always been the one to encourage me most, to help me to study, to learn about the world beyond that which we knew. His hopes and dreams – of becoming a great engineer, of building beautiful bridges, of making his way in the world – had rubbed off on me, on all of us. And now he was gone. Sadness infected us but as we did not know, could not be sure of what had happened to him, we each held the loss of Omar close and quiet to our hearts, fearful of allowing him to disappear for good.

It was easier to imagine his absence was temporary and so we all spoke of him in those terms: 'When Omar is back,' we would say, determined that one day he would be.

Other things began to change as the months passed. The villagers chatted less, were more watchful. Everyone was frightened of spies, of being denounced to the Taliban by their neighbours. Each petty grievance took on new significance. Those who had supported the Mujahideen stopped talking in public of resistance. Massoud was no longer winning and his men had retreated, they said.

The Taliban by now controlled large parts of the country and were about to take Kabul. Some said they had already captured the city and it was just a matter of time until the whole country faced Sharia rule. All this I learnt from Baba Bozorg. Rumours swirled about what could be said, what couldn't, about how you should act, about what was permitted and decent and honoured Allah, and what brought shame. Baba put away the radio. There was talk of hit squads, public order gangs who would watch over beatings, and amputations for alleged thefts. Stonings started to happen. Rumoured disappearances. Loved ones lost. It was the promotion of virtue, we were told. The people were to be controlled. This was the new order. The older girls and women all began to wear the burka. They were no longer to go out without their husband or father accompanying them. These were the new edicts filtering up to the village where we could not tell what was true and what was rumour. Even up here in the village, where surely it did not matter, could not make a difference, these rules were to be obeyed. Madar began to fuss more over our appearance. We were coached in what to say, what not to say in school, in how to behave.

Here, high in the mountains, cut off from the fighting, we had felt so far away from the chaos in the rest of the country. We had not believed it could follow us here. On market days we would learn which groups had taken over which parts of Kabul, how the resistance fighters pushed forward, how now the Taliban were winning. It seemed the shelling had intensified. People were being killed in the violence and many were leaving the city, running from this new order and all that it brought in its wake. Women could no longer work, could no longer go to university, older girls could not go to school. This news struck us as incredible but remote. It did not yet affect us or Najib, our teacher, who believed everyone – girls as well as boys – should receive a decent education and go and make something of their lives, do something to contribute to their country. This is what he would say to us over and over as we struggled with multiplication tables and verb conjugations and memorising stories of other people's history.

Then one day, Najib gathered together all the girls apart from the very youngest and explained apologetically that from now on we could no longer come to the school, that it would not be safe for us and that if we were to continue learning (and here he smiled in a sad way) we would have to do so at home. He added his sincere hopes that this lamentable state of affairs would be short-lived and that we would all be back to learning with the class soon.

None of this made any sense to me at all. What were we to do now all day long? How would we ever become lawyers or doctors or writers as Madar and Baba had encouraged us to be if we did not, could not learn? Surely this was all some sort of ridiculous mistake?

'Ha,' said Robina. She had never much cared for school though she enjoyed the companionship. Nas, like me, was bereft until Nazarine took to trying to teach the village girls, hidden from the watchful eyes of the new schoolmaster. Masha and Ara said nothing but they looked more and more fearful every day of what was to come, for they were leaving childhood behind and becoming women in a country where to be a woman felt like a crime.

Javad, however, continued to go out each morning to class. He would glance backwards at Ara and me – looking guilty at first, then, later, triumphant. Najib was replaced by a dour old man from the neighbouring village who taught in the *madrasa* style and with different ideas, ideas favoured by the new regime. The things Javad was learning began to change. Instead of geography and mathematics he came home talking only of religious study, of the new rules. He would take to lecturing us, sighing, saying we would never understand for we were only girls and it was his responsibility to lead us now, to guide us in what was right. Ara would guffaw with laughter at his priggishness and Javad's eyes would flash back in hatred and certainty. This gentle boy whom we had all loved so much and who had been so kind and full of fun changed before us. Everything changed.

Even the village games changed in the evenings. Children drifted away, unwilling to be seen as being too joyful, too loud and too active. Bike riding and kite flying stopped altogether. The volleyball court by the square slowly emptied out. The girls stayed indoors more. We began to seek out the shadows. We heard horror stories from other villages further along the valley of visits by Taliban enforcers who would break into homes and drag people from their beds. There were stories of people disappearing, being taken and brought before new local courts to confess to sins they had no recollection of having committed. The lines between what was right and what was wrong blurred and shifted so much that we were no longer sure of ourselves.

The village elders would talk long into the night, discussing what was to be done. Baba, who seemed fearful once more of choosing the wrong side of the argument, kept quiet as others planned and sent their sons off to fight this invisible enemy – fear. A fear so deep it dug right into our souls and could be tasted in the water we drank.

For Baba things were worse. The villagers whispered now behind his back about his rumoured Soviet-supporting past and his revolutionary zeal.

'Is it any wonder the boy turned bad?' they would say of Omar's disappearance.

Madar was tarred with the same suspected views as Baba. No one ever stopped to question her directly – not then. They did not believe her capable of holding her own ideas. Women were becoming shadows; shadows that did not, could not, would not speak. Like the others, Madar too became thoughtful and quiet and pale with anger at what was happening to her country.

Only Ara was unrepentant. She would run up into the mountains and scream 'Barbarians!' at the top of her lungs, until it echoed out over the valley. She would not wear a burka. She would not be silenced.

'All this,' she would repeat over and over, spitting disgust into the dirt, 'all this stupidity.' Her eyes would flash with rage. Madar would try to quiet her, to bring her indoors at least, to occupy her with sewing or reading (far from the doorway by faint candlelight flickering at the back of the cave). It was futile. Ara's will would not be dampened. I watched all this, uncertain which side to take, not knowing who to comfort and feeling a creeping danger coming ever closer to us.

Javad became even more zealous in his pronouncements. The boy who had once joked and laughed so easily, who had time for everyone and every creature, the boy who had once spoken of becoming a vet, who wanted to fix broken things, now spoke only of religion and duty. He became hard and judgemental. He was angry at losing Omar – though he would never admit to it. We were all angry and sad in our own ways but in Javad's case he blamed this loss not on the Taliban and their myriad rules, laws and cruelty, but on Baba and Madar, who had somehow let Omar go. He blamed all of us for not being a good enough reason for Omar to stay.

When Javad left to attend classes, Madar would bring Ara and I together and we would sit huddled at the back of the cave as she would try to teach us all that she knew, all she could remember from her own schooldays and her time at the university. We were taught in whispers. Now, however, we could no longer write anything down, keep anything anywhere other than in our minds. Just in case.

Mistrust grew in the village. We learnt to be careful.

One day the Talibs, young men with long beards driving blacked-out Toyota pick-ups, their white flags fluttering in the breeze, came up to the mountains, to the village. Amin had told Baba several days before that this would happen. He had arranged the visit, he said. We all wondered why. Amin was an odd, solitary figure. He had never married. Perhaps none of the village women found him an attractive enough proposition. It was not that he was ugly exactly, but given to fits of rage and strange tantrums that would, perhaps, make him difficult to love. And then there was the question of his gun, which he wore at all times slung on his shoulder.

'Shoot first, ask later, eh, Amin?' Baba joked with him. We would all snigger. Lately Amin had been coming to visit Baba more at the cave house. He would spend hours sitting outside with Baba in conversation, watching the comings and goings from the houses nearby. It was rumoured he was a spy for the Taliban. I do not know who first said it or how the rumour got started but I remember Ara and Masha whispering about it once and Nazarine shushing them and saying, 'He's a sad soul. An oddball is all.'

Well, now this oddball had invited the Taliban into the heart of our village.

Baba did not know what to say to Amin. He was fond of this old friend who as a child had been a loyal companion, taking Baba's side in arguments with older children, the two of them joined in adversity. Now, though, it was clear that their lives had followed different paths. At times I caught Amin staring at Madar as she worked in the house. This did not surprise me for she was very beautiful, but it was indecent and he was careful not to do so when Baba or Baba Bozorg were around. Sometimes, when he was not off teaching Javad how to shoot high up in the mountains away from the villagers or talking with Baba looking down over the village, he would help Nazarine carry water from the well. This was frowned upon by some of the villagers – after all, what was he to her? Tongues wagged in the way that they do when people need to have stories to gossip about, but in truth there was no impropriety to judge. Nazarine suffered from a broken heart, after all – and besides, it was clear she had not the least interest in Amin and rather tolerated rather than encouraged his behaviour.

In the days leading up to the visit, the men of the village gathered to discuss who would welcome the Taliban visitors and how they would be received. A meal was organised. But the atmosphere grew tense and unpleasant; no one wanted them there – except, it seemed, Amin – and yet hospitality would have to be extended. Baba Bozorg, as a respected elder, would lead the group. Baba and Amin would join him. A few of the other men agreed to join the welcome party. A lookout was established to keep an eye on the mountain road so that the villagers could be ready for their arrival.

'Let's just get this over with,' said Baba Bozorg to my father on the evening before the visit. 'Whatever he has to offer them . . . it can bring no happiness.'

Although they mentioned no name, it was clear they meant Amin. I began to fear for Baba and for Madar and to wonder what it could be that he could offer these angry men who wanted to rule over us all, why he sought to expose us all to such terrors. That night no one in the village, except for Amin, slept well.

It was early in the day when the pick-ups bringing the men snaked their way up the valley. Men stood on the back holding rifles, looking out over the valley, bringing the war with them.

'They are coming.' Up went the shout and the women all hid indoors, taking their children in with them. The men of the village formed a rather unwelcoming welcome party and waited in the square. Gloom descended and we all peered anxiously from behind the rags of curtains by the door.

The men spent a long time on greetings, introductions, the sharing of pleasantries and information, news of how well the Taliban's campaign was going in the rest of the country. Hospitality had to be extended. 'Let there be no bloodshed,' Baba Bozorg had warned.

It was clear the visitors did not trust us. A meal had been prepared and the Talibs all sat together, breaking bread and chewing their naan. After a while some of the men walked through the village led by Amin, who wore a tentative gloat of a smile. We heard them climbing up the hillside to stop next door at our neighbours' house. I thought of Naseebah and Robina scared inside, of Masha and Nazarine unable to offer them any protection. We heard raised voices, Nazarine crying. Madar looked like she could no longer breathe and we watched her on the brink of passing out in terror. The crying went on, then turned to screaming. We heard another man, my grandfather, I think, trying to reason with the men before they pulled Masha and her mother out of the house and led Nazarine down the hill to the square under the watchful gaze of the hidden villagers. Baba stepped into the house, gesturing at us all to remain silent.

'They will betray us,' hissed Madar, pacing now like a

caged mountain tiger. Baba shook his head, trying to reassure her.

'It is okay,' he said. 'Whatever happens, keep the children inside.'

She nodded, almost catatonic with fear. Javad smiled a glassy smile. Little Arsalan took to racing around the cave floor in small circles, annoyed at being penned up in the house. Maman Bozorg had gone next door to comfort the twins. Ara and I just looked at the dirt, thought of Masha and her mother and chewed our nails, nervous and silent.

How could these strangers have so much control over our lives? It seemed unreal. Then we heard Masha's screams rise from the square below.

'They will stone Nazarine,' said Javad, then added, 'She deserves it. Amin says so.'

Madar's arm suddenly snapped back and she slapped Javad with her full force. Baba grabbed her wrist but did not raise his voice to her, instead leading her away from Javad and putting his arms around her shoulders as she sobbed.

Javad rubbed his reddened cheek but did not seem angry or chastened.

'You cannot go against the law of what is right,' Javad said and then walked out of the house, Baba hurrying after him to ensure he would do or say nothing rash. I looked at him as he went, this brother I no longer recognised, so full of hate and vengeance.

'He is young,' Baba said to Madar as he went, his face full of shame. 'He knows no better than the nonsense they fill his head with.'

There was the sound of digging. They were digging a

hole to place Nazarine in. They were going to bury her alive in the ground. We saw her blue burka flutter in the breeze as the men pulled her towards the hole. Two men stood either side of Masha, who was sobbing in disbelief and screaming for them to release her mother. A crowd of men gathered to watch, drawn by the spectacle.

The screams rose once more and we peered down to the square. There they had tied Masha's mother to a post hammered deep into the ground – she could not possibly escape. They told her she was free to go – we heard them mocking her – but of course she could not get out, she could not escape. There was to be no mercy. One of the men was reading out a series of charges and affronts to decency. They called her an adulterer and worse. Amin stood smirking beside the strangers. Tears ran down Masha's cheeks; I could see her held between two of the men. But her mother Nazarine, a young widow so fragile she could not call out, did not lower her eyes nor plead for mercy. She had done nothing wrong. It was these men who were in the wrong. It was they who should be judged, yet no one stopped them. I could not understand why no one intervened. It was as if the whole village had frozen under their spell. Madar pulled us all away. The men started to throw stones at Nazarine's head. We heard them shouting at Masha. She was ordered to throw stones, told that it was Allah's will, that otherwise she would carry the sins of her mother. Masha refused. The only sounds were her screams and the thud of the stones as they smacked the earth. Suddenly Masha broke free and ran to cover her mother, to try to protect her. I watched her sprint away from the men and run across the square. I saw her wrap her arms around Nazarine's head which was now dripping with blood, her eyes dulled. Masha's screams filled the air. Amin raised his arm. The others had momentarily stopped. I saw Amin reach up high, something glinting in his hand. A rock was hurled through the air, a large jagged one; it caught Masha on the back of her skull and she slumped down next to her mother. It happened quickly. The small crowd shrank back. Amin stood, a sick smile on his face tinged with a look of surprise.

Nothing now could be done to save either mother or daughter. The Taliban men, young yet already accustomed to such scenes, just stood and watched laughing, joking with one another, watching the villagers. No one moved forward. Then eventually the men took their leave, one slapping Amin on the shoulder before they climbed back into their pick-ups and drove off, shots ringing out into the air. Everyone stood in silence, in shock at what had come to pass.

Masha's mother was still tied to the post, her burka, soaked with blood, caught in the wind. Masha lay there in the dirt next to her, her headscarf loose round her shoulders, her arms still thrown around her mother.

In the house next door we heard the wails of the twins. I longed to go to Nas and Robina, to hold them. I knew my grandmother was with them. I knew they would not have seen this – she would not have let them – but they would have heard everything. I should not have seen but I had . . . Now I knew. I knew what this world was we were entering. Instead, I held on tight to Ara. She was silent, pale. She said nothing. I could see something had broken in her. She had lost her only friend. She had let go of hope. It seemed as if around us time had stopped, and all I could hear was the whoosh of blood in my ears.

I understood nothing. I could not imagine what Nazarine might have done, what crime might be so terrible as to deserve such a murderous death. Was it her beauty? Could they not bear her beauty? Her youth? Was it because she taught the younger girls secretly, quietly, when learning was banned? Was it because she did not believe in their world, their lies? Was it Amin? That she could not love Amin? That she had refused him? In my heart I knew this to be true.

My mother climbed down the steps to the square. She was the first there of the women; some of the men still stood around looking shameful, not knowing what to do. Madar went up to Nazarine and pulled at the rope to untie her body. I heard her call for help. No one would help her. Then Baba stepped forward and between them they laid the broken bodies out on the ground. My grandfather called on the others to help. Now people busied themselves; a cover was found to wrap up the bodies. One woman washed Masha's face. Blood trickled down her head where one of the stones had smashed her skull. Ara and I trembled as we stood by the door of the house, looking down. I felt Ara falling to the ground and she let out one cry, just one, before dragging herself back inside, where she sat hunched over next to Little Arsalan, watching him turn in circles on the dirt floor.

Part Three

East to West, West to East

Chapter 9

I have told this story of our life in the Hindu Kush to Napoleon a dozen times now. He looks at me with such sad eyes when I tell him. We talk often about war and the stupidity of men. We share our stories, Napoleon and I; late at night when everyone is asleep, he will let me come out and sit with him in the staff quarters, the little box room he calls home at the end of the carriage. This is where we play cards, *Durak* usually, and talk politics and life. He is better at cards than me and has had more practice, but sometimes he will let me win. Everyone sleeps. No one disturbs us. He does not think I am too young for such conversations on account of all I have seen. He does not talk down to me, he just listens, and sometimes, when he has had a few glasses of vodka, with that same sad look still in his eyes he will tell me his own story and how it is that he came to be *provodnik* on the Trans-Siberian Railway. His story too is complicated and he needs to tell it, to have someone listen. So on those nights I listen as best I can, I listen to the words and to what is between the words until I can see Napoleon as a young man or as a child and I can understand that he too has a past he prefers to keep hidden. This is what we do for each other, we hold on to each other's secrets. We listen.

'I was born in Siberia a long time ago in the winter, in the forests, the *taiga*,' he says. 'Can you believe this wrinkled old man was once a child?' he laughs.

He always starts his story in the same way. Then each time he tells it he adds more details; more memories float in, or some parts get left out – depending on how he is feeling. I have shared only part of my story with him – as much as I can for now, as much as my mind will let me. And so we talk to each other about these terrible memories in the hope that if we share our stories enough times they will cease to have a grip on us and we will be able to move on with the business of living.

'Where was it that you grew up?' I ask, even though I know the answer, having heard the story before several times over.

'It was one of Stalin's work camps, a place where they sent what they called "enemies of the state". Not a pleasant kind of place to be born. I was a strange, wild little child, half starved, half frozen to death. But I survived.' He laughs at this fact as if it still surprises and delights him. His eyes twinkle with warmth, the lines criss-crossing his face.

'They sent whole families. Just uprooted from their normal lives, given half an hour to throw some belongings together, then herded off in long trains; I often wonder if it's where I got my taste for train travel. My mother would have carried me in her belly on a journey like that.'

I cannot tell whether he is joking or not. Napoleon tends to joke a lot about his past.

'A sense of humour helps,' he says when I am feeling teary and exhausted. 'That and distance.'

'Where did the trains go?' I ask him.

'The trains . . . they were cattle trucks mainly, not like this – you know, no luxuries.' He looks around at the carriage, pointing at the polished samovar with pride. 'They were taken to the edges of the country, to Siberia, where they could cause no trouble, where the prisoners could be destroyed and forgotten about and no one would care. This one place where I was born was for felling trees – freezing cold forest work. People kept near to starving. It destroyed them, you know – you saw them just waste away. I was the only baby born there that survived. Can you imagine? A child in the middle of all that.' He sighs. 'It was no place for a childhood.'

Napoleon looks away as he tells his story.

I try to picture this grown man, with all his wrinkles and sun-damaged skin, as a newborn baby lashed to his mother in the snow and ice and wind, dumped unceremoniously into somewhere so remote and far from all of life. The forests flash by as we journey back past the lake and I wonder what he must feel as we travel through Siberia and how close, if at all, we pass to this place he speaks about.

'It killed my mother,' he says then shakes his head and is quiet for a long while. He drinks his vodka and fills the small glass once more.

'No, I did,' he says in the end without hesitation. 'It was my fault. Keeping me alive killed her. It was impossible, you see. My father offered to work twice as hard – oh, they laughed at that. He didn't want her to have to do this cutting, lugging, back-breaking work. They just roared with laughter. Didn't care that she was pregnant either. They just wished us dead.'

He hangs his head and stares at his half-empty vodka bottle.

'She was very pretty, my mother, twenty years old. My father was crazy about her. She thought she'd made a good match. What did she know?' He smiles, a sad sort of a smile.

'He was NKVD, one of Stalin's henchmen. He would have done some awful things.'

'But then why would they take him? If he was one of them?' I don't understand how you can be on the right side, or on the wrong side but at the right time, and still lose everything.

'Paranoia. Stalin had so many people killed. You couldn't find reason in the actions of such a madman. My father thought he would be safe, that he was on the inside. He was a fool.'

Napoleon looks at his cards and places them on the table. '*Durak*.'

I have not heard this part from him before, this NKVD business. I had thought his parents were troublemakers maybe, not this – not on the inside. Then I think of Javad, how quickly he became someone cold and cruel, and I know it can happen.

Napoleon shifts in his seat. He wipes his eyes.

'They'd only been married a year when they were taken away – dumped in a cattle truck. Horrific, that must have been, that train journey.' He shudders. 'No windows, no air, no food. And when they stopped they'd pull out the dead. At each station.'

I place my small hand on his hand as it trembles – whether it is the drink or the indignity of the memories I cannot tell. He shakes my hand off gently.

I think about all those frightened bodies squeezed in, locked in the high cars, with little idea of where they were going or what would await them. And I look around the carriage and feel, not for the first time, immense happiness at the space, the warmth, at being able to watch the landscape roll by in the dark. It makes me feel less trapped. I feel almost safe, or at least safer than I have in the years since the time that Omar disappeared and everything started going wrong.

'How did you, did they, survive?' I ask. Despite knowing, having heard the answer before, I know he needs to tell me once more.

Napoleon turns as if to look out of the window but I can see he is watching me in the reflection of the glass, checking that I am listening. I turn the playing cards over in my hands. He lowers his voice.

'She . . . she gave herself to the soldiers, the guards. They would give her food and let me play indoors for a while by the fire while they . . . My father couldn't stand it. He took his own life. They said it was an accident. It was no accident. None of it.' He cries a little, quickly wiping away the tears with the back of his hand and I just sit beside him.

'The others in the camp despised her. They would spit at her, at me.' Napoleon looks away, his gaze catching on the shadows of the pine trees as we travel through the forest. I realise that he must feel fear every time the train passes through the *taiga*; it must all come back to him. I try to imagine him as a little boy – like Little Arsalan at the mountain house – crawling around, not understanding.

'One of the guards took a real shine to her. He was a right bastard but she played along. Got him to take us away in the end. That saved my life, I'm sure of it. She was heartbroken, crying all the time over my father, over her life. But I remember her smiling too sometimes, holding me and rocking me to sleep. I remember that even though she must have been going crazy inside.'

I nod and pat his shoulder as I stand to leave. I don't know what else to do.

'Will you write that in your book?' he asks me.

He has encouraged me to write it all down, to make sense of things.

'It's a long journey,' he says, 'what else are you going to do?' He keeps me supplied with pens and notebooks that he picks up at stations along the way and lets me sit in empty carriages where I can write or read in peace.

I think of Napoleon, normally so cheerful, always smiling, running up and down the carriage or polishing the samovar, busy collecting tickets, chatting to the passengers. I think of this kind man with his twinkling eyes and open smile. Then I look at this same man, sitting here broken, crying into his vodka, unravelling at the edges, the past flooding him, and I realise I have got to keep it together. For my family, for me, for whatever comes next – I cannot let everything fall away.

I give Napoleon a hug, leaving him quiet with his drink, and I wander back to the compartment to sleep, climbing into the fold-down bed and pulling the covers up round me, quiet so as not to waken anyone. I know there is so much more to his story but tonight I am tired. I haven't got the energy to listen as he needs me to – to absorb someone else's sadness. Normally it would comfort me to be of help but tonight my own memories push in and Masha's screams echo in my ears. I see her and Nazarine, I see Javad laughing. Their faces start to blur together. I pray for sleep. I pray to forget.

In the night I dream about Ara. She is in front of me, shaking me awake. I am heavy with sleep and cannot wake up. There is desperation in her eyes. She is trying to tell me something but I cannot make out the words. She is trying to tell me where she is. I wake with a cold sweat coursing down my back and look around. Of course, she is not here. Of course, I am imagining it. How will I explain to Madar and Baba, how am I to tell them that Ara has gone? And then I realise she is gone already. There is nothing to tell. I sob for the first time in months. I let the tears fall away from me. I stuff my fist into my mouth so as not to waken others sleeping. Still the salty tears drop down my cheeks. 'It is not your fault,' I tell myself. But this is not true. It is my fault. It is all my fault and now it cannot be undone. I stay awake until the sun rises.

The train has stopped to take on provisions and change over carriages. We are travelling west once more. At Ulan-Ude we had hoped that Ara would rejoin the train, that there was a possibility she would have come to her senses. But she was not there and so the train travelled on. Now we have arrived in Irkutsk – which some have called the Paris of Siberia. I think of Ara and her desire to go to Paris. Maybe she is here, I reason. From the carriage I can see the busy platform. Napoleon has told me: thirty minutes, no more. I get up in a hurry, taking my papers and money with me, and slip down from the carriage to explore, to see how much I can discover before the train pulls out once more. The exhilaration as I step away from the train washes over me. I could begin again here. This could be it. I could just walk away. The freedom has me floating along, dizzy with anticipation. The sun beats down already slicing the day in two and I shade my eyes. I am not used to the steady ground underfoot and I sway a little to catch my balance, so used have I become to the constant movement of the train.

These chances to explore, to be on new ground, are rare. Often I have not wanted to step down for fear of being left behind, but how can you be left behind when you have no end destination? And so I practically skip out of Irkutsk station in search of . . . I don't know what I am in search of . . . peace; belonging, maybe. It is hard now, this caring for others. Belonging is difficult too. I try to shake myself out of my sadness.

I hurry up towards the bridge crossing the Angara River, across to the east of the city. I imagine I am a tourist – a recurring fantasy I have these days. I do the things tourists do in Irkutsk. I look at architecture. I stand on the bridge and look contemplative, wondering if someone passing by will take my photograph. Not intentionally but that when they get home and look at their pictures I'll be there on the edge of the frame, a girl standing looking out at the water. I make the shape of a frame with my fingers and thumbs, a viewfinder which I peer through for signs of the Decembrists – Napoleon has been telling me about them, well-educated souls exiled to the city long ago, bringing their knowledge and ideas with them, teaching the local people how to read. He can see me as a teacher, when I'm grown-up, he says.

'For now, just be you, Samar.'

I have forgotten how to live for the future. It is all I can do to be present in the moment, to not let the past suck me back in. I run through the streets – there is a church, over there a monument to the railway builders, here a post office. I would like to send a letter, a postcard, but who could I send it to?

I make my way back to the station and the train that is ready to leave with or without me. I need to get back on the train. I need to keep it together. Napoleon stands on the steps of the carriage, a worried look on his face until he spots me.

'Hurry, Samar!' he shouts and gestures frantically for me to jump on again for we are off once more.

Chapter 10

After the death of Nazarine things between Madar and Baba were better. They stopped arguing and would go for long walks in the mountains together like a young couple in love. It was as if they were scheming out their future together and with it, ours. Even Omar's recent disappearance couldn't overshadow the happiness bubbling up between them. Whatever had happened with Arsalan at the yellow house was forgotten, forgiven. It had been left in the past and Azita and Dil were a team once more. I did not know whether to be scared or happy with this new madness. I did not know how something so sad could make them feel so alive. I did not understand then how death could remind them how life was worth living. How could they plan for the future when the Taliban were creeping in everywhere, stealing every last hope?

Ara was broken. She sat and grieved for her beautiful friend Masha and refused to leave the cave house. Even Maman Bozorg couldn't coax her out. Ara became pale and skinny; she stopped eating, stopped sleeping. At night if I woke I would often find her sitting by the door, looking at Masha's house and silently crying.

Madar and Baba had taken the girls into their care. Who else would look out for them now? They had no family left. It was as if I had gained two new sisters. But the twins were still in shock and we no longer played as before. They would spend a lot of time just sitting quietly, letting Ara braid their hair or sing to them – quiet lullabies sung in hushed whispers under her breath, for even singing was forbidden. Or sometimes we would all gather round Madar, who would recite poems or share hopeful stories of other places and people, tell us about strange lands, of scientists and musicians and dancers, and our imaginations would soar with hers. This was something they could not take from us – the freedom to imagine, to create new worlds beyond this one.

The shadows would flicker on the walls of the cave.

'*Migozarad*, the tears will pass,' Maman Bozorg would say over and over to no one in particular while handing round steaming glasses of thick, sweet chai and placing her hand on Ara's shoulder to remind her that life went on even though her friend was gone.

A gaping wound had infected the village – which was now divided into those who felt the Taliban actions had been justified versus those who felt only guilt for their own inaction or worse complicity, horror that they could have allowed it to happen, that fear had taken hold of them. Shame distracted us all.

It was at this time that Madar fell pregnant with Sitara. While her pregnancy with Little Arsalan had been difficult and sorrowful, this seemed to be a more joyful one. Madar carried herself as if she was full of happiness. Baba became ever more attentive. And we began to prepare for this new addition to the family.

There were other celebrations too that year.

I turned eleven, high up in the mountains, and Madar suggested we hold my first ever birthday party. 'Why not?' she said. She told us of some American girls, family friends she had met in Kabul many years ago when she was a child – how they had invited her and Amira to a party and how they had all celebrated with a cake, candles and singing. This seemed incredibly exotic to me.

So we prepared a picnic, carried in blankets up the mountainside. Baba stuffed the transistor radio to the bottom of the bundle and we all climbed up beyond the village to find somewhere far away from prying eyes and ears, somewhere we could dance and sing and be free. Only Javad didn't join us, and Maman Bozorg – because she complained the climb would be too steep, but I did not believe this. Although she was old she was like a mountain goat – sure on her feet. I knew she was staying to keep an eye on Javad, who was not to be trusted. She was trying to make him see sense, to talk him out of the madness that had come over him. He was, I realised, her favourite and to see him so cold must have frightened her to the core. We left them behind, waving as we went. Javad just shrugged and headed indoors to his studies. It was another thing to mark up against us all. His constant judgement was growing hard to bear. It saddened me. Some things you have to let go. Once you surrender them, they lose their hold over you. This was how I was beginning to feel about Javad.

On the surface things had not improved. We still could not go to school. The new edicts and rules continued to come, spread from village to village, from the towns in the valley below – though it was impossible to tell which were rumours and which were true. Safer to follow them all just in case. They included no music, no dancing, no singing, no nail polish, no pork, no satellite dishes (chance would be a fine thing in the mountains), no cinema, no chess, no masks, no alcohol, no television, no statues, no computers, no sewing catalogues, no pictures, no firecrackers. We heard later that they had banned kites and this made me sad as I remembered climbing up onto the roof of the yellow house to watch the sky over Kabul fill with these colourful creations, soaring in the sky, tethered down below but free as they danced in the warm Kabul light.

But somehow, although the list of banned things, banned behaviours, grew longer and ever more ridiculous, somehow we found a way to live within these new restraints. We found ways around them. We found ways to be free.

As we all climbed away from the village, with the sun shining down on us, the view widening out before us, I felt carefree and happy.

If we had only had Omar with us, then the day would have been perfect. By now we no longer believed he would just come home but we had heard no news of his death and so we had to believe he was still alive. Madar and Baba spoke of him less to us now – at first we had all talked often of our brother as if that would bring him closer to us. That had stopped as the months had passed. The sadness was too great to let it surface and so we each carried him in our thoughts, silent and longing, wishing for his safe return. As I looked around at my family, I imagined Omar walking along with Baba Bozorg, laughing with Ara, carrying the food, Madar leaning on his arm. I found I could no longer quite picture his face, or imagine him taller, older now, and so I pushed the thoughts away.

We set up our makeshift camp high up by the juniper trees that cloaked the higher ridges. Baba swung Little Arsalan off his shoulders and plonked him down in the middle of the blankets where he started to open all the parcels of food Madar had so lovingly wrapped.

'Not the baby for much longer, eh?' Ara laughed, lifting Little Arsalan up and away from the food, spinning him round until he dropped once more onto the blankets calling out indignantly, 'I'm not a baby! Stop calling me that.'

And we all laughed as it was true. Little Arsalan was no longer so little and soon he would no longer be the baby of our family.

Madar took shade under the trees that clung to the dry earth. She was quite heavy now with the baby and she could no longer run so easily after Little Arsalan, who became more and more intrepid with the passing of days, seeking out new freedoms and dangers. Robina and Naseebah were with us too, a part of our family now, and the three of us younger girls took to singing – at first quietly, listening to our voices echo out over the mountains, then more loudly – urged on by Ara, who set the pace, guiding our song. Baba Bozorg, Madar and Baba looked on, cautious and wary at first, then gradually beginning to relax as they realised how far we were from the village below.

I had now spent half my life in the mountains and found it harder and harder to remember Kabul and the yellow house, especially as we never talked about it any more. Before, Madar would remind us all what it had been like. She would tell us about the plants, the flowers, the park. Tell us how we had been. Not now, though. That life was gone forever. Here we did not have much but what we had was shared and we had each other. Before, when Baba was working or studying or whatever it was he had dedicated his days to in Kabul, we had not felt so much like a family. Here, with our grandparents, and now with the addition of Nas and Robina, even without Omar (who we all mourned constantly and quietly to ourselves), we were family.

Madar had brought grapes and plums, shish kebabs, carrots, tomatoes, ashak dumplings, potato salad, large flat naan breads and my favourite *bichak* – a birthday feast. After much singing and dancing and running freely over the hillside, we all collapsed in a heap on the blankets and ate, giggling and laughing, dizzy from such freedom. Even Ara was laughing and smiling – something I could not remember seeing her do in such a long time.

Baba gestured at us for quiet, a look passing between him and Baba Bozorg.

He stood up, a glass of chai in one hand and, smiling at me and ruffling my hair, said, 'My dear Samar – you are such a serious child, always thinking, always watching. We see this, you know.'

Everyone laughed, watching me squirm, uncomfortable at being the centre of attention.

'One day you will grow up to be a fine doctor, or a scientist – or an engineer, maybe. Perhaps a teacher, eh? Or even a writer.'

I smiled for a second imagining these exotic possibilities and then clouded over thinking, never, they will never let me, not here.

Madar held out her hands to us all, pulling us close.

'We want to tell you all something. It cannot be shared with others. It is a secret.' Baba glanced at Madar in complicity as he spoke.

'You understand? All of you? You promise.'

It was not a question, more an order.

We pulled in closer, startled.

'When the baby comes and is strong enough . . .' he paused. 'Then we will be leaving. We will be starting a new life. Outside of Afghanistan.' He delivered this idea to me, to us all, like a present packaged in shiny paper, this perfect daydream to unwrap.

I did not know what to think. My mind was a haze. All I could see was my missing brother.

'But Omar, how will he know where to find us?' I blurted out, angry that they had chosen my special day to upend everything once more into uncertainty.

Baba frowned. 'Samar, your brother made his own choices.'

Madar, more gently, added, 'He will find us. When he is ready – he will join us. *Inshallah*.'

I realised I would never see my brother again. We would be gone and if he came back, how would he ever find us?

'And Baba Bozorg and Maman Bozorg?' Ara asked, her dark eyes moist in the heat.

'No.' Baba shook his head, looking at his father who lowered his eyes. 'They do not want to leave.'

'I don't want to leave!'

I screamed it at him and then I got up and ran off, scared by the ferocity within me. I ran higher towards the cliffs and crags above, out of the scrubland and away from the trees. I ran to try and dampen down the feelings that seemed to push my heart right out of my body. This was my country. This was my home. Where could we go? Where?

I scrambled up higher, loose rocks tumbling away from my heels until I took shelter against the caves near the top of the mountain. I sat in the cool shade looking down at my family all still on the blankets staring up at me. They looked tiny in the distance. I caught my breath and looked out over the mountaintops. All I could see was land and mountain peaks stretching into infinity. Is that where they were planning to take us? Somewhere there? I shook in horror, thinking of cousin Aatif who had disappeared years before.

'I won't go. I won't.'

I dug my heels in against the cool rock face and fought back tears.

It was then I heard something move behind me in the cave. Startled, I peered in. We all knew the stories of bears and fear plucked at my chest as I realised how long it would take me to scramble back down to the others. Then there was a cough – low, short but unmistakable. This was much worse. While a bear could tear me apart, a person spying on us, watching us dancing and singing and listening to the radio, such a person could destroy us all. Fear took hold and I did not know whether to go towards the sounds or to run. I could do neither, so I stood holding my breath. It came again, a low, muffled cough. I could hold back no longer and, picking up a stone, I threw it into the cave before me. It bounced off the wall. I picked up another, then a handful of small stones and launched them one after the other into the cave.

'Hey,' a male voice called out. 'Stop it.' His voice sounded broken, hoarse and rasping.

I stopped and waited. Below I could see Ara waving up at me, calling me back. Baba stood with his back to me, angry perhaps. It was impossible to tell from so far away.

'Hey, come here,' the voice said. The cough came again, louder this time.

I went in, knowing it was a stupid thing to do but curious nonetheless. Inside, my eyes had to adjust to the gloom of the cave. There was a smell of something rotten that made me want to gag. Then a flash of movement from one side. I moved forward slowly.

'Who are you?' I asked. 'What are you doing here?'

The man began to laugh, a wheezy uncomfortable laugh.

I kept walking towards the sound of his breathing until I bumped up against a body lying on the ground of the cave. The stench was much stronger now and I nearly turned and fled but a hand reached out and grabbed my ankle.

'I need help,' he said. My eyes were growing more used to the dim light inside the cave. I could see he was injured and wincing in pain. I relaxed a little, realising he could not have seen us dancing. I nodded even though he could not see me in the darkness.

'I can bring help,' I said, pulling away, but his hand held tight to my ankle.

'Who? No one can know I am here.'

His voice sounded feeble now, not that of a grown man. He was a boy, I guessed – seventeen or eighteen maybe, not much older than Omar. And for that I wanted to help him.

'My mother, she is just below, she is . . . was a doctor . . . she has studied . . . she . . . she can help you.' I was not sure of any of this but I said it and I meant it and that was enough for this stranger, who let go his grip.

'Wait here,' I said without thinking. After all, where could he go? He could not move. I calculated the minutes it would take me to scramble back down to find Madar. She will understand, she will help, I thought. At that moment I felt great pride in my mother and I forgot about arguing with my parents. I forgot about the threats to leave. My mind was focused on helping this stranger, this boy in the caves.

The others watched me sliding and flailing as I cartwheeled down the mountainside, hurrying towards them. I avoided Baba's curious gaze and instead went to Madar and pulled at her clothes, the words spilling out of me.

'In the cave . . . there's a boy . . . he's sick . . . we need to help him.'

I babbled at her, pulling all the while at her *chador*. She looked at me, confused, and then seeing the panic in my eyes rose to her feet, righting her scarf around her head. The others followed behind.

'No, wait,' gestured Baba to Ara and Baba Bozorg. 'Stay with the girls and Little Arsalan.'

They nodded in agreement and Baba, Madar and I climbed back up to the caves at the top, taking water with us and Baba's *patu* – its wool the colour of mud.

It did not take us long – ten, fifteen minutes, maybe less – but it felt like an eternity, as Madar stopped along the way to rest and catch her breath. I showed them the mouth of the cave and pointed inside. Madar went in first, unafraid. Baba cast a glance around to make sure this was not a trap; that we were not in any danger. The boy was still there. He grimaced in pain. The smell oozed up and I covered my mouth and nose with my scarf. Baba told me to lift his feet and we dragged him out to the mouth of the cave so that Madar could him see properly. He was shaking with shock and I turned from him as I saw his leg had been eaten away with huge lumps of flesh pulling away from the bone. His skin was dry, covered in painful sores and welts. He was too weak to even cry out in pain as we pulled him across the stones and earth. He had been badly hurt and his leg ripped on wire or something designed to injure and maim.

Madar was talking to him in a low, soothing voice. She tore strips off her *chador* and having washed out his wounds, bound them tightly. She gave him sips of the water, no more.

'He is in shock,' she whispered to Baba.

'Will he . . .?' Baba asked her, his thought unfinished. She shook her head.

'But if we can get him to the village . . .?' He was still hopeful.

Madar looked at the boy once more and shrugged. She could do no more for him. We were too late.

I felt sick and moved out of the cave to take in deep gulps of air. She could not save him. I had been so sure she could help him. I believed she would save him. I did not know what to think.

Baba was sitting holding the boy's hand when I looked back at them. He was asking the boy many questions like who was he, who were his family, where were they, what was he doing up here, were there others like him, did he know one like him called Omar? The questions fell like soft rain on the dying boy. He was with the Northern Alliance – with Massoud's men. That much Baba gathered.

I had heard others speak about this Massoud as if he were some great warrior, some great hero – the Lion of Panjshir. Someone ready to fight the Taliban. Is that where Omar had gone? Was he too lying somewhere in the dust, bleeding to death? The thought sucked the air out of my lungs.

Madar was doing what she could. Her hands shook. I had never seen her shake like that before. I knew she was thinking of Omar or of this boy's mother. Perhaps that was it: somewhere down in the valley he had a family. It hurt me to think of it. It hurt me that we could do so little for him. When she had done all she could, she sat and prayed. I bowed my head and I prayed too. I did not know what else to do.

The sun was getting low. If we did not start off soon we would be lost out there on the mountainside for the night. Baba signalled to Madar to go. He pushed me with her.

'I will stay,' he said.

We went, reluctant, with backwards glances, sliding back down the steep incline to Ara and the others. Madar leant on me from time to time to avoid slipping and damaging the baby. I wondered, would she have done more for him if she hadn't been pregnant? I pushed the thought away. Below when we reached them once more, Little Arsalan clung to Madar's ripped *chador* and squealed in delight to see her again. Baba Bozorg raised an eyebrow but asked us nothing. He did not want to frighten Nas and Robina. They had seen enough loss and death. They looked at me, questioning, then chastened by Madar's expression they helped Ara pack up without saying a word. We all made our way back down to the village in silence, no longer joyful and singing. Dusk chased us down the mountain paths until we reached the cave house once more, the celebrations over.

When Baba returned in the morning, his *patu* soaked in blood, he looked ashen and frozen to the bone. Madar wrapped her arms around him and I saw him cry like a child in her embrace. It was the first time I had seen my father cry and I knew the boy was dead.

That was my eleventh birthday.

Chapter 12

The days in the mountains passed, seasons shifted and soon it was time for the baby's arrival. Madar took to cleaning the cave house with a vengeance. We were all pulled into the swirl of activity and preparation with her. Ara and I helped by beating the rugs outside, watching the dust fly through the air, washing clothes, cleaning, more washing, clearing – making space as best we could. Grandfather and Baba had knocked through a passageway into the house next door, which had lain empty since the stonings. We would often still choose to all huddle together, none of us comfortable to sit in Masha's old home except for Javad, who didn't seem to care and liked to be apart from us when he could. He spent less and less time with the family and more time with the mullah who now taught the boys. Javad was eager to be away from Baba's disapproval.

Until finally one day Javad was no longer with us at all. He had gone to study at one of the *madrasas* near the border. Baba and he had fought bitterly but in the end it was Madar who said, 'Let him go. Let him see for himself what fools they are.'

When he left, she watched him disappear down the mountain track in an open pick-up truck driven by three Taliban, only a few years older than him, until he became a dot in the distance, leaving her with a look of disbelief and horror on her face. She had lost two sons to different worlds. Her hand balanced on her growing stomach, Madar turned and went back inside.

When Javad left I was glad to see him go, but the thought that I could wish him gone so easily tortured me. True, we had often bickered but he was a part of me, my life. Now . . . it had become impossible with him glaring at us all the time, criticising, lecturing. Only a couple of years older than me but repeating the ideas of men he admired, not understanding what he was saying. Baba shook his head in sorrow. Neither Omar nor Javad would learn from his mistakes.

In the evenings, we would sit by the fire and Madar would read from the *Book of Kings* and tell us stories – stories for the baby, she called them – of princes, princesses, spirits and strange happenings, and we would gather at her feet to listen to her spin magic in the night air.

'The *Shahnameh*, these stories hold the secrets of man's heart,' she would tell us. 'All his greed, his heroism, his hopes.' She would recite the story of Father Time, the sadness of death and loss, yet how the sun would nonetheless rise once more. Her voice would rise and fall, sad and happy all at once, the world cupped in her words, and I would sit enthralled, imagining different times, different stories to my own.

These were my happiest moments. I remember them now and it is like watching someone else sitting by the low light from the kerosene-lamp, the flames from the fire dancing in the night sky, the girl with her head cocked to one side, leaning on Nas's shoulder, feeling the beauty in her mother's voice and the images she conjured at the cave house.

Looking back I do not know who that girl is any more.

The baby came in the night. Madar's breath was thick, a grunting animal sound muffled in the dark, Baba holding on to her. Maman Bozorg was shaking me awake and sending me to fetch help in the village. Then running off again to fetch water. The fire was stoked and we watched in awe and horror as this new life pushed and howled its way into the world. When she finally came, she was wrapped in the warmed cloth and passed to Madar and Baba, whose eyes shone with such happiness and hope.

'Sitara,' Madar called to the mewling bundle in her arms. 'Sitara.'

'Our little star Sitara,' Baba agreed.

We had a new sister. The village fell to celebrating with us. For forty days there would be celebrations, shots rang out and echoed through the valley. A stream of visitors came to coo over the baby, to bring food, to offer help. Our family seemed to expand to encompass everyone on the mountainside. There could be no music or singing or dance but there was laughter and joy to welcome this new addition into their midst.

Sitara's birth was bittersweet for me. On the one hand I loved this dark-eyed little baby who howled and giggled and held you in her gaze so steady and sure. But then, each day she grew stronger, each day Madar recovered her strength, I knew would bring us closer to leaving. Since that day of the picnic, Baba had said nothing more, not even about my outburst, but it was understood that the plan was decided upon. I began to see my parents' happiness differently. They were happy because we would be leaving. They had never committed to this life with our grandparents. This had always been just a stopping place.

I had become obsessed by news of the resistance. I would try to gather any information I could glean from conversations at the well, in the square, in the market. Listening, I was always listening. I would overhear snatches of conversation between Baba and Baba Bozorg late at night. The men were in the hills . . . they were pushing back the Taliban on several fronts. The world was waking up to our problems.

Baba Bozorg would share what he knew with me, sensing my interest. Knowing it all led back to Omar, he tried to reassure me with heroic tales and optimism.

At night I would dream about Omar. I would picture him deep in the mountains surrounded by other boys and men like him: all exhausted from the fighting, their shoulders weighed down from the constant rifle-carrying. This is what I imagined. I would hear him call out to me, 'Samar!' It was as if he were so close I could just reach out and touch him. But he was not close at all and when I would wake, his voice, his image would disappear. I do not know if Ara or Madar or Baba shared these dreams; if we were all lying there at night talking in the shadows to Omar, whose absence grew like an ache in my heart.

In the summer Javad came back from the *madrasa*. He was dressed differently and now carried himself in a purposeful way but he was still a little boy trying on a man's clothes. He congratulated Madar on Sitara and he would sit on the floor and play a while with her and Little Arsalan, who took to clinging to this returned brother's legs. In those moments I could forgive Javad the hatred in his voice when Masha was killed, forgive him his threats and chiding. I could remember sitting with him in Kabul watching kites dance. In those moments Javad was still my brother, returned.

But he was also a spy. Baba made this clear to us all. Javad was not to be trusted. You could tell it hurt his heart to say this to us. And so we played a double life, never mentioning the plans to leave in front of our brother.

'You cannot tell him,' Baba said.

We did not need to ask why. By now Robina and Nas were a part of our family. We played together, shared together, fought together.

'Will they come with us?' I asked Madar, who nodded quietly.

'We won't leave them behind,' she said and I believed her. I always believed her. Why shouldn't I?

Chapter 13

The train carries on towards Tayshet then on to Krasnoyarsk. We have left behind the 'Blue Eye of Siberia', Lake Baikal, and Irkutsk (and no, I could not find Ara there). The train has been passing through beautiful countryside – the tall hills and cliffs by the Yenisey River eliciting a series of furious camera clicks from the passengers who hang out of the window.

Baba has gone for his daily walk on the train. Javad has gone along with him. Madar is talking to a couple sitting further down the carriage. She looks so graceful, the sun glinting off her long dark hair. She seems so self-possessed, so regal. I watch her from behind the pages of my book as she gestures and laughs and I can see how she enchants these travellers, how exotic she must seem to them with their drab European jeans and T-shirts. They cannot see how they appear to us, strange too with their pale freckles and sunburnt skin and their noisy voices and their sense of entitlement, believing that the world is theirs to travel through, to explore. They are free to go where they please. They are not running. When this journey ends in Moscow, they will travel on to their next destination then home, with photographs and stories of their great adventure. No worries for them, no decision to make about where to go, where to live. Yet I sit here thinking, where will take us in? How will we begin again?

As I watch Madar, her fine-boned hands circling in the air, her easy smile and the way she shines her full gaze on these tourists, I realise I do not know my mother very well. I know what she has told me, what she has chosen to share, but there is much left unsaid. She is a person other to me. Is that how Baba sees her, how Arsalan saw her? I stumble over this thought. More and more I wonder about Arsalan and his role in all our lives. I remember his presence at the yellow house. His gaze as it followed Madar constantly. The way they would speak together. I wonder why he wanted to help us so much. I know what we were told, about his debt to Baba, how Baba had saved him. And yet . . . there must be some other reason. I am sure of it. What were we to him? I have no answers, only questions and doubts.

Some people believe you are born into your family and then you are stuck with them – for good or bad. Others make their family as they go. Napoleon is like this, adopting us, taking me under his care. Is that what we were to Arsalan? An adopted family he couldn't have for himself? I watch Madar and it is as if some larger part of who she is remains hidden to me and to everyone else.

Still, it comforts me to see her here, especially now as memories come flooding back; it helps me to feel the rocking of the train and to picture Madar talking with these strangers, gathering up information about the life we are about to live, abroad somewhere new, somewhere that will take us. She is gathering up friends along the way to help us. This she has taught me: to know how to seek help, to know how to take it.

I am reading Tolstoy again. Anna has just told her husband Alexei Alexandrovich that she is in love with Vronsky, and that their life together is over; it is all a lie and she cannot live a lie any longer. I am engrossed as they pull apart their life together over one conversation, one set of unshakable truths that can never be taken back.

When I pause and look up again, Madar is not there. Just the couple remain, staring out of the window at the hills as we pass by. I look around for Madar. She is gone. The woman raises her arm and smiles at me. I wave back and return to my book. Even though I know what will happen, even though I have read it a million times, I discover something unexpected there every time.

I keep going, writing it all down with Napoleon's unfailing enthusiasm and blessing for the project. 'Tell your story, Samar,' he smiles at me in passing. He brings me fresh pens and more paper every couple of days. It is he who gives me the encyclopaedia, an old and well-thumbed edition, a little outdated now. Still, he has busied himself with reading it on the long journeys and is now passing it along to me. I do not know how to thank him. It is a long time since I have had such kindness from anyone without expectation. He shrugs it off.

'Just keep writing,' he laughs.

We don't talk much about what I write; it is enough that I do write. I tell him the parts I can, the parts I need to say out loud.

I can hear Little Arsalan and Sitara in our compartment. They are fighting over the radio – twisting the dials this way and that. Soon Madar will put an end to it, pull them apart, wrap them in love and admonishment in equal parts. Baba and Javad return bringing cups of warm chai from the samovar. The noise fades and I return to my scribbling, the thoughts coming faster now since Ara disappeared.

Writing it down helps me to hold on to the past, to make sense of it. Although some things have no sense to them at all. There can be no reason, no justification, no explanation. These things must just be borne.

Chapter 14

In the cave house preparations were underway for the 'great escape', as Ara jokingly called it. I could tell from her eyes she was ready to leave the mountains. To find a new home. This had never been home to her. She had watched us all as an outsider – watching her world shrink and grow smaller, fearful of what lay ahead. She had been ready to leave for a long time.

I still struggled to believe we would leave behind Baba Bozorg and Maman Bozorg. After all those years apart, to have finally made a family with them, to have been accepted by the rest of the villagers, even for Baba's Communist dalliances to have been diplomatically forgotten, and now we would start running again.

Madar seemed happier as each day passed. Sitara was growing into a happy, strong child. Baba seemed anxious – worried about leaving his parents once more. He would sit outside the house with Baba Bozorg talking quietly late into the night. They did not want us to go but they would not stop us.

Madar tried to reassure me.

'You will have Robina and Nas with you,' she would say as if by way of consolation, and while it was true that having these two friends cheered me on, I would always be on the outside.

'If Omar comes back, your grandfather will know where we have gone,' Baba said to me one evening.

It came out of nowhere and surprised me that he had not forgotten. I shrugged my shoulders, unsure what to reply. But I knew then that it was final, that we would soon be gone and that this mountain life was over. I was growing up. Things would have to change. I could see this in Madar's eyes as she watched Ara and me anxiously, and I knew it to be true. How could I hope to become a doctor, a teacher, an engineer, or anything else here? What kind of future would we have? Madar had taught Ara and me all that she knew. We needed change whether we wished for it or not. And she was anxious over Little Arsalan, keeping him away from the school, fearful of what he would learn there, frightened that the Taliban would steal him away as they had Javad.

This was the only sticking point between my parents in their discussions and the reason for our delay – Javad. Madar was of the view that we should take him with us, that eventually he would come to his senses and that we had to get him away from the poison of these men. Baba would let her speak, would listen as he always did, but then would shake his head.

'We cannot take him against his will. He would betray us before we made it out of the country. You must see that. He is lost to us.'

She could not believe this to be true and so a stalemate ensued, with Madar holding out for signs of change from Javad. They never came.

And yet it was Javad in the end who saved me.

A second Taliban visit was planned to the village. It had been put off several times due to the heavy rains as winter thawed but now the Taliban were soon to arrive. People became nervous again, remembering Masha, Nazarine and the last official visit. Whatever it was that they wanted, it could bring no good. The elders gathered to discuss how to handle things. The old mullah sat listening. Javad had stayed close to the conversations, following it all with excitement.

The twins grew quiet and fearful. Ara too began to cry and shake uncontrollably at the slightest mention of the impending visit. Only Baba Bozorg and Maman Bozorg seemed unmoved.

'*Een ham migozarad*,' Baba Bozorg would say, 'this too will pass,' his face lined with many years of the sun's warmth and the wind that gusted over the Hindu Kush.

'They can't come,' said Ara. 'We can't let them. Do something, Baba *jan*,' she implored.

I looked at Baba, who sat, his forehead furrowed, gazing out at the valley's gathering storm clouds. If he had heard Ara's plea he did not acknowledge it. Madar was fussing over Sitara, tickling her under the chin and watching a wide smile break over and over as the baby giggled, unaware of what was below in the valley, coming ever closer.

'Of course our brothers will come and we will welcome them,' said Javad, throwing down a challenge to the rest of us.

Madar moved away from her son, fearful perhaps of what she would say or do. I watched as Maman Bozorg looked at Javad with such sadness. He was becoming a stranger even to her who had tried so hard to hold on to the kind, joyous grandson he had once been. That was long ago now, when we had first arrived in the mountains and when the Taliban had been no more than a distant rumour.

We heard a low rumble across the valley. The sky had darkened and the storm clouds chased the horizon.

'There will be no welcome,' I said, my voice trembling as I stared at Javad. 'Look what they did . . . have you forgotten Masha? Nazarine? Have you forgotten what happened?' I shouted at him.

Javad looked taken aback, not used to me rounding on him with such ferocity. Ara was crying and went to Madar who handed Sitara to her to hold. Then Madar came towards Javad and me, ready to intervene yet saying nothing, just watching as her family split apart.

'You should be ashamed,' I tell him.

'Samar!' Baba called out sharply. Madar moved towards me with her arms outstretched.

'Samar,' she called me back to her. But I wouldn't go to either of them. I would not back down. Ara had moved outside with Sitara. Javad stared at me but it was as if he was looking right through me, as if I was no longer there.

'You can't stop them,' he said, 'but you will learn.'

Madar cried out in horror.

Thunder rumbled across the valley and below the villagers in the square started hurrying back inside their homes.

We stood at the mouth of the cave house looking out at the damp valley, our mood as dark and sodden as the clouds overhead. I wrapped Omar's abandoned *patu* round my shoulders.

'Now you will see,' Javad taunted us, a gleeful smile playing around his lips. 'Now you will all see.'

Below, a small convoy of vehicles was winding its way up the steep mountain road, the wheels scattering loose rocks that bounced down the mountainside as the pick-up trucks came nearer, their flags whipped by the wind. Down there in the valley everything looked so far away.

'Stop it!' I screamed at Javad, lashing out at him, wanting to swipe the smug smile off his face, remembering Masha's mother, remembering her screams and the look on her face when they took her down. I swore not to be afraid any more.

'You know nothing,' I shouted at him. 'You're just empty. You say what they tell you to say, repeat words they give you. You cannot even think for yourself.'

In that moment I despised Javad and saw only weakness in my parents, who stood there, letting him spread hate and fear as they watched and waited for the right moment to leave him behind, all the while saying nothing, letting him believe he was right. I looked at them all, disbelieving. 'Stop it!' I cried once more at Javad, at all of them. Madar's eyes pleaded with me to be quiet, to say nothing more.

'You can't stop it. No one can,' he said. At that something broke inside me and I found myself running from him, from all of them, climbing up the mossy mountain paths behind the cave house and away over the bare hills towards the pines on the higher reaches. Let them come, they won't find me when they do, I thought, and I raced on, stumbling over the rocks, startling the goats and sheep dotted about the mountainside, letting my anger fly out in all directions.

I could hear Ara calling out after me telling me to come back, and then she was climbing too, still carrying Sitara who was clinging on to her side. Her voice was tossed about in the wind, her words lost to me. I kept going, climbing higher, moving away now from the village. I ignored the dark clouds. I knew where I was going, back to the cave and the dead boy soldier we had failed. I was going to find the Northern Alliance, the fighters, to join them, to find Omar. In truth I didn't know what I was doing but I knew I was not going back, that Javad could not be right. They had to be stopped. This was my home and I was no longer afraid. No one would take it from me – not Javad, not the Taliban, not Madar and Baba with their dreams of starting over. I would be free. I would find Omar. I would stay here in the mountains. It would all be okay.

I said these words over and over as I climbed, sweat dripping down my back, shielding my face from the sun that now broke through the clouds as they raced away, taking the threatened storm with them. Off in the distance I could hear a series of intermittent rumbles echoing round the valley. The storm would pass us by after all – we would be spared, I thought. The muddy earth was starting to cake over. Days of heavy spring rains had made the earth squelch and then crack underfoot. I slipped and slid away from the village, the mud clinging to my clothes, tingeing them a reddish brown, seeping into my sandals.

As I looked back I could just make out Ara as she struggled with Sitara, but she would not give up; her shouts still came, though distant now. Why could she not just let me go? I clambered on up higher.

I had almost made it back to the highest caves now. The world looked so different from up here. Only goats and eagles, vultures, the red of the rock underfoot, the air so clear and the view . . . one amazing unbroken horizon. Hauling myself up over the lip of the last of the overhanging cliff edges, I made it to the mouth of the cave. Of course the boy was gone now, buried by Baba long ago, but I lowered my head and prayed for him that he had found some peace. I scanned the valley, seeking out the village far below and the twisting road that led up to it. Somewhere down there the Taliban were coming ever closer, bringing their hatred and fear. They cannot touch me now, not here, I thought. And so I cursed them: for banning me from learning, for splitting my family apart, for making Omar leave, for turning Javad against us, for destroying Masha and Nazarine. I cursed them for the fear they brought to everything they touched.

I looked out over the valley, which had grown silent. The birds had stopped singing and then, with startled cries, they flew in all directions. The earth began slowly shifting beneath me and I lost my balance, righting myself, leaning against the cave wall. At first there was a small shudder, then another stronger one. Small stones started to roll down the hillside. I heard a low rumble, no longer that of the storm, but coming from the belly of the earth. It grew louder until all I could hear was a torrent of rolling, crashing stone. The mountains were moving.

Down in the valley I saw the cliff face above the village start to break away and then huge drifts of rock and earth collapsed and a slurry of mud raced down towards the village. I called out but of course they could not hear me. I couldn't outrun the deluge, I couldn't warn them and the earth trembled and cracked between my feet. I held on to the rock face. Small stones rained down and hit me. Deep cracks formed in the cave walls behind me. I skidded back down, rolling, falling. Below I could make out Ara and Sitara, who had still been chasing after me. They had stopped now halfway up the mountainside opposite the village on the far gully. Ara had collapsed to the ground and was cradling Sitara in her arms, trying to protect her, watching in horror as the village was swept away by waves of earth.

'Madar!' I cried. I screamed her name over and over and she was all I could see, then Baba and Maman Bozorg and Baba Bozorg's faces, then Little Arsalan and Javad. I pictured Omar, but he was not there. Panic welled up inside me.

I thought of the twins, so unlike each other yet almost one and the same now – why were they not with Ara? I tried to think: where are they all? Will they be safe? Please, Allah, let them be safe. I will go anywhere, do anything, just let them be safe, please . . . please . . . Another low rumble and a crack and another wall of mud swept down, breaking away from the ridge above the village, clouds of dust and crushed rock rising. I put my hand over my mouth but the scream didn't come. There was nothing left – the whole village was submerged. I ran back down to Ara. The tremors continued, still rippling through the valley, smaller now. I fell and cut my legs, my arms, my face. I pulled myself up and ran again, almost rolling down the mountainside, willing myself back to them.

Ara stood back up in shock, her hands over Sitara's eyes. Even though Sitara was too young to understand what was happening, she still tried to protect her. I grabbed hold of Ara and shook her.

'Come on,' I cried, half pushing her down the mountainside. It was as if she had frozen there.

'We have to go.' I pulled at her. 'Ara . . . they are down there, we have to help them.'

She followed me down in a daze.

When we got there the cave house was gone, everything was gone. Nothing felt safe underfoot. Nothing looked the same. The earth was still sliding, settling. We could see a few of the villagers – those that by some similar miracle had also escaped – standing staring, digging, pulling at the rocks. I hunted for any sign of Madar or Baba. I screamed out their names. This screaming grew and grew until I did not recognise it as my own. I clambered on the rocks, trying to see where the house would be underneath all of this. It was impossible to tell.

A scrap of yellow fabric poked up between the rocks. Could it be Madar? Is that what she was wearing this morning? I wondered. I cursed myself for not paying more attention, for not knowing. I climbed over to it and started pulling, screaming all the while. The rocks were heavy. I couldn't move them alone. I called to Ara for help and together we pushed as best we could at the rubble, trying to pull clear the rocks. Was it Madar? I could not look, I was afraid to look. But it was not her. It was someone else's mother, a woman who had lived a little further down in one of the mud houses by the square. Sitara was still clinging on to Ara's hip; she started to cry.

We were choking, covered in mud and dust. No one could help us find them. I gazed blankly at the other survivors. Everyone was in shock. A man sat on a broken piece of wall, now just rubble, and sobbed.

I cried out, 'Madar . . . Madar!'

Nothing.

Ara stared through me. Sitara howled into the dust. The earth still trembled underfoot. We were alone and Madar could not hear us.

Part Four

Migozarad! This too shall pass.

Chapter 15

I write this and flip the notepad closed. It is dusk and we are close to Tomsk. Napoleon brings me tea, steaming from the samovar, placing it on the table next to me. I nod in thanks, barely aware he is beside me. The train is quiet now, everyone settling into their narrow fold-down beds for the night. I am shaking. Napoleon puts his hand on my shoulder but I hardly notice it there. In my mind I am still in the mountains.

As I look at the words on the page once more, there can be no turning back.

I look to the carriage where I had pictured Little Arsalan and Sitara squabbling earlier, to where Baba and Javad had passed by me laughing, carrying glasses of warm tea, only moments before. I look to where I had pictured Madar sitting talking to fellow travellers and I feel empty now, like I have let go of them. I can no longer picture my family beside me but I am not yet ready to say goodbye to them. They have carried me this far.

Yet they are no longer here.

'Stay with me!' I call out, my voice loud in the empty carriage. 'Stay,' I plead. I need them with me for us to begin again – somewhere new, somewhere safe.

I am not ready to make this journey on my own.

'I'll stay, Samar.' I glance up and Napoleon is still here, watching me, as he says to me: 'Write it down, write it all down.'

And so I open my notepad once more and I continue to write, to get it all down on paper. I cannot tell whether I am trying to expel the memories, to cast them from me, or to trap them between the pages.

Chapter 16

Ara and I held the silence taut between us, afraid to break it, fearful of the truth, unable to say, 'They are gone.' We looked at each other. Sitara's cries were becoming ever more plaintive. We were all covered in dust from the earthquake and the digging, our nails muddy with earth.

'Ara!' a woman called out. It was Jahedah, a solitary woman disliked by most of the villagers. It was said she was cursed so she lived on the edge of the village far from everyone. Like us she had been spared. We recognised her by a limp that she tried to hide by walking slowly, shuffling along. She gestured to us to follow her and she took us away from what had once been the village, clambering over rock, boulders, crumbled walls. We navigated our way carefully around the destroyed remnants of what had been our home. There was no sign of life. Nothing. It was as if the earth had swallowed them whole.

Jahedah took us to her mud house away from the destruction. She lived on the far side of the grove of poplar trees the old man had planted. The trees were uprooted, their trunks smashed by the force of the landslide. I could not see the old man amongst the survivors. I hoped he had been far away down in the valley – that he would not see what had become of his work. Cracks fissured the mud walls of Jahedah's home but it still stood. Ara looked uncertain, unwilling to be buried in mud should another tremor hit the valley. But Jahedah, more confident with us now, offered her water for Sitara. We all drank, and stepped momentarily out of the glare of the sun, grateful to be shown care. She could see we were in shock too. She had no family left of her own, having lost them all to freezing mountain winters and weak constitutions, and as she had been so roundly disliked by the villagers she had had no one to lose in the earthquake. This gave her an air of invincibility. She mothered us, fussing round Sitara, who still clung to Ara, unwilling to let go. She could see that we were struggling to make sense of our loss and failing.

There was a glint in Jahedah's eyes that made me uneasy. I tugged at Ara's sleeve, saying we should go. Ara looked at me, eyes flashing, as I rejected Jahedah's hospitality. Then Ara could see the way I was silently pleading with her and we gave our thanks and left. Jahedah was staring at Sitara, holding out her arms to her. We backed away and then once outside again we ran off. We would not be separated and we would not lose Sitara to a cursed crazy woman. There was still hope that we would find Madar or Baba or Javad alive, or Little Arsalan – my heart tightened as I could not bear to think of them all, of my grandfather and Maman Bozorg lying buried under all that mud and rock and dust. The fear they must have felt when the land collapsed. Would they have had time to react, to know even? Would they have seen it coming down the mountainside?

They would have had no time to escape. I knew this and yet I hoped.

I remembered how the wall of mud had just broken away and swept down towards the village. I saw it over and over in my mind. Hope and sickness rose together in my throat. Ara was talking to one of the men who was standing gesturing down to the valley. It was Najib, our old teacher.

'Help will come,' he said to us, uncertain. What else could he say, what else could we all believe?

We had lost everything. Only a few hours earlier I had been ready to leave forever, to go off in search of Omar, to leave everyone behind, and then this. What had I done? I could hardly look at Ara. Sitara was just a little bundle of red mud and dust in her arms. We looked around at what the village had become. Where should we start? Where would they be underneath all this?

My throat burned; my legs felt weak and my forehead clammy. I felt myself falling away, collapsing to the ground until Ara was there, slapping my cheeks, calling, 'Samar, Samar!' She was pulling me up. Najib sat behind me, propping up my back to steady me.

'It's okay, Samar.'

Their worried faces peered into mine. I wanted the darkness to swallow me up. My eyes rolled back.

'Samar! No!' Ara held me so that I could feel her heart beating. So that I could know we were alive. We sat still together for a long time until I could breathe again, until my heartbeat steadied and matched hers.

Below, the cave houses had slid far down the mountainside, knocked out of the way and pulled along by the torrent of mud and rock. My family was gone. My grandparents' home. All our belongings. Gone. Everything gone. I had nothing, only what I was wearing, old clothes belonging to Javad and Omar's *patu* wrapped round my shoulders.

I knelt forward in the earth, my nails scratching at the dirt. I did not know what I was looking for. I opened my mouth but no sound came. I pushed a handful of the soil into my open mouth and tasted it there, heavy on my tongue. Ara held on to me. Sitara reached down to me.

I was not alone.

Chapter 17

I pause from writing and look out of the window of the train. The carriage has become noisier, full of people drinking and talking, striking up new friendships and journey friends. The air is warm and muggy as the heating blasts out from the sides of the carriage by the seats. I find I can tune out the voices and laughter of my fellow passengers. When I go back in my memories to the earthquake and all that followed, it is as if I am there once more. I let go of this world and return to the mountains. My world, the world that I knew, ended that day and I feel as if I am forever stuck there, watching and waiting for a sign, something to tell me it will all be okay, it can all be erased. If I tear the page out of my notebook, will that undo it? I press my hands to my eyes, cupping my lids with my palms.

Outside, the evening light is a warm golden colour, bouncing off the sea of grassland as we pass by. The carriage lights come on. I become conscious of other people's eyes on me, watching me as I sit here alone writing. So I am glad when Napoleon passes down the corridor and nods at me.

'Here, Samar.' He passes me a bowl of steaming broth. 'You can't forget to eat, girl.' He gives me a look, disapproving and affectionate at the same time. His shirtsleeves are frayed and worn at the cuffs. I notice this and the way he taps his fingers on the table. It seems to help him think through his thoughts, underline them in his mind. I gesture to the seat beside me and he sits down once more.

'Can't stop long,' he says.

When the distances between stops are endless then he can sit and talk, sometimes for hours at a time, especially late in the evening when it's hard to make him stop talking. For now, the train stops here and there, picking up provisions and passengers. He sees the pages filled with writing in my notebook and nods approvingly.

'Keeping busy,' he says.

I nod back. It is good to have someone watch over me. Someone to confide in. Someone who trusts me with their secrets. I am wary of the other travellers, their happy tourist faces, their intrusive curiosity. Napoleon is different. He has become family. Almost.

Napoleon has told me more about his own childhood, about the camp guard who took his mother in so that he could have her to himself and beat her with an iron bar and no one would know or care. He describes this man to me with such quiet hatred.

'An utter bastard,' he says, 'and he used to love making me watch, always wanted me to see him hurting her . . . I'd be closing my eyes and shouting at him to stop and he'd say, "Watch this, boy – watch or else she'll really get it." I'll never forget the shame in her eyes,' he goes on, 'that she let him do that to her in front of me, that she let him beat her like that. She was broken by then, her spirit, her body, her mind. That's what he thought. Then one day, he'd had a skinful to drink and was throwing his weight around, slamming her into the wall, punching her on the head, and then I couldn't take it any more and I . . . grabbed what was next to me, the iron bar that he'd let go of so he could punch her better, and I hit him across the back at first – I was only seven at the time, no strength in my arms, just a lot of hate in my heart. Well, he didn't care for that and he swung round with it and came straight at me, lungeing and swinging, and I was running away from him, hiding under the table legs, screaming at him to stop. He caught hold of me and I remember his fist drawing back, the stink of drink on his breath, darkness in his eyes and then his fist smacking into the side of my head. All I could see was my mother standing behind him, holding his gun, her hands steady, and she shot him in the back. Put a hole right through him. I passed out after that.'

'Then what?' I lean forward.

'Well, when I came to we were in the back of a wagon heading to the border. All that time she'd been planning, you see . . .' He looks out of the window at the landscape blurring past.

'She'd been hiding away money, enduring beating after beating, so we could get away from him. In the end we just left. She wasn't going to rot for that bastard. We must have looked a right pair. Though so many people drifted then, so many lost souls, that we were just two more oddities.'

'Where did you go?' I ask, slurping up the last of the broth.

'We joined the nomads, trying to get by unnoticed, which was difficult. Even after all the beatings she was still a very beautiful woman. He never touched her face. People noticed her, remembered her, and I looked a right sight with my head cut to pieces. Still have the scars.'

I look at Napoleon's face from the side, and see there at the hairline a gash that runs from eye to ear. It is faint, silvery on his weathered skin, but it is still there after all this time. The past stays with us, I think, marking us in ways seen and unseen.

'So we went wherever we could hitch a ride to, with whoever would take us. It didn't really matter as long as we were alive and free. When you have your freedom taken from you it takes a while to learn how to live again. I didn't know any different, but she did. She would say it was too late for her but not for me. She wanted a different life for me. A free life. And look at me now.' He laughs – a bittersweet laugh.

He tells me this and I sense how they would have felt, he and his mother – the fear of always running, unsure of where to go, who to trust, how to start over. I know this feeling too.

'You know, Samar,' he tells me, 'you can always begin again.'

We sit there for a while in silence. Around us the carriage is lively with Russians singing and drinking and a Belgian couple are joining in and trying out the few Russian phrases they have picked up along the way. The woman says, '*Etot muzcina platit za vse*' ('This gentleman will pay for everything'), and the man shakes his head and says, '*Eta dama platit za vse*' ('This lady will pay for everything'), and there is much finger-pointing and merriment. The carriage fills with a party mood and the drunken woman is singing again, this time out-of-tune Edith Piaf songs. There is the waving of arms and clinking of glasses.

Napoleon takes up his story again.

'Most people were kind. They did what they could – when you think, no one had anything left to give away except kindness. We made it as far as the border . . . We crossed and that's where we stayed,' he says.

I nod. 'What was it like?' I ask him but he needs little encouragement. In his mind he is back there already.

'It wasn't much of a place to live. We shared strangers' tents . . . In the middle of all this space and emptiness. That said, we had a roof of sorts over our heads, a warm fire, food, shelter. It felt safe. Safer than before.' He smiles at me. 'Sometimes it is good just to stop – to be in one place. And at least there was no one to tell us what to do. No one swinging iron bars!' He laughs as he says this and shrugs his shoulders as he looks at the passengers in his charge.

'Time heals,' he says, looking at me, watching the sadness steal over me.

'Not everything,' I say.

In that moment I feel so old. He doesn't contradict me. I stare out of the window at the reflections of the lamps playing tag like fireflies against the moving shadows. It is so bright in the carriage in the evenings; the lamps are lit all along the side walls of the compartments, reading lamps dot the carriage and overhead white and blue lights dazzle from the ceiling.

The smell of cooking – potatoes, rissoles, fish, fried eggs – wafts down the carriage from the dining car and I realise how hungry I am. I have learnt to exist on so little, so little food, sleep, love. I have pared everything back to the essentials to just get by – jettisoning everything else. It is not good to need things.

Further along the carriage the Belgians are calling to Napoleon, wanting coffee, not yet having figured out how the samovar works.

Chapter 18

In the days following the earthquake Ara and I tried to find our family – if we could even find their bodies, if we could be sure of what had happened to them, that would have been something. Could they have survived? If they had been inside the cave house would they have been safe, perhaps? Trapped but alive. Waiting for help to come. Did anyone ever survive such a thing? This thought haunted my sleep.

Sitara stopped crying – stopped making sounds. Her babyish babble dried up and she would spend the day with a yearning look on her face for Madar. Ara was lost, feeling responsible for the two of us, not knowing what was ahead, how she could protect us. She had no answers either. We just clung to each other in the dust.

It was days before help arrived. We built a shelter from what we could gather amongst the debris. We scavenged food. At night we linked our arms together for safety, afraid to sleep, not knowing what would befall us. We prayed for the dead. We prayed for help. We did not know what else to do.

We were alone, almost. Najib watched over us, always hovering nearby making sure the others left us in peace, keeping Jahedah from stealing Sitara in her madness and grief. However, Najib too was unravelling, muttering to himself more and more each day. We grew ever more scared.

Ara and I tried to console Sitara as best we could. She

had water and whatever food we could scavenge or that the others would share. Only a few of us from the village had survived. We became a reluctant family, united against all that the earthquake had taken away. Two of the older women had been driven mad now by the aftermath and wandered around in a slow daze all the time. We avoided them as much as we could, taking Sitara up to the shelter of the trees near the top of the mountain during the daytime just to be away from the village, or what was left of the village. In the evenings Jahedah kept following us around, her eyes fixed on Sitara. The others worked together to build shelter, to hunt food on the mountain-side, to keep a fire going. They would talk long into the night, sharing stories of all those disappeared. We tried to remember each person, each family, and share what memories we could of them. It was a way of burying our dead, of remembrance. How do you mourn the dead when you cannot bury them? Cannot clean the bodies. Cannot even find them. Do not know if they are there or else-where. It is an impossibility. Everything became impossible.

We were all in shock. We functioned, we made do but we were not really there, not understanding the enormity of it all, unwilling to accept that this was now our life.

Eventually our thoughts turned to what to do next; the situation could not continue as it was. Soon we would run out of food, we had no real shelter, we did not know where was safe any more. We wondered about help and if anyone knew or cared that dozens of people lay dead, buried on the mountain. One day a helicopter buzzed overhead. We stood looking up at it for a while, then two of the men started jumping up and down in excitement, waving their arms in the air.

'They see us!' the men cried.

The helicopter hovered and dipped lower before spinning off and away and we were all left wondering, have they seen us and still don't care?

When help finally came, it was in the form of one large truck covered with tarpaulin bringing aid workers, some bags of rice, water and two weary-looking men with guns hanging off the side, with a small jeep following behind. We were their last stop in the valley. There was no real doctor, no team to lift the rocks that crushed our family or the others. Nothing like that. We were too far away, too unimportant.

We had begun to live in a blur. The aid people wanted to help us. They were glad to find us, glad someone had survived – and here was a tale of two girls and a baby sister. A small foreign camera crew had followed the aid workers in the jeep up the mountainside to capture the devastation and they put TV cameras in front of us like we were a sort of happy miracle story against all the grief and loss. 'How do you feel? What will you do next?' We tried to answer their questions. We were so hungry, cold and numb. We had lost everything, everyone. No one seemed to care. We had survived – wasn't that enough?

But they couldn't leave us there. So we were bundled onto the back of the truck, all of us, and promised a better life in a camp in Pakistan. Just across the border, they said, as if we could have walked had we wanted. We would see. We would be treated well there, given water, food, shelter.

These were the promises they made. Yes, it was basic but it was a start. It was something and we were to be pitied. Isn't that what they thought? We let them take us. What could we have said – no? All I could think of when I thought of Pakistan was the *madrasa* and Javad, and I feared being taken somewhere where they might want to change our minds, to make us forget all that was true. Jahedah refused to leave. She ran off into the hills and the truck tired of waiting for her. Najib, too, climbed down.

'I will find her,' he said.

'We cannot wait long,' the workers said, gesturing at their watches as if time made sense here.

He nodded, understanding. And us? What now? Ara and I had nothing. Nothing. We could not run. What about Sitara, how would she survive? I screamed when they put me on the truck. Bundled up in Omar's old *patu*, leaving behind Madar and Baba, our family, I felt the earth pull apart once more. I was not ready to leave them, buried there underneath the landslide, lost forever. Ara was silent. She stared ahead, Sitara on her lap. I don't think she even shed a tear for the twins, Nas and Robina, lost beneath the rubble, these twins who had clung to her for the last year – who had treated her as their sister, their mother, their world. Perhaps they were at rest now, reunited with their own sister and mother. No, Ara had no tears left. When Najib did not return, the truck left. We sat in the back, watching the ruins of the village recede from view until it was gone altogether.

As we left, grief broke wide open inside me. A grief in waves so deep that I could not touch the bottom. My hands searched for Ara to hold me. My nails dug into her arm as she rocked Sitara gently, saying over and over, '*Migozarad, migozarad, migozarad.*' Maman Bozorg's voice filled my ears as I cried and shook, pulling the threadbare *patu* round me. The others on the truck shifted away from my tears as if they were contagious. Ara soothed me, stroked my head until I could no longer cry. Allah had ignored my prayers. I had brought this upon us.

The truck took us back down the twisting route that we had taken to the village from Kabul all those years before when we had travelled through the night. It stopped every once in a while, the men on either side at the back with rifles keeping an eye out for trouble. The truck passed the same stopping points, the same views, the same dangerous bends in the road, the same rusted shells of Soviet tanks, the same rows of small flags, fluttering green, marking the graves of those who had fought. When it reached the outskirts of Kabul it kept going, routing us further away from the city (too dangerous, they said), taking us away from everything we knew and loved, until eventually it crossed the border where we arrived at what was to become our new home – a huge refugee camp with tents stretching on for what looked like miles into the barren earth. We were in Pakistan. Our new home. The camp. A hell on earth.

The camp was made up of rows of densely packed muddied tents, marked UNHCR, each about two feet apart, each with enough space for five, maybe six people but often holding eight, nine or more.

'You are lucky,' said one of the foreign aid workers, a blond-haired man with white teeth. 'This place is better than some of the other camps. You'll be okay. Just stick together.'

He nodded at Ara and Sitara, lifting us down from the back of the truck. Behind us weaved a long line of people walking, carrying all that they could with them, looking dazed and broken. We, it turned out, had arrived in style.

'Earthquake victims' privileges,' the man joked.

We didn't laugh. He led us to one of his colleagues, a harassed-looking young woman with a clipboard but no pen.

'No family,' he mouthed at her. She sized us up.

We were taken to a long row of tents all marked with the aid agencies' symbols and then into one giant tent full mainly of other children like us, children who had lost everything. There was an aid worker at the entrance and a few adults standing around keeping watch. We were given a space to sleep and live, a tiny cramped corner with no privacy, the lights shining constantly overhead. Later we learned this was to try and keep us safe, so that we were not hidden away. The camp was a place in which it would be easy to disappear completely. After all, no one cared. We had ceased to matter. No one was interested in who we were any longer, what our stories were. We counted but only as numbers on a list of displaced, of refugees.

The days took on a routine. We would go to fetch food, spending hours waiting in queues, especially in the first few days when we did not understand the systems and rules and had no one to ask. Ara, who had been so silent since the earthquake, began to talk to everyone in the camp. She shared Madar's skill in finding friends, finding help. We tried to make sure Sitara had food, had water. We asked the older women for help and advice. They shooed us away like flies. Sitara learnt to walk in the dust, wobbling between tent poles and lines of washing. When she took her first steps a joyous smile bubbled up and she clapped her hands.

There were hundreds of people in the camp, thousands, an endless sea of seated figures, boys darting around outside, the girls mainly staying in the tents for safety. There was little sense of order. Many people had given up, unable to make a life there. We were not welcomed by the local people, who saw us as bringing problems, disease and unhappiness. Nor were we welcomed by the aid workers, who were overwhelmed and overworked, unable to care for so many lost souls. The workers warned us to stay close to the tent, to not wander far.

There was no school although there were different temporary classes that one aid agency or another would try and put in place. They never lasted more than a few weeks, then other more pressing needs took over. The staff were no longer available to help teach and the children drifted away. We were instead to be pitied and sporadically filmed by foreign journalists or visitors, who would walk around the camp looking at us, fascinated and aghast. We could not often wash and our clothes quickly became threadbare. Our hair got matted. We no longer looked like ourselves. I would think of Madar, of how particular she had always been, the hours she spent brushing and braiding our hair, and I shuddered to think what she would say if she could have seen us.

Ara became bitter and angry all the time. She blamed the Taliban, the Russians, the Americans, Baba, Madar, everyone for our misfortune. I did not fight with her. She was all I had left and I did not want to lose her too.

'Your daughter is pretty,' said a young woman who passed by us one day, pointing at Sitara. Ara looked at her, first in confusion and then in horror. 'No, my sister,' she called after her. The woman, who had a kind face and sad eyes, came back and stopped to talk with us. 'I'm Hafizah,' she said. 'I help out here.' She gestured at the tent and we began to talk, to tell her our story.

'So you're from Baghlan, eh? It was my husband's home too, before . . . the Taliban took him.' She looked at us. 'It is not good to be alone. If you need help, ask for Hafizah.' She let us be, taking with her the two girls who followed her around. Like us they were orphans. She had taken them on as if they were her own. We later came to know them. One of the girls, Parwana, was closer in age to Ara although she looked older, taller. The other one, Benafsha, was younger than me, a pretty little girl with blondish curls and green eyes. She reminded me of Robina and it made my heart hurt to look at her. After that first conversation, Hafizah kept an eye on us. She made sure we had food to eat each day. She checked that Sitara was bathed and kept as clean as possible given the circumstances, and that we got to see the visiting doctors. Slowly, we let her in, cautious at first and then, seeing only goodness and care, we let ourselves believe she could be a new mother. She could look after us.

People do terrible things when they think no one is watching. At night we heard screams, cries from other corners of the camp. We would see children looking red-eyed and dazed in the mornings. We heard stories. We heard about young girls, no older than Ara, some even the same age as me, selling themselves to strangers for money, being sold or being taken and raped. The same thing happened to some of the boys too – the pretty ones, the ones with no one to protect them. This all seemed impossible but we would see their faces and know it to be true. Ara warned me never to go out to the queues for food or the washroom alone. We were to do everything together. We were to protect each other and Sitara above all else. Some of the young girls had disfigured faces, a punishment for their behaviour, a marker to indicate availability. Who else would take them now? We would see girls carrying babies of their own. Hafizah would warn us against talking to them.

'You don't want to hear their stories,' she would say.

Instead we would play with Benafsha and Parwana, our newfound friends who had set up camp next to us with Hafizah in the main tent. We played quiet, hopeful games like *Sang Chill Bazi*, making do with pebbles instead of toys, Benafsha tossing a pebble into the air, grabbing for the others on the ground, then Parwana, then Ara, then I – over and over, until a victor would emerge. Or we would tell each other stories, share memories of home, invent happy tales under the damp canvas. I would whisper to Benafsha how Ara, Sitara and I would escape the camp, how our brother Omar would find us and we would all return to the yellow house in Kabul once the fighting was over. She would squeeze my hand and agree it was a fine plan.

On sunny days, if Hafizah would let us, we would play *Aaqab* with some of the children from the tent. Parwana would be in charge.

'Come, Samar.' Benafsha dragged me with her. We were to be pigeons, pecking the dusty ground; Parwana was the eagle. She had climbed up onto a container that sat by the end of the row. Taller now, she looked out round the camp before jumping down and chasing after all of us, catching as many as she could, her arms reaching out.

'Run, Benafsha,' I cried out, laughing, dancing away from Parwana, the other children fleeing in all directions. We landed back 'home' safely, a corner of the row by a tall flagpole. Out of breath, laughing, free.

In those moments I would remember that I could still play, imagine, make friendships – even laugh – that life could continue. When fear crowded my dreams at night I sometimes babbled in my sleep, and Benafsha would reach out and hold my hand.

'It's okay, Samar,' she would whisper, and I would hold tight to this young girl I did not know.

The days blurred one into the next. Months passed. There seemed no likelihood of ever leaving the camp. Its numbers swelled each week, more new people arriving in trucks, carts or on foot – the same mixture of hope and fear in their faces as we'd had when we first arrived ourselves. We had less and less space in the main tent. Hafizah asked for a tent for her and the five of us children. We too begged the aid workers, 'Please let us have this, please!' until they gave in, overwhelmed by the desperation in our eyes and in need of the space we occupied for other orphans who, unlike us, had no one to show an interest in them. Hafizah was given a small tent on the end of a row, a way down from the larger open tent we had been living in, that tent where the light of the lamps had burned through the darkness until dawn and where you could not close your eyes in the dark and forget where you were, not even for a single night. We yearned for the darkness, to close our eyes and shut everything out.

In our new home, Hafizah told us each to take a corner. None of us wanted to lie next to the flaps at the entrance to the tent. In the end Parwana reluctantly set up her bedroll nearest them. Ara and I stayed to one side with Sitara in between us and Ara against the edge of the tent. Benafsha curled up close to Hafizah on the other side. At nights it would be bitterly cold and we would heap all the clothes and blankets we had available over us all and huddle together for warmth. Plastic sheeting covered the dirt on the ground and kept us dry from rains. Hafizah used the space outside the front of the tent to cook on the days when she had fuel, and we would sit inside the tent or just outside with her in the daytime, always aware of strange eyes on us.

Belongings were stolen on a regular basis in the camp. Nothing was safe unless you attached it to your person and even then light-fingered thieves would steal what they could. Ara wore a gold necklace, a gift from Madar, from her old life. She had to hide the chain under her tunic or it would have been stolen on sight. We learned these things by watching what happened around us. We learned a new way of living so different from our time in the mountains and the freedom we had felt there. Even when the Taliban started restricting everything we could do – even then we could still run up into the hills and feel free. Here, as the months passed, we felt only desperation.

We grew weaker. The food was bad and infrequent. The water was never clean. People were constantly ill. Many died. They were buried in land to the back of the camp, not far from the tents. The foreigners, charity workers, did what they could but it was never enough. Ara would often give away her food to Sitara and me.

'Eat,' she would say, her dark eyes watching me, ravenous, not caring about the grit in the rice and the flies that surrounded us. Sitara worried us both and she worried Hafizah too. Her belly stuck out, her eyes seemed large and lost in the hollows of her cheeks, patches of her hair, soft baby hair, fell out in clumps. She had black welts on her legs. She stopped walking and would just sit on a blanket, a weary old-woman look in her eyes.

At night, in the snatches of sleep that I would allow myself, Madar appeared in my dreams and I would see her searching for Sitara and calling out to her. She did not call out my name, nor Ara's. I could hear Javad's laughter and remembered his last words to me, 'You can't stop it. No one can.'

I woke drenched in sweat and fear. But he was not there. He was never coming back. They were all gone. Our one last hope was Omar – we knew he was out there somewhere, fighting up in the hills. At least this was what we wanted to believe and we allowed ourselves to dream and talk of a time in the not too distant future when he would come to the camp, find us and take us away, and we could be some sort of a family once more.

'Do you think he will remember us?' I asked Ara.

'Of course.'

'But what if he is different now?'

She shrugged.

'We could go back, all of us . . . to the old house.' I placed the thought in her hands. Ara considered it then shook her head. 'We can never go back, Samar. Never,' she said.

I did not want to believe this.

I could still remember the yellow house and playing in the *kala*, the scent of the flowers by the door.

'There were rose bushes, honeysuckle – do you remember, Samar? And the trees you could hide behind or the tallest one, by the gate – that was the one Javad was always trying to climb,' she said. Ara would tell me about it over and over – how the walls were a pale yellow, the roof flat, looking over the city, white against the blue of the Kabul sky. And then I would see us all. There were Omar and Javad playing, Ara laughing with them – we were all playing . . . racing around the garden, chasing each other, collapsing onto the grass with laughter.

Madar sat in the shade. She was reading and humming a tune to herself. Arsalan and Baba were over by the door. They had taken two kitchen chairs and a small red table outside and they were drinking chai and talking in hushed voices. I remembered all this. I wanted to break through into this memory and to be there.

I needed to escape the camp. I got a mad, glazed look in my eyes and ran a fever. Ara fretted. Sitara too was weak and ill. The hours passed and I worsened. Hafizah told Ara to go and find the doctor. Ara hesitated by the door of the tent. She did not want to leave us alone. She did not want to go alone. Dusk was falling and it was not safe for her to be out there on her own. The others had gone to get water. Hafizah waved her away.

'Go, Ara, to the main tent; there will be someone there. It is urgent, she is very hot; she's ill and the baby too,' she said, nursing Sitara who was limp on her lap.

Who is ill? I wondered and then realised they were talking about me.

I started to float out of my body and spin around inside the tent, moving up towards the pole in the roof that held the sheeting above us. The yellow house was spinning now too. I lay down on the cool grass and pulled at tufts of it between my fingers. An eagle was circling overhead, its graceful flight entrancing me. I was thirsty. I called out to Madar for a drink. She didn't look up from her reading. Ara had gone . . . I couldn't see her now. Omar and Javad were play-fighting on the grass beside me.

'Has Ara gone to fetch water?' I called out.

Hafizah was soothing my fevered forehead but I was no longer in the tent. I was up in the mountains with my grandparents. I was in the cave house watching the lamp flicker. Maman Bozorg was holding my hand and stroking my forehead.

'There, there, Samar,' she said. 'You need to sleep. This pain will pass.' But I could not sleep.

Baba Bozorg was shaking me.

'Keep her awake,' he said, his tone sharp.

I heard a rumble outside, like distant thunder, low at first then louder, then the cave house was collapsing on top of us and I was suffocating. I could not breathe. My hands grabbed at my throat and the darkness covered everything.

It was days before I recovered and when I did Ara was missing.

I opened my eyes and I was in the hospital tent. A foreign nurse was looking at me, holding my wrist. She smiled. There were people around the bed.

'Look, she's . . .' said one. My eyes hurt to look up at the light. I pulled my wrist up to shield my eyes but my arm was attached to wires, a drip funnelling liquid into my body. At first I did not know where I was, then I remembered. I closed my eyes once more. My throat burned.

'Ara,' I called out, my voice weak. No one said anything.

'My sister,' I said. 'I have to see my sister.'

The nurse squeezed my hand. She leant down towards me so that I could see how sorry she was to tell me.

'Your sister is dead,' she said softly. 'She was very ill too. It is a miracle you have survived, you know.'

I felt tears wet on my cheeks.

'Ara . . .'

The nurse looked at me.

'No, not Ara . . . not that sister. It was the little one, she is with the angels . . . Sitara, no?'

Sitara was dead. My eyes stung as relief, then shame, then quiet loss flooded through my body. Sitara – not Ara. I would mourn Sitara in time but I had held out so little hope of her surviving the hell of the camp and now she would be at peace with Madar – of that I felt sure. It was better that she was not here.

The nurse squeezed my hand again. I closed my eyes.

Soon it was no longer the nurse but Madar holding my hand. 'It's okay, Samar. Rest, sleep,' I heard her say.

'But Sitara . . .' I needed to tell her.

'Shush now, Samar, it's all okay.' Madar's voice rocked me back to sleep.

The voices became soft murmurs around me. Then later they were lifting the stretcher they had placed me on and were moving me somewhere else.

'Tell Ara,' I mumbled as the nurse let go of my hand.

They needed the bed for someone else closer to death. They needed the space for another miracle.

'You had fever, Samar, brain fever like the little one,' the nurse said. She looked at me.'This virus, it has taken many lives. It was a good job your sister – Ara, isn't it? It was good that she came to get us. You were close to . . .' She stopped and said no more, afraid of frightening me further.

'I want to go . . .' I almost said *home* and it overwhelmed me completely. I could not go home. I no longer had a home or a family to return to. All I had left was Ara and the hope that Omar would come back.

Why is she not here? I thought, looking around. There were other children in the hospital tent too – some of them feverish, some with wounded limbs; all of them weak, ill, worse off than me perhaps.

I was afraid to ask and afraid not to. 'My sister, Ara, is she coming today?' The nurse was busy helping another little girl to sit up. The girl's face was wrapped in bandages. I could see burns on her skin. The girl clung to the nurse.

'She hasn't been in in a few days,' the woman said to me. 'Before, she came every day and would sit here all day with you. She brought in the little one too – but it was too late for her.'

My heart sank. Ara had not been to visit in days. What would keep her away? She would never leave me there alone. I was sure of it. Perhaps Hafizah made her stay away for fear of catching my illness. Yes, I thought, that was it. That was all. When I return to the tent she will be there and we'll be together again. I cheered up at this thought.

'We can't help you any longer, I'm afraid,' the nurse said. 'It's good news – you can leave. You are recovered, more or less.' I nodded blankly.

'You were feverish for many days, a long time, talking a lot. But the crisis has passed. You will be fine now once you build up your strength again.' She smiled. It was a hopeful, sad half-smile.

I did not want to leave.

'I don't . . .' My words faded to nothing. These nurses and doctors, they could not keep me here and Ara was waiting.

I wondered if I would be able to find my way back to the tent in the never-ending sea of canvas. I asked for the tent of orphans, figuring I would be able to find my way from there. They pointed me in the right direction and the nurse, her face lined from nights without rest, told me, 'Be safe.'

I half walked, half ran, still weak and uncertain, heading towards the orphan tent, passing row after row of smaller tents, rows that stretched far into the distance – blue, green, white tents, the white turned dirt red from the soil and dust, thin blue UNHCR logos rippling on the sides as if this offered some protection. Men and boys stood all along the side of the path watching me run. Some smiled, others just stared. I had to slow down to catch my breath. Having spent countless days lying down, the exercise left me winded. The rows blurred in front of my eyes and I felt faint.

I bent over, gulping down deep breaths of air. My chest hurt. Behind the sea of tents the mountains rose up, pockmarked with dark green trees. The sky was streaked pink and orange and the air felt chill on my cheeks. I sensed movement around me, someone trying to take my hand. I broke into a run again, hurtling towards the safety of the tent for orphaned children. When I found it a woman ushered me inside.

'I need to find my sister,' I said, shaking my head and running on. I now knew the route well and weaved between the last remaining rows before sliding to a stop.

The tent had gone. There remained only a patch of flattened earth and the outline of where the tent had been. I fell to my knees and touched the ground. My mind went blank and I began to cry. Then I thought to ask the people in the neighbouring tent – they must know something. They could not all just have disappeared. I went to the flaps of the tent and called in, 'Hello?'

A man with dark curly hair wearing a *pakol* poked his head out. I did not recognise him. He looked at me intently and, seeing I was alone, beckoned me into the tent. I pulled away and then ran off again back towards the orphan tent. There they took me in. I spent the day sitting on a mat with blue and green flecks and gold running through the cotton. I rocked back and forth thinking, someone will help me. They have moved tent. Why? Where are they now? Here in the camp people did move from time to time – sometimes a better spot became available, sometimes a tent was replaced, sometimes others needed the tent and families were forced to share. Sometimes people left. Or got sick. Or died.

I decided to return. This time I asked one of the women aid workers to come with me. She was tall and pale-skinned with hair the colour of marigolds. She took my hand and we went back to the place where the tent had been – where my home, makeshift as it was, had been. I asked one of the other neighbours, in the tent behind where ours had been, where they had gone.

'Ah, Hafizah said she was going back to Afghanistan. She'd had enough of the camp. When the little girl died – I think it broke her,' she told us.

I was in shock. I stared at the woman. How could she leave without me?

'And Ara? My sister?' I asked, biting my lip.

'Oh . . .' The woman looked down. 'She went missing.'

'Missing?'

'Hafizah looked for her but she never found her. She was due to come back one evening from the hospital tent. They wouldn't let her stay there at night with you so she would come back and forth to see you. But one night . . . she just didn't return,' said the neighbour, who was a young woman yet looked so old.

'What can you do?' she said, seeing my face. 'Have hope. She'll turn up.'

She looked at the other woman with me, the worker from the tent. I saw the nervous glance they exchanged. Ara would not be coming back. I thanked her. She gave me a gentle hug and we returned to the main tent once more.

I hardly slept that night under the bright lights. What I realised was that I needed to find Ara. I *had* to find her. So in the morning I started by asking other children. I spoke to every child I could. I asked about Ara, I described her, her dark eyes, her pretty face, her cackling laugh, her strong temper, her beautiful singing. They all shook their heads and looked away. I asked a group of girls who were known to give themselves to the soldiers and the men of the camp. They told me to stick with them but I declined. They had not seen her. I felt relief – I could not picture that for Ara. She would never give herself away like that. She would sooner starve.

I asked a group of boys. A look of recognition flickered in the eyes of one of them, younger, shorter than the others, when I talked about Ara. He looked at me longer than the others did. Then, saying nothing, he took my hand and gestured to me to follow him.

'That's Aaqel,' the others said. 'Mute. Doesn't speak.' I nodded. I was not scared by this silent boy and could see he knew something. He led me away from the rows of tents, out past the mud houses that some of the men had started to build on the edge of the camp, realising a return home would not happen soon. Aaqel took me down to the riverbank. We scrambled over the cliff edge to the river below. Other children played in the riverbed. The water was grey and muddy, and low. The new rains had yet to come. Some boys were jumping across the low sludgy water, hopping from rock to rock, and one waved in recognition at Aaqel.

We kept going along by the river and then he pointed to something floating in the water, billowing fabric caught up by boulders and tree branches.

Fear shot through me. I saw a flash of fabric like Ara's scarf. We picked our way through the wetness, my feet squelching in the mud, my ankles damp. The boy held back as I leaned down and turned over the body. It was Ara. Her face was bruised and bloated but it was her. I turned away from her, a sickly bitter taste rising in my throat. Aaqel looked away.

'It is her,' I said even though he knew already. 'Help me . . . please.'

Together we lifted her swollen body and laid it down by the bank. Her face looked so shocked. I could not think about what had been done to her, how she came to be here, who I should blame. Anger burnt me. All I could do was hold her in my arms and weep. Grief flooded out of me. I cried for my beautiful sister who wanted to see the world, who dreamed of living in Paris, of falling in love one day and walking freely along the boulevards and who dreamt of becoming a famous singer. I cried for Madar and Baba, my grandparents, Javad, the twins, Little Arsalan, all buried and lost on the mountainside. I wept for Sitara taken by illness and I cried because I did not know if Omar was alive or dead. I cried for myself and for Aaqel and all the children trapped here in this forsaken hellish place.

I shed no tears for Hafizah, who I blamed for Ara's death and who had abandoned me. It was good to have someone to blame.

We sat there for what felt like only moments but must have been hours as the sky darkened. Aaqel looked at me. We would bury her. I remembered Madar's gold chain and I knelt in front of Ara's body so he could not see as I checked, running my fingers around her neck. Ara was still wearing it. Somehow it must have remained undiscovered when she was attacked. They did not want her gold. My fingers looked for the clasp and I freed it from her neck.

I decided then that I would not stay here to rot and die. The necklace could not save Ara but it would save me. It would serve to take me far from the camp.

We buried her by the riverbank and Aaqel stayed with me. Some of the older children helped. We all dug with our hands – we had little else. The mud slid dank between my fingers. When it was done I knelt beside the upturned earth, covered now with stones. I placed a stick between the stones and tied a corner of Ara's ripped scarf to the top, where it fluttered in the breeze. We prayed that she would find peace. Aaqel held my hand and the two of us stood there as the darkness fell.

I said goodbye to Ara. I said goodbye to the camp. I was empty inside; numb. My tears had emptied me. It was time to go home.

Part Five

After every darkness is light.

Chapter 19

Arriving at a refugee camp is easy. You are brought by truck, by need, by desperation. You follow long columns of other lost souls carrying all they can salvage of their old lives on their heads, their shoulders and their backs. Leaving is more difficult. Many people stay years, live whole lives in the camps. They have lost all hope of ever returning home. They forget in order to survive.

I would have to find a way to escape. At night I would dream of the yellow house in Kabul. That was my last hope. It was where I was sure Omar would go if he tried to find us once he realised the village was gone. He would come back. I believed he would. I told myself this over and over. Who else could I consider family? My mother's parents had long ago disowned us all. I would not be welcome there.

There was only my aunt Amira left. She had fled to Moscow or St Petersburg in Russia. Madar had spoken of a place in Moscow where Afghans live, where you can smell the naan bread baking in the street, which Amira had told her about in a letter she had long ago sent to the yellow house. She had talked of how one day we would visit her in Russia. *Inshallah*. One day. Perhaps that is where Madar and Baba had planned to take us. Amira might help, might take me in, but that seemed almost impossible. How would I know her, how would I ever find her? No, the yellow house was all I had left.

I joined the short queue of people leaving the next morning after prayer. We waited in line in the early light. We were not so many and I hung close to a family in front with lots of children, hoping to blend in, looking down and staying away from the guards. I was still too young to be on my own without drawing attention. They would want to keep me in the camp until someone could claim me. I could not allow that to happen. I wrapped my headscarf tight around my face and kept my eyes down at the barriers. The adults spoke with the guards.

'Where? Bamiyan . . . that's where we'll go. We'll take our chances,' the father said and the guards shrugged. On the opposite side a queue of people were waiting to get in. The father told the guards that the camp had been a mistake. The men nodded, not caring, expecting to see us back soon enough. They waved us through. I kept my eyes down until we were out of the camp a distance along the dirt road. The mother turned and, seeing me tagging along, pulled me away from her children.

'You are out now,' she hissed at me. 'You *can't* stay with us. Understand?' she spoke to me slowly as if I were stupid or uncomprehending. I stopped and let them walk on, startled by her anger.

Soon enough another group came along and I stepped in beside them. There was an old man in a green and red striped *chapan*; his son, a man not yet old but beaten down by living in the camp; and the son's wife, her hair streaked a silvery white, her eyes still full of warmth.

'We are from Hazarajat – and you, child? Where is home?' the old man asked me, his voice gentle and low.

'How is it you travel alone?' For a moment I did not know how to answer his question. What could I say?

'Kabul,' I said, 'I am from Kabul. I am returning to my family's home, to where we used to live.'

They nodded, tilting their chins forward, understanding somehow. They were no longer so curious as to how it was I had come to be in the camp alone. They had heard too many sad stories. I did not need to tell them mine. It was enough that we all walked together. I did not want their questions or their pity.

I was still weak from the illness and heartsore to leave Ara and Sitara behind but each step took me closer to Kabul, further from the camp, and I kept going one foot in front of the other, stopping only for water and short periods of rest. The sun beat down and it was hard to keep going in the heat but I would not be defeated. Every few hours aid trucks would drive past in the opposite direction, sometimes stopping to give us more food and water, picking up anyone ready to give up and return to the camp.

They were a strange group, these foreigners – from many countries, all choosing to be here in the dirt and dust, looking at us with compassion at best and despair at worst. I wondered what it would be like to be able to drop in and out of a country's problems, to pass through just helping out how you could and to feel gratitude or guilt that this was not your life. There were good people at the camp, some of the people. I knew that to be true. But they could all leave. They could all disappoint you. I was angry at them for failing Ara. Mostly I was just angry.

I was terrified at first that we were walking in the wrong direction, walking further into Pakistan, but the aid workers pointed us in the direction of Kabul. Remembering the long journey to the camp in the truck I could only guess ahead at the miles, the long days I would need to walk to cover the distance.

'How are things there in the city, in Kabul?' I asked the workers who passed us bringing the latest refugees to the camp, who waited a short while to see if we would return with them. I felt braver now we were further from the limits of the camp.

They would shake their heads. 'Not good.'

We were warned to watch for bandits, for shooters, for wild animals that might attack, warned off the open main road, told to cut through the mountain paths where we could, warned to watch for mines. We nodded, by now just putting our faith in Allah.

Would the yellow house even still be there, I began to wonder, or would it have been shelled and destroyed like so much of the country? I had to trust that it would be there, untouched, that some things do not change. I had to believe in something.

Walking during the day was tedious, but we stopped only to share the little food we carried between us or to find water in the mountain streams. The horizon was a blur before us but at least we were moving. Nights were terrifying. We would huddle together for warmth and to feel safe. The old man was kind and made sure his family welcomed me along with them. They would go on to Hazarajat, he said, and I realised we would have to part ways sooner or later. They would not risk getting too close to the fighting in the city. For now, though, it was good not to be alone out here on the long road back.

The old man reminded me of my grandfather. I allowed myself to remember Baba Bozorg and Maman Bozorg and the way they had welcomed us all into their world. I thought about Baba Bozorg rounding up goats on the mountainside, striding across the uneven mountain terrain surefooted and proud, and how he was full of questions for Baba and wanting to know all his son had learnt and could share, believing Dil would live a better, easier life. I felt a knot in my throat at the thought of Baba. The yearning to see them all, to bury my head in Madar's neck and smell her hair and warm, comforting scent, was so strong it stung my eyes.

I started to talk to them, my absent family. Silently, at first, in my mind as I walked, I had long conversations with Madar, Baba, even Javad. There were many things I realised I wanted to ask him. I imagined playing with Little Arsalan, chasing him round the hillside. I remembered Madar reading to us all, her voice spinning out into the night. I could not think of Ara or Sitara, not yet. I pushed those memories further to the back of my thoughts and focused instead on creating a world in my mind where we were all still together, where there was laughter and hope. It was this that carried me forward and I felt myself growing stronger each day, leaning on them when I tired, looking to them for encouragement. They willed me on.

The road was full of potholes, its surface broken and with patches of cracked tarmac. Mainly, though, it was just a dirt road with few markings. Scrubland stretched out on either side and beyond, in the background, purple- and rust-coloured hills. I hurried through this emptiness, eager to make it back to Kabul, to a life that I had bathed in a warm golden glow of hope.

The walk was difficult through the mountain roads. The old man could not go very fast and we made slow progress. Hunger shadowed each step. I tried not to think about Ara and Sitara or the camp, or Aaqel's eyes when I left, just standing there watching me go. I pushed it all away. I just kept the yellow house in my mind.

The son and his wife talked about the life they would build together, a simple life in the mountains, somewhere peaceful where they could live and grow food and be far from the fighting. They would make a family. It was as if they too had decided to ignore all that was happening around them and that life would be peaceful simply because they wanted, needed it to be so.

I started to tell them about Madar and Baba, my family.

We all want to believe these happy endings are possible. Is it so much to ask to be happy? That is what I thought.

Things had got worse, we heard from other travellers. There were a lot of fighters on the route to Kabul. We would need to watch out crossing the mountain pass between Khost and Gardez. No one crossed there unless they needed to. We stopped at a small village on the way

– the old man needed to rest. We all did. We sat in the shade of a stand of cedar trees and the son went to find us more food and water. We relied on the kindness of others. A village elder came out to see us; he had questions about the camp, about life there. He was surprised to see us, he said – most people stayed away from the road to the city.

'Haven't you heard?' he asked. 'There is no Kabul any more. Everyone is leaving – heading to the mountains, the camps, Tajikistan, Iran, wherever they can get to to escape.' They would not leave the village, he said, though he had heard of young Taliban supporters burning whole villages to the ground.

'Where would I go?' he said.

Even though they had little, they welcomed us and we were fed and able to rest. This contact with other people, without fear or danger, made me lightheaded. My heart had grown so hard in the camp.

I found myself thinking of Ara and Sitara. I wanted to curl up in a ball and stop moving. To wait until the waves of sadness swept over me and I could see again.

The two old men were talking routes. The village elder told us, 'Avoid Khost if you can. There are different militia there. These fighters . . . they are violent. They think nothing of killing ordinary people. Women, children. They don't care. It is impossible to pass by the gorge without them seeing you. You would be easy targets. They take recruits.' He raised an eyebrow, looking at the old man's son. 'And they take women.'

A chill passed through me.

If we were not to go by the mountain road to the city then how were we to get there? The others would travel on beyond Kabul but I sensed the old man had wanted to help me as best he could. His eyes clouded over and he sat trying to puzzle it out as we rested from the midday sun.

After talking a while with the village elder, then pushing himself up off the ground, the old man said, 'We will go by Sharana and Ghazni then. Even on a mountain, there is still a path. It will take longer but in the end it will be safer.' We all smiled in agreement, all reluctant to end our journey prematurely at the hands of mountain bandits and militiamen.

I knew they would take me as far as they could. Then I would be on my own.

We thanked the elder for his hospitality. The villagers gave us naan stuffed with *qabuli pulao* and water to take with us as they wished us a safe journey. A small group of young boys waved us off in the dust. And it began again, the long walk.

The mountains crowded over us on either side and we went as quickly as we could, eager to put some distance between us and Khost. We were now walking away from Kabul in order to get there. I thought about how strange the world was, how back to front. I took comfort from the steps of the others beside me. No one complained even though we were all exhausted and our feet were chafed by the stony ground, our heels bleeding in the cheap plastic sandals given out at the camp. We were far from there now, back on Afghan soil. I felt my shoulders relax as I walked taller. I felt free again and I drank in that sensation, using it to keep going even when my body wished to stop.

We had walked for several hours more and the road had been quiet. No aid trucks, no checkpoints. Just red dusty tracks, narrowing, stretching up into the mountain passes; shrubs and gnarled trees dotting the landscape. On the mountainside, large boulders clung to the dry dusty earth. Spring was almost here but there had not yet been heavy rains. I thought of my grandparents' village and hastened my pace. I did not want to get caught out on this journey by falling boulders or mudslides. I would not die that way. I had lost enough already to the hand of nature.

The old man's breathing was heavy and laboured. He clutched at his chest. We stopped. He leaned on his son, a friendly open-faced farmer from the mountains, tired and worn thin from his months in the camp.

'We must stop,' said the son.

The old man could not walk any further. Another road was in sight below us.

'We rest here . . . we pray. Help will come,' said the woman.

I did not want to stop but I did not want to leave these people who had let me journey with them. I scanned the horizon looking for vehicles – someone, anyone we could ask to stop and help us. There was no sign of life. And then, after what felt like hours as the day was cooling into dusk, we saw something approaching along the road below, kicking up a small cloud of dust in its wake. It was a truck with men with guns. Our hearts sank – we could not hide and besides the old man was too unwell and weak to move. Instead, the son pulled me with him down the hillside into the middle of the road.

'We will wave them down,' he said. 'Don't worry. They would not shoot a child.'

I was not so sure but I went with him and we waited, waving our hands in the air until the truck, coming closer, saw us and gradually slowed.

The driver peered out cautiously at us. Then from the back a man jumped out and walked in our direction. He looked at the four of us; saw the old man lying in the dirt further up the hillside. He judged the situation.

'Please,' said the son.

The man held up his hand in a weary signal. He did not want to speak. He was still weighing up whether they would help us or leave us here on the roadside. Not speaking to us made the decision easier, for it was as if we did not exist. The old man called out in pain. I felt for Ara's gold necklace underneath my scarf. The driver revved the engine, keen to keep going. Everyone was afraid of ambush, of being targeted.

'Help us,' I said. '*Komak!*'

I stared in the man's eyes. He looked at us all once more. He kicked at the dirt and then climbed up with us to where the old man lay and helped lift him. He and the son carried the old man down to the back of the truck where he was laid down on tarpaulin. The truck was full of crates. Poppy seeds. Opium. We did not care. We would say nothing and take our chances. The man knew this and so we all climbed in next to the old man.

'We are going to Ghazni,' he said.

I thanked Allah. This was our second piece of good fortune. The driver passed back oranges for us to eat. I fell asleep quickly to the rocking of the truck, exhausted from the walk, exhausted from hope and fear. I imagined Madar was stroking my head, soothing me. When I awoke the truck had stopped in Ghazni. It was night. The others had gone, abandoning me to rest and I was alone once more.

I was sad that they had left me without saying goodbye. I had wanted to thank them for their kindness, for letting me walk with them, but perhaps it was easier this way than us taking leave of each other in the daylight. I knew the old man did not want to let me go on alone to Kabul. I wondered if he had survived the journey. People kept disappearing. I was becoming numb to it.

I lifted up the tarpaulin and slipped down off the back of the truck, its crates now empty, even the driver gone. Pulling up my headscarf I started to explore the city of minarets. The buildings were asleep and I stepped lightly to avoid making any noise. I did not want to startle the empty streets.

I found a well and, leaning on the pump, drank for a long while. I washed the dust of the long walk out of my hair and my face. Here there seemed to be no fighting. I sat for a long while looking up at ancient city walls and the night sky. I thought of Ara, her body face down in the stream. It was so easy to disappear. I shuddered as I remembered her face, the horror in her eyes. This was not how I wanted to think of my beautiful sister. I wanted to remember her laughing, eyes sparkling; Ara singing and dancing and full of love and hope. That was what I would choose to remember and I made this promise to myself. I would take my family with me – they would guide me. My fingers ran over the gold chain around my neck. From Ghazni it was a two- or three-day walk to Kabul.

I decided not to part with the chain unless I really needed to. I would walk to the city. I had come this far. Allah or good fortune had protected me. I would be safe – I would reach the yellow house. Convinced of it, I sought out the road markings, wandering through narrow streets until I found where the road widened and travelled one way to Kandahar, the other to Kabul. Although it was night and pitch black save for the stars, I walked on towards the city. It was a cold night and it was good to keep moving, one foot in front of the other, each step taking me closer.

Chapter 20

I look up from my writing and rub my eyes, which are sore from the bright lights overhead. The train rocks a little, side to side, tilting on the track. The air inside the carriage is warm, muggy, but outside it is cold – the end of the winter months. Around me in the carriage the other travellers play cards, drink and tell each other their own stories to pass the time. At night the atmosphere on the train changes. It becomes charged and lively. Instead of looking outwards, the dark of the night forces us all into companionship. Some of the travellers – the Belgians, one of the Russian men – have tried to get me to talk to them but I stay quiet, my head buried in my book or my notepad. I avoid eye contact. I do not want to have to share my story with these people for whom I will be nothing more than a curiosity to be pitied. Napoleon is different. He cares. He shows his own wounds. He offers no false hope or empty promises. It is enough that he comes and sits near me and that I know I am not alone.

When I think of my journey, how it is that I am here now on this train, that I have a chance at a new life far from all that has gone before, I look back and I see that girl outside Ghazni. She is standing in the road looking up at the stars, listening, waiting for what they may tell her, how they might guide her if she could only hear them. If she could only quiet the rush of her heart long enough to hear.

It is odd to piece together your past – to write it down as a series of impressions, events, moments in time. For a long while at first I couldn't write anything. I could only look sideways at what had happened, imagining it happening to some other unlucky soul. And yet, it is not all sadness. It has not destroyed me yet. Anger can only take you so far. So when I feel most lost I choose to remember those things that help me survive. I choose love.

Chapter 21

That night no animals attacked me, no strangers approached me. I had the road entirely to myself with the stars, silent above me, leading the way. I walked at a steady pace and when the early-morning light swept away the night I was a long way from Ghazni, climbing higher in the mountains towards Kabul.

The road was open and I knew that my presence would not go unremarked upon in daylight. A young girl out walking on her own in the middle of nowhere was sure to draw attention.

My pace slowed as I would have to veer off the road and hide behind rocks and scrubland at the sound of approaching vehicles. With no one to protect me, I chose to protect myself. Ara's death had taught me that I would not be easily trusting of strangers. The day passed like this, with me dipping off the road each time a truck or car came into sight. By nightfall, exhausted and weak, I had covered little ground and so I decided to find shelter for a few hours to rest and sleep. I sought out a mountain stream to drink from and ate small, careful bites of the naan I had carried with me since we had stopped at the village on the road to Khost. My stomach ached but I no longer cared. The darkness protected me and when I woke several hours later, stiff and cold, I began my walk once more, hurrying now, undisturbed by passing vehicles and curious eyes.

As I walked in the dark I imagined Madar and Baba alongside me, urging me on, each taking one of my hands and swinging me gently between them.

'Come, Samar, it is not far now.' They swung me high, shaking away my sadness.

They led me through the nights. In the daytime I slept, sheltering away from the roadside. Madar and Baba stayed with me throughout.

It was like this that I made it to the outskirts of Kabul two days later. My feet were cut and bleeding, my sandals rubbing against the skin. I was on the point of collapse, having had so little food for several days. The city seemed like a mirage in the valley, dipping near then far as I walked towards it.

From all sides of Kabul shelling and gunfire could be heard. Buildings were burning or gaped wide open to the sky. For hours I walked away from the main city arteries, circled the outskirts of Kabul, watchful, working slowly towards the north, then walking into the city, getting ever closer to Shahr-E-Naw, to the old park and to the yellow house beyond. My body ached and I wanted to stop but the sound of shelling to the far side of the city kept me moving. The trees were long gone and there was little shelter as I moved from the shadows of one building to the next, hurrying across open roads now mainly empty of cars and buses and bikes. Kabul was on fire, everyone fleeing or having fled already, those that remained clinging to the shadows. My heart was beating hard in my chest. If the house were not still there what would I do, where would I go?

As I eventually came closer to my old neighbourhood, I began to run, not caring now who might see me. I had to know. I passed what had once been the park where I had played with Javad, Ara and Omar. I kept going until suddenly I could see it: the yellow house, still there above Shahr-E-Naw.

It was only when I reached the *kala* walls that it occurred to me that someone else might live there now. I paused for an instant, my hand silently slipping open the gate. The house was quiet. I saw no sign of it being occupied though there seemed to be damage to the roof and one of the walls. Once in the courtyard I slipped round the side of the building to the low window and ran my fingers along the frame. The window opened with a gentle shove and I hoisted myself up and in through it, landing on the other side. The room was in half-light. A layer of thick dust covered the tiles and the window ledge. I tiptoed through the house from room to room. It had been looted, most belongings long gone, things taken almost tidily, removed rather than ransacked. The dust was everywhere. I saw no signs of anyone having been there for a long time. In the kitchen the dust swirled in the light through shell damage to the wall. I stepped carefully. I had learnt all about mines from the children and adults in the camp on crutches, limbs ripped from them with one careless misstep. The kitchen door to the garden creaked on its hinges as I pushed it open.

The garden was more overgrown and wild than I remembered it; the grass had grown high and the trees shaded more of the patio now. A fine film of dust covered everything here, too. There in the centre stood the almond tree, full of early blossom, its petals white and pale pink and around the base of the tree, undisturbed, were the leaves of the saffron flowers Madar had planted so long ago.

I went and sat underneath it, hugging the bark, letting the earth spring up under my fingertips. I laughed. Sheer joy escaped from me. It was almost too much that the house was still here, the tree, the garden. I lay down on the earth looking up at the sky as I had done so often before, and felt happiness and love flood through my aching body. Now that I was at the yellow house my body collapsed in on itself, no longer striving for a goal. I fell asleep outside, half hidden by the long grass, a small, slight figure curled up in the warm morning sun. I still had Omar's old *patu* wrapped around me and when I awoke dusk was not far off.

I decided to stay sleeping outside. Most of our belongings had been taken but there were a few old blankets left and I wrapped those round me too. Under the tree, even with the gunfire in the city, I felt safer than at any point since the earthquake.

As I slept I dreamt about a time when we were all together at the house and Madar was singing to me, a sweet low lullaby, and her hands were stroking my head. Then in the dream she was digging in the soil, pulling up the flowers and digging with her hands, the soil catching beneath her nails. I woke as the sound of something moving in the long grass startled me. I watched, then I saw a golden-eyed cat scale the wall and disappear over the other side. I was relieved it had gone.

Madar's hands digging . . . The image stayed lodged in my mind and I thought back to those last days before we left the yellow house. There was the arguing between Madar and Baba, her gathering up . . . what? I could not be sure.

I looked up at the window above the courtyard and the image of me as a small child, standing years ago staring down at the tree in the moonlight, came back to me. There was a box. She'd had a box with the flowers. What had happened to the box?

I started to pull away the saffron, to find where the earth was looser and would shift under pressure. At first the earth was hard and I kicked at it with my heels to loosen it. Then I dug down under the roots of the tree without knowing why until my knuckles connected with the hard wooden surface of a large box. This was what she was doing. This was what she had wanted to hide. I remembered now, her dropping it into the hole, wiping her face with the back of her arm, planting the flowers on top. What was it that was so precious she had to protect it, yet did not want to take it with her? My hands were shaking now. I could hardly believe that in the midst of all the chaos and destruction this place had remained intact. Something real I could touch. A small miracle.

I pulled out the box with only the light from the stars and the intermittent flashes of shelling to guide me. The box was heavy. I struggled with the lock, eventually picking up a stone from the ground to prise it open. As I lifted off the lid I saw a cloth wrapped around . . . I hesitated. Would Madar approve? Would she want me to find this whatever it is? I thought about it for a moment.

When you die I do not believe that you disappear into the dirt. You are buried, yes. But your soul, that part I am not so sure can be held even by the heaviest of earth. Even though Madar was lost to me, although they were gone, I could still feel my family's presence with me. And in that moment, a breeze shook loose clouds of blossom from the tree. Either Madar was standing there shaking it to tell me to stop, or shaking it to tell me to hurry up and open it, or she wasn't there at all. Having given the matter some thought, I decided that she would like me to open it.

I unwrapped the cloth, frayed and yellowed, as quickly as my fingers would let me, stiff now in the chill night air. Little plastic bags of photographs spilled out, letters, papers, money. It was a box of hidden treasures. Madar had buried her secrets there under the almond tree.

It was too dark even with the moon overhead and the occasional flashes of rocket fire to read the letters. I put them to one side. I opened one of the bags of photographs and squinted at the images. Some were old, sepia-coloured; others were pictures of us children when we were younger, and Baba and Madar, some of Arsalan. It was hard to make out the images. I ran my fingertips round the edges of the pictures and traced the outlines of the figures. Each layer of the box's contents brought new finds. There was money, thick wedges of notes tied together, again safely covered with plastic. Money for some reason she had refused to take with her to the mountains. I was confused and exhausted. These were things she'd wanted to keep, to protect. Had she thought she was coming back? Why hadn't she brought this box with us? I dragged the box just inside the door of the kitchen, out of sight of prying eyes. In the daylight the neighbours, any that remained, could look down over the garden. I did not want to draw attention. I kicked over the soil again, filling the hole once more, righting the flowers that had come loose.

I could not sleep despite my exhaustion, too tired, too excited by the find. I sat by the tree, my eyes half shut, waiting for the dawn light so that I could read the letters and see what it was she could not take with her. I wanted to see what it was she would not destroy. I felt close to her here holding these papers, close to the others seeing their outlines fuzzy on the photographs. It was something. An unexpected happiness.

Throughout the night the sound of shelling erupted like a firework display over the city. In the end, exhausted, in the last hours of darkness I slept.

Light cracked open the day. The yellow house glowed a pinkish gold as the sun slanted over the mountains. The air was fresh but I was not too cold, the *patu* still wrapped round me. It had been a deep sleep, the first in many nights since the walk to Kabul had begun.

To the back of the house was a well. I went in search of water early to avoid being seen. The roads were empty and in the daylight I had my first good look at the city: huge gaping holes like uneven rows of blackened teeth where buildings had once stood, the smoking shells of former homes, a grey-bluish smoke sending signals all over the valley. The main arteries of the city, usually clogged with traffic and carts and people on bicycles hurrying to work, were all empty. It felt like the city had been deserted. Looking around at the neighbouring houses, they too looked abandoned, as if the people who once lived there had just walked out one day and never came back. I tried to remember Madar's friends and the children I'd played with in the garden. I could picture faces, recall voices, shadows reaching down to pat me on the head, laughter at us children as we played together in the *kala*. All that was gone now.

The water from the well pumped cool and fresh. I washed my face and hands and drank. It amazed me how little I needed to survive, how used I had become to going for days without really eating, with hardly any water, just hope and anger, one fuelling the other.

What I had hoped for I hadn't yet found. There was no sign of Omar at the yellow house. No message, nothing to signal he had been back to Kabul, that he was okay, alive, searching for us all. Wherever he was, it was not there. This was a heavy disappointment. The plan would have to change. If he hadn't come to the city I would have to find him instead. The much hoped-for reunion would have to wait. I believed he was still alive mainly because he did not talk to me like Madar and Baba or the others. When I closed my eyes I could never see him or hear him. So he had to be out there, somewhere, I reasoned.

For now I would have to make do with the treasure box instead. I hurried back round to the house and let myself in, looking around to check no one could see me. I pulled out the box once more to a shady corner of the garden and sat in the long grass obscured from view.

I looked first at the photographs. There was one picture of all of us and Arsalan squinting into the sun. He was standing behind us as we all lined up in front, his arm resting on Baba's shoulder, Madar sitting beside us in a chair. This was before Little Arsalan was born, when it was just Omar, Ara, Javad and me. A friend of Arsalan's had come by the house that day and he took a whole roll of pictures of us playing outside, with one of Javad sitting by the door looking very serious; one of Omar, Baba and Javad with Arsalan; one of Ara, Madar and I; one of me sitting in the courtyard laughing in the sun. I touched their faces.

Now I knew why I was meant to come back to the yellow house, that Madar had brought me here to be close to them all. I touched my hand to my heart as I let go of all the sadness I had carried since the earthquake, since the camp. My shoulders shook as I let my tears fall in the long grass. The dusty saffron drank them in.

Blinking in the sunlight I found another older photograph – this one was of Madar as a young woman. She looked incredibly beautiful and different in it. She was not wearing a headscarf. Her head was uncovered as she looked proudly at the camera. Her hair was long and loose and her eyes, dark like Ara's, stared into the lens. A slight smile played at the corners of her lips. On the back was written, 'My Beloved'. I looked once more at the picture, surprised. She seemed young – sixteen, maybe seventeen, not older than that. I realised that this would have been before she met Baba. How, then, could she be the 'beloved'? Who had written on the back? Grandmother? From Madar's accounts I did not imagine her mother called anyone 'beloved', much less Madar. Why, then, did she have this picture? And why hide it? I puzzled over it, uncertain and troubled.

The next picture was fuzzy, an image of a group of young men. I looked at it more closely. Two of the men had rifles slung over their shoulders. They were dressed in khaki short-sleeved shirts and trousers with heavy boots. Looking at the faces of the men I saw one looked like a younger version of Arsalan, one a lot like Baba. And there at the corner of the image, blurred and hard to make out, was a young woman in the same clothing, looking away from the camera, her hair tied back in a long plait. The image was grainy but it looked like Madar. This image made no sense to me. I turned it over. The back was unmarked, undated, but the picture had a crease down the middle like it had been kept many years in a shirt or trouser pocket. I stared at it for a long while, the faces blurring. It was them. I was sure of it.

I flicked to the next image in the stack. It was of Arsalan as a young man, the same intense strong look, the same smile in his eyes. Written on the back it said: 'To my beloved Zita'. My mother's nickname, the name he had always used for her. I looked at the picture, turning it over and over, tracing the writing with my fingertip dark with soil from digging that the water from the well could not wash out, buried deep even under my short bitten nails. I looked back to the photograph of Madar as a young woman. The handwriting was the same on both. I rocked back in the grass and exhaled, the air punched out of me. My mind was whirring.

Surely Madar and Arsalan had only met as students at the university? That was what Madar and Baba had told us, time and time again. How could it be that they knew each other before then? And what were they to each other? And what of this other picture, the three of them in uniforms of some sort? None of it made sense.

I had always understood Arsalan to be my father's friend. Hadn't they met as boys in the mountains? Didn't Arsalan support Baba's education? Bring him into this other world? I thought back to all the conversations at the yellow house between my parents and Arsalan. Never once had Baba and Arsalan spoken about fighting together. They had mocked the Mujahideen, the constant fighting between tribes and factions, been cautious of them – hadn't they? Didn't Madar and Baba secretly support the Soviets as students – the talk of equality, of the common good? Or was that not the truth? Had the truth been something else? I realised I had never thought about or questioned this part of my parents' lives, never considered that they had lives of their own, secrets of their own. They had told us their story and I had believed it. Why wouldn't I have?

I thought back to Arsalan's death, his body hanging from the almond tree. What had happened? Why?

The questions rose up inside me now, one after the next. My head began to ache.

Ripping open the plastic bag of letters, I tipped them out in a stack across my knees. I flicked through them, trembling as I held the words and paper in my hands, knowing that just the act of doing this, of reading and of looking at these photographs was somehow illicit. I glanced up. From my hiding spot deep in the shade and long grass I felt sure I could not be discovered and yet I felt uneasy. I couldn't decide whether it would be worse for me if the Taliban found me reading, or if Madar could see me opening these letters, letters she had never intended me to read. Anxious and curious in equal parts, I read the first note that had tumbled out. It had clearly been folded and read many times.

My Beloved Zita,

I miss you every moment of every day. I count the days until we can be together again.

You should be here with us all. We need your warrior heart to lead us. We are sorely lacking, I fear, without you. You, who always knows how best we should act.

My love,
A

I opened the next letter, hands shaking.

My Beloved,

I do not know when or if I will see you again. Things have gone badly here for us. We have lost many of the men. Dil and I worry that we will never leave. I count the days away from you. I wish you were here with us and then know it is better that you are not. You are safe. That is all that matters. I have given this to the boy. If he manages to get it to you, look after him. He is very broken.

I miss you, my love.

A

I pictured Arsalan – the way he would look at Madar. I remembered him leaning over her in the doorway. The close way they spoke together – an unhappiness at the heart of it. I remembered him and Baba arguing. How sad Madar became around him. Did Baba know? He must have known. Yet how is it that she married Baba? And us – where did we belong in all this? What had seemed so clear became clouded in my mind.

The next letter in the pile had been read many times over, its creases worn thin, the script small, dense, spidery.

Z,

The boy brought your news. Now I understand why you did not join us. Forgive me. The Lion needs me here. I must not leave, now we are so close to freedom. I am sending Dil to look after you. You cannot do this without his help. It is a question of honour, not pride. Trust me. Talk to no one about this. Do what he says. He will explain everything to you. He owes me that much and besides, he is in love with you already. I will make this right somehow.

A

Baba owed Arsalan? I struggled to understand, to make any sense of it all. What of the story of a friendship forged on the mountainside? How could they be away somewhere fighting when Baba had said he was at the university, that he met Madar in the meeting in the caves? What was Arsalan sending Baba to do? What news? I turned the ideas over and over in my mind. I should never have opened the letters. There was a reason she had buried them. All love has its secrets.

My stomach ached with hunger. My head hurt. I wanted to read more and yet I wanted to burn all the letters, be done with it all.

When I thought of Omar's face, now I imagined I saw Arsalan in his features, not Baba. Yet we were all so alike, at least Omar, Javad, Ara and I. We all looked like Madar – even if Ara was more beautiful and fine-boned than me. And what of Little Arsalan and Sitara? I wondered. They were darker, more serious, with Baba's eyes and stubborn resolve. I knew nothing. Was certain of nothing.

I pored over the images of us all at the yellow house. I could not understand the world of adults. It felt as if my whole family had been a lie built upon lies.

I kicked at the tree and pulled on its branches, scattering blossom over the courtyard. I kicked up the dirt and the flowers, fighting against all the hidden half-truths, the things we were never told.

What of Baba's love for me and mine for him? Was it the same or not? Baba Bozorg? Maman Bozorg? What family did any of us have? I felt grief yet at the same time I was not sure what it was I was grieving for. Something precious had been lost forever.

I looked again at the photograph of the young men in khaki, at the girl at the edge of the picture, not looking at the camera. Was it Madar? I could not tell. I thought of Madar and her warrior heart.

I hoped I had inherited that too. I would need it for what was to come next.

Chapter 22

The train has jolted to a stop.

I can hear the other passengers standing up, stretching in their compartments, some coming out into the corridor to look out of the windows.

'What's happening?'

'Why have we stopped?'

Everyone asking each other the same thing, hoping someone will have the answer.

Napoleon is walking up the carriage. 'No need to panic,' he says, his voice booming up the corridor. 'Just some animals crossing the track. The driver will have them cleared out of the way soon and we'll get going again. Please stay in the carriage. We won't be stopping long. Don't want to lose any of you!'

The tourists laugh, craning their necks further out to see if they can see what is happening at the front of the train. Occurrences like this become small events to be enjoyed on the journey, highlights of the trip. They break up the endless rolling panoramas and bring all the travellers together.

'Will he do it?'

'I don't know – those deer can be stubborn.'

'Is it deer?'

'I think so.'

And on it goes, the carriage knitting together a story of what is happening even though none of them, not even those with binoculars, can actually see what is ahead due to the bend in the train, the curve of the track. So instead, we fill in the details for ourselves.

Eventually the train starts up once more, a slow jerking movement at first, sending some travellers bumping into each other and against sharp door handles. Rather uncomfortable for some, I imagine, watching a fat tourist grimace as he topples forward.

'Okay everyone, we're back in business,' Napoleon says, sailing down the corridor, surefooted from years of train travel, watching the clumsiness of his charges with a mixture of compassion and good humour.

'Here you go.' He puts out an arm to steady the man, whose eyes are pinkish from early-morning vodka.

Laughter echoes round the carriage and everyone is merry once more, the adventure having ended well.

As the train passes by the pine trees, on the verge below I see the deer casting off into the forest, except for one – a fallen wounded animal, the ground bloodied around it. I look again but it is gone behind us now as the train picks up speed. The *taiga* is no place for the weak or wounded. I think of the vultures that will soon descend and work over the carcass, picking it clean.

I pick up my story where I left off, back at the yellow house.

Chapter 23

My hopes of finding Omar in Kabul were fading. At night the shelling and fighting got closer. It was time to leave. I decided to take as much of the money, the letters and photographs as I could hide about me, the bags twisted and tied under the old *chapan* and salwar kameez that I wore. It had once belonged to Javad but was worn thin now and frayed at the sleeves. I considered leaving the letters. I was tempted to burn them but something stopped me.

'I will show them to Omar,' I thought. 'He will help me make sense of it all.' I was convincing myself that it was just a question of time before I tracked him down and we would be reunited. A pair of Omar's worn boots still lay upstairs, overlooked and long abandoned. I put these on too, blowing out the dust that covered them. They were still too big for me, but they reminded me of my brother and they were something to keep.

I looked at myself in the mirror. It would be difficult to pass unnoticed on the streets of the city. I looked at my long hair before pulling it back from my face. Now I looked more like Javad. I climbed on a broken chair in the kitchen. Balancing carefully I reached up to the top of the door and there, still hidden undisturbed on the ledge, was Arsalan's knife. He used to keep it there – in case of attack, he said, though he would never say who he feared was coming for him and in the end it had not helped him at all. My fingers grasped the handle and the leather sheath as I stepped back down, wobbling on the chair and holding the knife away from me.

I went to the mirror, now tarnished and dusty. I hacked at the ends of my hair, slow and careful, avoiding my ears. As long pieces dropped to the floor I tried not to cry. This was a new beginning, I told myself. After a while I checked my handiwork. The cut was rough and uneven but I looked just like Javad. I decided I would take his name. I imagined inhabiting the life of my brother. It felt fraudulent at first. I practised walking and talking like Javad, Javad as he was before he took up with the Taliban. I prepared to let go of Samar: a girl on her own in the Taliban's Kabul was too hard to protect. I would keep Arsalan's knife with me in case. I kept Ara's chain covered by the *chapan*, and the headscarf I wound round my neck instead, covering the lower part of my face as I had watched Javad do in the mountains.

I decided to venture out in search of food. In truth I had no idea if the marketplace would still be there with the men with carts of fruit and nuts, the butchers' stalls, the spice-sellers, the stacks of naan freshly baked – all faint memories now and if it were still there, would it have anything to sell? Kabul was a shadow city now.

Omar's old bicycle had been abandoned, hidden deep in the bushes to the back of the garden. It was rusty, its green paint peeling, but it worked. I got on and memories of Baba Bozorg teaching me how to ride a bicycle up in the mountains, not long after we had first arrived there, came flooding back to me. Him calling out encouragement to me as I fell in the dirt over and over with Javad laughing at me then helping me right the bicycle that belonged to one of the village boys. However, despite the laughter and tears I had stuck with it until I could cycle round the village square without falling off. Baba Bozorg slapped me on the back like a boy and said, 'Well done, Samar.' How proud I had felt.

Omar's bicycle was still a little tall for me and I wobbled at first then gained confidence circling round and round the almond tree. As long as I didn't have to stop suddenly I reasoned I would be all right. Once sure of myself I made my way out of the *kala* and down the hill, freewheeling and picking up speed as the bicycle bumped along, its wheels somewhat flat and rapidly losing what little air they had left in them as I bumped over stones and potholes.

I stopped by the park – or what remained of the park. The city was in chaos. Buildings were destroyed on almost every corner. The streets were eerily quiet and empty now, shelling in evidence everywhere. I remembered the old Kabul, the Soviet soldiers with guns on their shoulders walking about, but a sense of order, of containment in the city. People moving about their daily business. Not this emptiness that there was now. On the horizon I saw buildings burning. I realised I did not know this Kabul nor how to navigate it. I needed to find help.

I headed over to a well where two boys stood leaning on the pump, filling plastic yellow containers full of water. I approached slowly. One was carrying a rifle. They did not look like Taliban but you couldn't always tell. There was no one else around and they seemed bored and unthreatening so I went up to them. I nodded in greeting. They looked at me warily. Having obviously decided I posed no threat, the taller of the boys waved me over.

'Nice wheels,' he said, looking at the bike. I smiled, though not too much.

'What's your name?' said the shorter boy.

I tested out my new name. 'Javad. You?'

'Mati,' said the shorter one. 'He's Abas.'

We stood for a while in silence as they filled the containers, Mati holding them steady. Then the older one, Abas, pushed down the pump, keeping pressure on it so that I could drink for as long as I needed to once they were done. The water tasted metallic, not like that from the mountains. I thanked them.

'Hungry?' Mati asked.

I shrugged.

The two boys looked at each other, exchanging thoughts silently.

'Why don't you help us with the water?' said Abas. 'You could balance these either side of the handlebars.'

I thought about this. It was clear they were fighters, though I did not know on which side or what the sides were or indeed how many there were of them. But I knew enough not to ask. If I did not help them they would take the bicycle anyway. I could see it in Abas's eyes.

'Sure.'

We loaded up Omar's old bicycle and I pushed it slowly over the rough broken road, trying hard not to splash too much of the water. It was difficult and heavy work but I did not want to seem weak so I did not complain. Mati lugged a third large lopsided container and Abas walked ahead of us, his eyes darting round, looking for signs of danger. As we crossed a wide road I sensed people watching us from the shadows. We made easy targets. Also sensing danger, Abas gestured at us to head down a narrow side road. Shaded now by the shells of houses and shops we wound our way deeper into a maze of narrow alleys until we came to a wooden door in the wall of a building that remained standing. Abas knocked on the door, a quick three taps. It opened slowly and a man's face peered round.

'Who's this?' he asked.

'Javad,' said Mati, as if we had always been friends.

'He's a good guy,' he said.

'*Salaam*,' I offered.

'Hmm . . .' The man looked at me, uncertain, returned the greeting and then opened the door, ushering us inside and helping to lift the buckets off the handlebars. I thought about leaving the boys there, just wheeling away, but something told me I would not make it very far so I stayed and trusted in Allah. Besides, where else did I have to go?

Inside the house was dark. There were a few men. Mati told me to leave the bicycle by the door; I was reluctant to let go of the handlebars but he smiled and whispered, 'Don't worry. You're with us now.'

I took off my boots and washed my hands in a dish on the window ledge. We knelt on the edges of the mat on *toshaks* next to the men. I could smell cooking – *mantu* – and my mouth watered. I realised how long it had been since I had eaten an actual cooked meal. When they brought out the food I nearly fainted with happiness. I listened to the men talk and realised I had been lucky. They were with the Northern Alliance, Massoud's men. I wanted to ask about Omar but I stayed silent, trying not to draw attention to myself. The room was hot and smoky and the men talked in hushed voices. One kept guard by the door.

It seemed there were many different groups fighting in the city and the outskirts but it was the Taliban who were winning.

'For students they are well equipped,' said one of the men.

'Not students any more,' said another.

'Islamabad, foreigners,' said a man from the corner of the room by way of explanation. He was taller and more serious-looking than the others who deferred to him.

'We are to head back to Jurm, tonight – we can be of little more use here,' said the same man, who seemed to be in charge or at least respected. There was some murmuring and a sense of relief. I wondered how long these men had been hiding in the city, what they had been doing. How it was that people fought such a war. I thought of Kabul, how it used to be, how it was now, and I did not understand why you would destroy something you sought to protect.

'We'll go at nightfall. There is a truck ready,' he said. The men nodded their heads in agreement, clearly happy to be leaving the chaos behind.

'What about Javad?' Mati asked.

The men looked at me. I lowered my eyes.

'What of him?' said the tall man. They owed me nothing. Apart from the bicycle I was of little use to them.

'My brother is a fighter with Massoud's men,' I said. 'I want to find him. Will he be where you are going?'

The man looked at me again, closer this time.

'His name is Omar,' I said. 'I need to find him.' They watched me now.

'We lived in a village in the mountains in Baghlan. Omar disappeared. They said he joined the Alliance. He wanted to fight,' I started to explain.

The men nodded approvingly.

'And you, little man, do you want to fight?' the leader asked me, holding my gaze steady.

'Yes,' I said, not knowing what else I could offer.

The man slapped me on the back and the others laughed. Mati smiled.

'Tonight then you will come with us to the mountains.'

And so it was decided.

That afternoon passed in heated discussions about what was the best course of action for the country, for the people, all argued in whispers and hisses, someone always watchful of the comings and goings on the roads bordering the alley outside. I listened, hoping to hear something that would lead me to Omar.

As darkness fell we were told to rest. The men would wake us when it was time to leave. Usually there would be a lull in the shelling when everyone grew tired, even the soldiers, and before the night tripped towards dawn, then we would leave and take our chances.

That night, however, the shelling was relentless and the men kept watch two at a time, flares exploding like constant fireworks outside. When on the rare occasion footsteps would come near and then pass by in the alleyway we all tensed, the men waiting with their guns ready.

All apart from Mati, who slept through it all on the floor. One of the men knelt in a small room off the main space where he prayed constantly. It seemed as if he thought that if he stopped we would all be killed.

I pretended to close my eyes and sleep. The whole time I could feel the man who was in charge watching me as if waiting for something to happen. In the middle of the night we were told to get up and prepare to leave. One man opened the door, keeping watch in the alleyway for a signal that the truck would be there waiting for us.

'What about the bicycle?' I asked.

The men thought about it for a moment. It seemed wrong to leave it behind.

'Leave it,' said the tall one in charge. 'It will draw attention.'

Omar's bicycle, it appeared, was destined to remain in Kabul.

For the second time I left the city in the back of a covered truck, this one too heading for the mountains.

Even though I had been so little – five, nearly six years old – I could still recall the fear and excitement we had all felt the last time I had left Kabul, the desire to get away from the yellow house and Arsalan's death. I remembered too the Mujahideen stopping us at the checkpoint and Baba laughing with them. Now after Madar's letters and the photograph I began to look on that differently.

It was hard to tell where allegiances lay. All these factions fighting each other, each one convinced that they and they alone were right.

I thought about when Omar had left us behind in the mountains. Baba had not been upset at the time – if anything he had seemed proud. It was as if Baba – and Madar, too – had known Omar would make that choice.

I began to see signs, secrets in everything. I began to mistrust my own memory of events. When Omar disappeared after Arsalan's death he was gone for several days. Where? Doing what? And who were the men who had come to the house, these men we had never seen before – what had they wanted? What had they expected to find? Question after question filled my mind.

It was a tight squeeze in the back of the truck. Two narrow wooden benches lined each side. In the middle between them lay a straw mat. That is where we sat, the men on the benches either side of Mati and me. The truck smelt of animals.

The driver was a short burly man with the exhausted look of someone who has not slept for days, his shoulders hunched over the steering wheel, his eyes twitching furiously, watching for signs of mines, rockets, ambush. He passed old rifles to each of us. They did not look up to much as weapons went – perhaps if the enemy comes near, I thought, I could hit them over the head with them. Otherwise I did not think they would serve much use.

'Take this, just in case,' he said, handing one each to me and Mati. Abas had his own already.

Unlike my brothers I had never held a gun. I copied Mati, cautious. I had no desire to shoot any of my fellow travellers or myself by mistake. Up in the mountains Amin had taught Omar and Javad how to shoot – target practice high up in the hills where they could not disturb or inadvertently injure anyone. After Omar left, Amin continued with Javad, who was a good shot with steady hands. They would go up walking in the mountains, taking Amin's gun with them and come back in the evenings carrying whichever unfortunate mountain creatures had been too slow to avoid their aim. Now I wondered about the conversations they'd have had on those long walks, the poison Amin would have poured into Javad's mind.

It infuriated me how these men had taken my brother, who had been so gentle before, and had filled his heart with hate. I was angry at Javad for letting them, but angry at Baba and Madar too – at all of us, for letting it happen, for just standing by and watching. It was not fair to lay all the blame at Javad's feet.

It was a slow leave-taking of the city, the truck trundling along, the driver cautious and careful on the uneven roads, the surface pockmarked from the shelling. We could see nothing, the driver having closed the canvas at the back as if he were headed back to his supposed farming life in the mountains. No one spoke.

These men had grown accustomed to always being ready for the worst. It was as if they constantly expected it to happen so that it would not.

When we had safely wound our way up the mountain passes far from the city, the men began to relax somewhat; they started to talk again, to joke with Mati and me. Abas sat alone on the edge of the bench to show he was no longer a child, unlike us. It amazed me how quickly I had become Javad, had sloughed off my old skin as Samar and how this was not questioned by the men. Smaller, skinnier than Mati, with my hair short behind my ears, I had become the image of my brother. The truck rattled its way up the hillsides, swerving into the bends and turns, the driver hurrying now to put as much distance as he could between the city and his cargo.

After a while, far from the city, we pulled back the canvas, tying it back at the sides so we could all look out over the valley and watch the sun slowly coming up. One of the men passed around bread. We all ate, hungry and grateful.

The sky took on purples and pinks, a rose-gold light bathing the valley below. I felt a quiet happiness realising I was no longer alone.

By now we had entered Massoud's territory and everyone was calm.

'You are with the Alliance now, Javad,' Mati smiled at me.

In that moment I wanted so badly to start over, to be this boy Javad they spoke to, to let go of Samar and all that had gone before. Would it be so terrible? I thought. I could fight with them, make a new life here, but I already knew in my heart it would be a lie and there had been enough of those already. And besides I could not stay a child forever. Looking at Mati, feeling my heart quicken at his kindness, I knew then I could not stay. I just needed to find Omar. Then everything would be better.

I had not really slept since leaving the camp, only snatches here and there. I had not been able to close out the nightmares. I would see the mud sliding down the side of the mountain, rolling towards our house. I would dream of Nazarine and Masha screaming, of Ara floating face down in the river, of Sitara sick and feverish, of Arsalan swinging from the tree. It all jumbled together in my mind and I couldn't separate myself from what had happened. I would dream, too, of the dying boy in the cave and wonder who had been so cruel as to leave him there like that to die alone, injured and scared. Or I would dream of running, running past rows of empty tents, endless rows stretching out into the desert no matter which way I turned. I would wake choking back tears, crying out in my sleep even though no one could hear me and even if they could they wouldn't care.

It all seemed so far from Madar telling me that anything was possible, that I could do or be anything I wanted if I worked hard enough for it, dreamed for it.

'After every darkness is light.'

I looked up at the man who'd spoken. He was the man who had spent all his time in Kabul kneeling in prayer, trying to protect us.

I was not sure if he was directing the saying to me, to all of us or to no one in particular.

He had noticed my faraway look and the way my hands tapped against my knees over and over to remind myself that I was still here. I was still alive.

There were so many things I wanted to ask these men, to find out, so that I could find Omar. If he had joined them someone would know something, would know where he was or where he had been. I tried to smile at the man. I was afraid to speak, to draw attention to the lie I had become. Later I would talk with Mati; he would help me.

The truck drew to a halt, the driver banging on the side to signal we were to climb out. My legs were stiff from sitting so long. The bags felt sticky against my waist and the knife blade in its sheath pressed hard against my thigh. In the back of the truck I saw bright blue stones rolling under the mat as the last of the men climbed out. I picked one up and closed my fist around it. When I looked up Abas was watching me. He looked away and said nothing. I put the stone back down and felt shame.

It was good to walk on the mountainside, to breathe in the fresh air and have the sky once more wide overhead; for there to be no shelling, no fighting. We were told we were to wait, that a second truck would soon pass by for us.

'Don't wander too far, watch for mines,' Mati called out to me.

'Where are we?'

'On the way to Jurm. Some will go on to Feyzabad,' he said. I looked at him blankly. This was not my grandparents' valley but further from Kabul, higher.

'Badakhshan. We are travelling to the roof of the sky,' he said laughing.

The mountains towered over the valley. Below stretched out green fields and orchards, the land lush and fertile.

'And where am I to go?' I asked him.

Mati looked at me.

'You can come with me. I am going back to my family. My mother does not want Abas and I to fight any more. She has threatened to leave my father if we do not return so we have been summoned back.' He laughed again.

I was touched by his kindness and drawn in by his smile. For a moment I let myself imagine this possible new life, a quiet life in the fields, but I knew it was a dream.

I shook my head. 'No, I must find my brother, Omar.'

Mati looked at me, disappointed but understanding.

'Ask Abdul-Wahab,' he said, pointing in the direction of the man who had given the earlier orders. 'He knows everyone. If it is possible to find your brother, he can help you.' He hesitated. 'Just know he will expect something in return.' He said this quietly so the others could not hear.

I nodded, not really understanding what he meant.

After a while of sitting in the sunshine, we heard the second truck approaching uphill, its gears pulling as it made each corner turn. The men held their guns ready. Even here, in Massoud's own territory, it paid to be cautious. The driver called out. Recognising the man, Abdul-Wahab went over to greet him and soon we were all back on the road once more, heading towards Jurm where I would have to say goodbye to Mati, the closest thing I'd had to a friend since the camp.

I felt sadness at the thought of saying goodbye once more, then relief that I no longer felt only emptiness inside, that I could still care, could even feel strangely alive. Mati smiled at me and my heart quickened as I held his gaze.

Somehow the pain of all that had passed had not yet quite overwhelmed me.

Chapter 24

I look out of the train window at the falling light. Outside, the Siberian steppes stretch on, endless and seemingly empty. It is a deceptive emptiness, I know. Out there the ground teams with life hidden from sight – hidden from the train that passes by, never stopping.

The other passengers weary of taking photographs. They are now content to let the colours of the evening sky wash over them as they look out of the windows. It is so vast, this space around us.

'Madar, do you see?' I whisper this so that the other passengers do not hear. Madar smiles at me, rocking Sitara on her lap. I picture them there opposite me. I allow myself this and I am not alone. Perhaps Baba has gone for a walk along the train. Perhaps Ara is making friends with other travellers, with Javad pulling at her sleeves, trying to drag her back down the carriages to Madar. These are the thoughts that travel with me. I hold tight to them.

When I look at other places, that's when I find myself thinking of the landscapes of home, the crisp blue of the sky, the majesty of the mountains, the rivers gushing through the Hindu Kush. I think of the beauty of all that I have left behind and all that I may never see again.

Chapter 25

'Javad,' Abdul-Wahab beckoned me over, 'come and sit up front with us. You can tell me more about this brother of yours.'

I looked back at Mati, grateful that he had spoken for me, had been willing to help without really knowing me at all. I clambered in beside the driver. As the truck wound its way over the mountain passes and down once more into the valley I explained the story of Omar leaving, the men coming to the village and how then he was gone. It had happened a long time ago, I knew, but I was sure Abdul-Wahab could help me – after all, Mati had said so. I smiled at the older man, wishing under my breath that he would be able to help.

'I will see,' he said. 'We will ask but you should know there are many fighters, many boys – young men like your brother – in many parts of the country. It may be impossible.'

He saw the shadow cross my face. 'Everyone has lost someone,' he added.

'I have lost everyone.' I said it quietly. He seemed to sense my determination and resolve. 'Someone will know,' I said.

'And if he is dead?'

'I want to know that too.'

He looked at me for a long while, a smile playing at the corners of his lips.

'You are very determined, Javad. We need young fighters. Why not come with us, be with the men? There is a training camp. You could learn; we will search for your brother. What do you think – interested?'

I did not know what to say, how to explain to him that although I was desperate, although I had lost everything, I was still no warrior. War had taken everything from me. All I wanted was peace, to find Omar and get away from the fighting as far as Madar's buried money would take me. I wanted to start over.

'Think about it,' he said. 'We will be staying near Jurm a few days to rest. You have time to think it over.' He leaned against me as he spoke and I felt sure he could feel the belt under my *chapan* and the secrets I carried with me.

The truck bumped and sped along the road down to Jurm. Green fields, poppy fields spread out either side, stretching far into the distance.

Abdul-Wahab said nothing more to me, talking now with the driver. I relaxed a little. It felt good to be watching the countryside roll by – to be sitting up front in the truck, travelling forward, to no longer be walking alone. My body was getting stronger again, recovering with the sleep and the food and the company of the men.

I found images of Ara and Sitara coming back into my mind and I pushed them away. I was not strong enough for that, to think about what had been, how things had ended for them.

The men were laughing at a joke in the back of the truck, Mati making everyone smile. I knew my heart would hurt to take my leave of him. Yet it was good to know that in the midst of all the chaos we could still laugh.

Jurm twisted through the valley. The houses were small, low. Along the way bright stalls sold nuts, fruits, the vegetables grown in the valley. It was a place where life continued in defiance of the Taliban.

'Things are different here,' said Abdul-Wahab, laughing, watching my face taking it all in.

As the truck drove through the village a woman and man came running forward, calling out. The driver slowed. I tensed again, imagining an ambush. But the truck came to a stop and Mati and Abas jumped down off the back. I watched them in the side mirror, Mati being lifted up by his father and swung around, his mother crying, happy laughter shared between them all. She did not wear a burka and her headscarf sat loose on her shoulders as she hugged Mati to her.

'Why did you let them go?' I asked Abdul-Wahab.

'They did not want to stay.' He shrugged. 'You cannot force people to fight; they have to believe it for themselves, choose it.'

He looked at me intently once more. Mati came bounding up to the side door of the truck and banged on the window. I opened the door and leant down towards him. We embraced and wished each other luck. '*Zenda bosheyn!*'

'Long life to you, brother,' Mati said, squeezing my shoulders hard. I let go and slammed shut the door and he went running back off to his parents, the four of them receding in the wing mirror as the truck drove on. I looked down. Ara's necklace had slipped out from under the collar of the *chapan* and was shining now on my chest. I quickly covered it with my hand, trying to shove it back underneath the cover of the scarf. Abdul-Wahab was watching me. I looked at him and down again, fearful now. He said nothing and pretended he had not noticed. But I remembered Mati's words: 'He can help you. Just know he will expect something in return.' I cursed myself for being careless.

We journeyed on towards Feyzabad where, as dusk fell, the truck stopped outside a compound with a large courtyard. I followed the men, not knowing what else to do. Until I heard about Omar I would stay with them, I reasoned. They could not make me fight if I did not wish to. And I had questions I wanted to ask them.

Chapter 26

Napoleon has come to sit beside me in the carriage – it is time for his shift to end and the *provodnitsa* will take over for a while. He does not much like her and they are forever fighting over who will take the night shift, who the day. She is a mean-spirited woman and always criticising the travellers in the carriage, sighing and rolling her eyes at the stupidity of people. Napoleon in contrast jollies everyone along, so we all share one great big adventure.

I have told him about Mati and my time in the mountains. Not everything, though. I did not tell him about Abdul-Wahab. I do not know why. I have shared so much with Napoleon, so many secrets. He knows all I have cared for and lost. He does not judge me for having left my country, for fleeing. The things I have told him, it has felt as if I'm talking about someone else's life. They are things that happened to Madar, Baba, to my family, not to me.

But this I have not told him. I have not told anyone.

I am trying to put it all in order, to keep my mind in order. What is here, now, and what was then? It is harder for me to separate things out . . . I struggle, thinking of Abdul-Wahab; I see Javad's eyes disapproving; I see Madar holding out her arms to me.

I think about writing it down now in the notebook – I am on book number four and filling them so quickly

Napoleon jokes that we will run out of paper before the journey is done.

I write in smaller script, making full use of the paper left to me. I want to tell it all. Even this.

Chapter 27

That night I was to sleep in the courtyard. The men had put out mats and there were blankets and a fire. We all sat around it late into the night, the men I had travelled with talking to the people from this compound near Feyzabad who had welcomed us in. I was listening to it all, learning much about Massoud, this 'Lion of Panjshir' that I had heard Omar and Baba speak of so often in the mountains.

I learnt about his campaigns and ideas, how he had first pushed back the Soviets, then the Taliban, how in places like this under his control the Taliban's rules and courts held no sway. Here there were schools, even for girls. There were doctors and teachers too. It was a part of Afghanistan fighting to hold on to those things we feared would be lost forever to the Taliban.

'Javad,' Abdul-Wahab called me over to him by the fire. He sat me next to him and said to the older white-bearded man to the other side of me, 'Here is the boy, Javad. He is looking for his brother, let him tell you his story.'

He looked at me. I squirmed, uncomfortable with the attention, sensing all ears now listening to the story I no longer wanted to tell to strangers, but knowing that if I did it might bring me closer to Omar, and that I really had no choice. I began once more. I described the men who had come to the village. I described Omar, how he had just disappeared. I even spoke of the boy dying in the cave. I told them how I had lost everything, that Omar was all that was left, that I needed their help. The men leaned in, listening all the while as the flames from the fire danced in front of us. The old man rested his hand on my arm. 'You know, Javad, life continues whether you are happy or not. It is in looking back that a man knows his worth. Massoud . . . he tells us this and it is so. Better to have no regrets.'

In my pocket I held tight to the old photograph of what I thought looked like Baba, Madar and Arsalan in uniform. I had taken it out to look at earlier that evening. My fingers rubbed against the sharp edges of the picture. I did not know whether to show it or not. The men were shaking their heads, saying how it would be impossible to track down this lost brother.

'Javad, many of the fighters who come to us, they change their names, they become warriors, not sons or brothers. You have to stop thinking of family in order to fight.' Abdul-Wahab smiled at me, a thin unpleasant smile.

'Don't listen to him,' said the old man. 'All things are possible, are they not?' As he said this I thought of Madar and the tears welled up behind my eyelashes. I blinked them away and took out the picture. I showed it to the men, then reluctantly to Abdul-Wahab, who looked angry that I had kept a secret to share with these strangers first and not him.

'Can you tell me what this uniform is?' I asked.

The men all passed the photograph from one to the other.

'Where did you get this?' one asked, looking at me with renewed interest.

'It belonged to my mother,' I said, not wishing to lie.

'And the people in the picture?' Abdul-Wahab asked me, his voice tense.

'My father, his friend, I think, and my mother.'

I had said it. I could no longer take it back. The men stared at each other, then at me, suspicious now.

'Who sent you here?' one asked, the tone less friendly than before.

'No one sent me. I am looking for my brother.' I looked at the men, their faces closing around me.

One man from the compound called Abdul-Wahab apart from the others and they took to muttering far from the fire, arguing over something. I sat nervously, rocking back and forth, wishing I had never shown them the picture that had filled my mind with so many unanswered questions.

Panic rose in my throat. I had drawn attention to myself, become a problem for these men, a problem that would have to be dealt with, yet I had done nothing wrong. I had only asked for answers.

'Come with me.' Abdul-Wahab stood tall over me, his face dark.

'We want to know who sent you amongst us. What are you doing here? Who are you spying for?' He put his hands on my shoulders, pressing down hard. I did not think to run. There was nowhere to escape to and his grip was tight.

'I'm not lying!' I yelled. I pointed to the picture again.

'Look, that is my father, this other man is called Arsalan. My mother is, was, named Azita.' The men hesitated. The elder raised his hand.

Then another man beckoned Abdul-Wahab back.

'Arsalan, you say?' The old man looked at me.

I nodded, tipping my head forward. '*Baleh*, yes!'

I decided to tell them everything that could be of use to them, everything that would stop them from letting Abdul-Wahab take me. So I told them about the yellow house, about my parents' stories of the Communist meetings in the caves, of my father's friend Arsalan, of the men coming to the house, their questions, Arsalan's death. I did not say anything about the letters or Madar. I did not want to betray her honour and besides I did not know, could not know for sure if what I feared was true.

'Your father's friend was a powerful man,' the old man told me, his eyes wet, after he had listened to what I had to say. I could feel him looking at me anew, watching my face lit up by the flames from the fire. I willed him to believe me.

'I am sorry if we have frightened you. We have to be careful. There are always those who would betray us or seek to bring harm.'

Relief flooded through my body.

'This man, Arsalan, he was a great friend to our leader. A real warrior. I knew him well long ago when he was a young man. And your parents . . . they too were brave.' He seemed sad as he said this. 'You know, Javad, not everything is always as it appears.'

I looked at him, wondering if he knew – if I had failed to disguise the truth.

'Allah in his wisdom has led you to us. We will help you find your brother. *Inshallah*.' He looked at the other men, who were all in agreement now. I sighed, thankful for my good fortune.

'We may need you to come with us,' he continued. 'This photograph . . . there is more to this story.' He looked at me intently. 'Is this the only such picture?'

I thought about the bags tied around my waist, the other photographs I carried, but it was the only *such* picture. It was no lie to say so, so I replied, 'Yes, the only one.'

'Good.'

Abdul-Wahab moved to protest but the elder waved him away.

'It is good you have brought this child to us. We will take young Javad with us tomorrow. We have much more to talk about.'

Abdul-Wahab gave me a look of hatred and I was left unsure as to what I had done to so enrage him.

'We'll leave early in the morning,' the old man said to me. 'Make sure to be ready after prayer.'

He passed the photograph back to me. I thanked him as he led away Abdul-Wahab, who continued his protest just out of earshot.

Exhausted, I found a mat to lie on, a little distance away from the warmth of the fire and next to a couple of young boys from the compound who were already asleep, shadows from the fire dancing over their sleeping faces.

I just lay down, closed my eyes, threw Omar's *patu* over me and wondered where it was they wanted to take me, who it was they wanted me to see. Perhaps it would be Massoud himself. They had given me no answers and yet they knew much more than had been said. I would have to be patient. That night I felt alone once more. Thoughts of Mati and Abas at home with their parents flitted through my mind and my heart ached for Baba and Madar and all that I had lost. I slept lightly.

Still, I did not hear Abdul-Wahab until he grabbed me by the throat and pulled me up off the ground, his hand over my mouth. He dragged me away from the mats, my boots kicking in the air and pulled me towards a gate on the edge of the compound beside which was a low mud hut. He opened the door to the hut and pushed me inside.

His hand reached out and hit me on the side of the head. The blow hurt, a ringing sound echoing in my ears. I fell backwards and heard the door close behind him. It was almost completely dark inside. I wanted to cry out but he came towards me and covered my mouth with his hand. Then, in that moment, I could not understand his anger nor that I had made him look foolish and uninformed, nor that I had captured his interest and that he was someone used to taking things that he wanted without question – but I knew that, if I did not get away from him, did not get out of the hut, everything would be over. I would never find Omar. I would never be free again.

I pushed back against him as his hands pulled at my clothes. I bumped up against something wooden – a narrow table. He held me over it.

'Come, come, little Javad, let's see what other secrets you've been hiding.'

His breathing was heavy, his voice hoarse. His hands sought me out. I reached down and found Arsalan's knife at my side, and pulling it loose from its sheath I turned the blade towards him. I could see nothing, only feel him pulling at me, his breath warm and tangy against my face. I jabbed forward with the knife. Nothing. He came closer once more.

'Now, now, Javad,' he said, pushing one hand against my mouth, the other searching between my legs. Panic welled in my chest. I kicked forward, swinging at him with my legs, hearing him curse me in the darkness. One kick landed on him and he loosened his grip for a second. In that instant I bit his fingers. As he steadied himself holding on to the table I raised the knife once more, this time finding him in the darkness. I plunged the knife in. He howled out in indignant pain as I slipped away from him, my hands searching in the darkness for the latch of the door. I wasn't sure, but I thought as the door swung open and I ran out into the night that I had stabbed him through the hand, pinning him to the table. I ran through the gate and out of the compound, not looking behind me. All I could hear was my heart pounding in my chest. I ran. I did not know if he would come after me or send others to hunt me down. I just ran.

Chapter 28

It is strange to relive these moments, writing them now with an unsteady hand as the train travels on towards Moscow. I look at the words in my notebook. A tourist, a tall fair-haired man, walks past, lurching a little from side to side as the train curves westward. I shield the page from prying eyes. I don't know why this moment with Abdul-Wahab disturbs me so. In the end I escaped. He didn't hurt me, only my pride. I fought back. Perhaps it is that that scares me most in all of this – that when it mattered I was prepared to fight, to protect myself, to hurt someone else in doing so. This troubles me and I still feel shame. Shame for what happened. Shame for not preventing it.

I relive how I felt that night, cowering under bushes away from the compound, listening, waiting for them to find me, terrified of what would happen to me once they did. This was where my search for Omar had led me. It was many days later that I stopped shaking.

I write all of this down too.

Napoleon will tell me later, 'Samar, you did nothing wrong.' I will listen to him say it and I will not believe him. I will feel that perhaps not all secrets need to be shared. Now he too carries my shame.

Chapter 29

No one came for me that night. I do not know how Abdul-Wahab explained his wound or my disappearance but by some small miracle they either did not come for me or failed to find me and I made it far from the compound on the road between Feyzabad and the border.

I began my journey out of Afghanistan.

I could no longer believe that I would find my brother, that there would be a joyful reunion. For the longest time after the earthquake happened it had been something of which I had dreamed. When I had run up the mountain away from my family I had run in search of Omar. That was at the heart of all that had happened since to my family and I suppose I had hoped that if I could find him, that one right would undo the wrongs. But Madar was mistaken, not everything is possible. You cannot always go back.

In the darkness of that hut I had to let go of Omar. I let go of the dream of ever going home.

Instead I would head for the border and make my way to Europe, to Russia, to a new beginning. I had had enough of the fighting and anger in men's hearts. It was the only way I knew to bring me closer to Omar – the only journey left to me to take.

I still had the money – Abdul-Wahab had been uninterested in what I carried about me. I would use it to get out of Afghanistan. I would start a new life. I would go forward.

I would not go towards Iran. No, I would go north, cross into Tajikistan. I had heard the men talk a lot about this country bordering Badakhshan – about the people there, about how the Lion of Panjshir was loved there too. How nine times the Soviets had tried to force their way into the valley, how nine times he had driven them out. I remembered, too, the geography lessons with Najib, him drawing on the chalkboard, his desire to teach us all about the world beyond our borders – the many countries, peoples and cultures different to our own.

I thought of the railway Omar had so often spoken about – the Trans-Siberian – linking east to west and west to east. Before he had disappeared he would often show me the map of the journey in one of Madar's old Russian travel books, a map which Omar's fingers would trace as he spoke. I remembered too my mother's sister Amira who had fled to Moscow when the Taliban came, no longer protected or on good terms with her parents, long after Madar had disappointed them in her choice of life.

I let go of the dream of finding Omar before it could destroy me. Instead I began to think of Amira and the possibility of finding her still in Moscow. I focused on how I was to make this journey, how I would escape Afghanistan and make a new life for myself with no family, no papers and only money to help me. But I had faith and I was not alone. I would call on Baba and Madar, on Ara and Omar, on Javad and Little Arsalan, and on Sitara – all of them, to help me. Nas and Robina I let go. They would stay in Afghanistan with Masha and their mother. They could not make this journey with me. My heart tightened as I thought of them and my grandparents. They too would stay buried on the mountainside but the others I would take with me. I would not make this journey on my own.

Taking my chances in the early-morning light I hitched a ride with the first truck that would stop for me on the road to Ishkashim. The driver, a kindly man with pink cheeks and a long drooping moustache, opened the door and I climbed up beside him.

If he was surprised to see a young boy alone walking on the remote road he didn't show it. I said I would cross at the Panj River if I could find someone to take me. I asked the driver where he was going. He spoke of the Ishkashim market and its weekend bazaar held on a strip of land in the middle of the river, a no man's land between the two countries. He would take me as far as the town and I would have to find someone else to help me make the crossing. I thanked him for his kindness. I was still shaking, my mind fixed on putting distance between me and Abdul-Wahab. The driver watched me.

'You will need papers,' he said.

'I have no papers.'

He thought about this for a while.

'Have you money?'

Cautious, I nodded.

'Well, then, we can get you papers.'

He laughed at my wide eyes, my disbelief at my good fortune in finding someone willing to help and equipped to do so. He didn't ask me where I had come from or why I wanted to leave. Instead he just drove, his eyes smiling, chuckling like he had discovered a good joke on the side of the road.

As we drew closer to the border town the countryside became rockier and flatter all at once – behind us now were the peaks of the Hindu Kush and the Karakorum mountains; before us the hills lay bare and then the land stretched out towards the Panj River, which snaked between the two countries. The people we passed were farmers or nomads, riding on mules or horseback. The driver would wave and they would smile back as we all navigated the rough mountain roads together.

'Things are getting better there,' he said after a while of no oncoming traffic.

'Where?' I asked.

'Why, Tajikistan,' he said.

This had not occurred to me. I had thought only of the fighting in my own country, not in others. I had forgotten that the Soviets were on the retreat everywhere, that countries had changed names, regimes, ownership. I did not want to substitute one war for another.

'Better?' I asked, nervous now.

'There is peace, of sorts. Better for business,' he laughed, and seemed cheerful about this. 'Even talk of a bridge.'

I smiled back. 'A bridge?'

I thought of Omar with his sketches, his plans and hopes. I thought of the train – the line that he had traced long ago at the cave house, the Trans-Siberian journey he had spoken of, the great adventure he was sure it would be.

In Ishkashim the driver took me to meet someone who could get me papers. It would take a few days but they could help with visas and a passport for a price. I agreed, willing to try anything. We met in a small shack near the traders' stalls where a thin wiry man with a long beard greeted us and took us inside. Anxious, I stepped from foot to foot, my eyes on the open doorway the whole time.

'Here's our traveller,' the driver said, introducing me.

'So, you want to go to Tajikistan?' the man asked.

'No, I want to go to Russia.'

'Ah, a true traveller.' The man laughed a little. 'You know that is a very long journey indeed? Very expensive.'

I nodded.

'And you will go alone?'

'Yes.'

The two men looked at me. I stood as tall as I could. They laughed for a long while but they took the money offered and they helped me all the same. They found me drivers, trusted people, someone to fake papers; they bought me a bag of Western clothes from the market stalls, Chinese copies of things labelled Gap and Old Navy. They fed me, let me rest there a few days and when all was ready they wished me well and sent me on my way.

I do not know why they wanted to help me. Perhaps it was just good business for them. I did not know, could not tell any more what was kindness, what was necessity. I realised I had grown used to not trusting anyone.

A new driver took me by jeep across the river at one of the lowest points, the wheels of the 4x4 turning slowly in the water, the jeep bobbing along where the water was deeper before reaching the shallow bank on the far side. There, once through the crossing point, we were in Tajikistan. I looked behind me in the window and said goodbye to my homeland.

The driver waited with me on the Pamir Highway, where I was switched to another truck, this one colourful, painted with mountain scenes. Soon I was sitting up front once more with yet another new driver. This one was called Cy and he was happy to have me travel with him.

'A first-class traveller, I hear,' he joked. He was friendly, gruff but cheerful enough and told me about his country. We spoke mainly in Russian, understanding each other that way and I was glad of Madar's many lessons and of the hours spent learning and whispering new words in the cave house in the mountains, the hours spent drawing stories in the dust. We were to travel a long distance together. He had the radio on and we listened to music as we went, humming along to the songs. After so long of being forbidden to sing, the music tumbled out of me and I felt the beginnings of a new freedom draw closer.

It was a long journey from one border to the next but the beauty of the mountains and the sky surrounded us as the truck rattled across the passes, and I drank it all in.

I tried not to think about what I had left behind or might never see again.

'Why do you want to go to Russia?' he asked me.

'I have family there, my aunt in Moscow,' I lied. Or perhaps it was the truth. After all, I did not know for sure. I hoped to find Amira there. It was easier to sound certain.

'Oh,' he said. 'That is good. Family is important.'

I scrunched up my fists under my thighs and looked ahead, unblinking.

'And your family?' I asked him, keen to move the conversation away from talking about Baba and Madar or my brothers and sisters and all that was lost to me.

'Three sons,' he said proudly. 'All healthy, strong boys. The eldest two work, the youngest is still at school. It is hard for them now; everything is changing. We don't know what the future will bring.'

'But they'll stay?' I asked.

'Yes, of course. Things here . . . they are bad . . . but they are better . . .' He looked in the rearview mirror as he said this. I nodded, understanding.

'Besides, if they go who will look after me in my old age?' he laughed.

I thought of Baba and felt a stabbing pain inside. I thought of Arsalan. The confusion rose up in me again. I started to tap my leg once more, marking time. Cy looked down and noticed but said nothing.

The road was tricky in parts where rocks had fallen and sometimes we had to stop and get out and roll them back off the road so that the truck could pass. On some bends the surface of the road crumbled with the weight of the wheels, and small stones and gravel would bounce down the mountainside behind us. The driver was calm, unflustered. He had driven this road many times before. The inside of the truck up front was filled with icons and good luck totems – he had all bases covered just in case.

'How will you get to Moscow?' he asked me after a while, marvelling at the distance I was prepared to cover alone.

'By train. There is a train that runs east to west, the Trans-Siberian,' I said. 'I want to go on that train. It was something my brother . . .'

My voice trailed off. I had said too much and began to look out of the window instead.

'Look,' he said.

I followed the sweep of his arm to the side of the valley below. Several riders were chasing each other in the vast open spaces that dipped down between the hills and mountains, one dragging the carcass of a calf, the others trying to catch it from him. On the backs of the horses we could just make out the colourful saddles of the riders, the way they circled each other like dancers. I watched, mesmerised at how free they were.

'It's a game,' the driver said.

'I know, *buzkashi*,' I said. 'We used to have it too.'

'They are practising.'

'Tell that to the calf.' He looked at me, smiling, and we stopped a while and stood by the side of the road looking down into the valley, cheering the men on, waiting for a victor to emerge.

It was good to stop. Everything since the earthquake had been constant moving from one place, one disappointment, one hope to another.

One of the *chapandaz* was wearing an old Soviet tank helmet to protect his head from the whips of the other two and he leant far to the side of the horse, sweeping forward to pick up the calf from his opponents.

'He is good, this one,' Cy said, approving of the man's skill and speed, the way he judged the movements of the other two who tried to outwit him. He swept in between them, leaning low and grabbed the headless calf, his horse cantering away from the other two, the man waving his catch triumphant in the air.

'What are the rules here?' I asked.

'Here? There are no rules. It's each man for himself and the bravest will win.'

'Then what?'

'Ah, then they play again.'

He roared with laughter, his voice echoing out round the valley. I laughed too and the tiredness slipped away a little.

'When you get to Osh, what will you do?' Cy asked as we climbed back into the truck.

'I will look for someone to help me,' I said.

He smiled at my determination. We had long left behind Khorog, crossing the river once more with the truck pulling hard against the flow of water. High in the mountains we looked down towards Lake Karakul and the crossing into what was now called Kyrgyzstan. All this Cy explained to me. We had spent the nights sleeping in the truck, wrapped in blankets and sheepskins. Once we had stayed in the small home of a woman he knew along the way, a widow who had welcomed us in, unsurprised to see him. She let me sleep in a low chair by the fire. In the morning it was hard for them to waken me and I left half asleep, still drowsy from the heat.

I continued to keep my guard up but these people were kind. You could see it etched on their faces, the lines all turning upwards from lives of laughter lived in the mountain sun and wind.

When we finally arrived in Osh I realised that I had slept through the frontier checkpoint buried under a pile of old coats. I peered out, woken by the noise of the busy streets.

'Welcome to the Kyrgyz Republic!' Cy said smiling.

After all that had gone before, this part of my journey seemed so uncomplicated, so straightforward that I smiled too.

That happiness was not to last.

Chapter 30

Napoleon is drunk. I find him slumped in the corner of the box room at the end of the carriage, an empty bottle rolling beside him on the floor.

'Get up,' I hiss at him.

If the *provodnitsa* finds him or a passenger complains it will bring trouble.

'Napoleon, get up.'

Nothing. I slap him on the cheeks, lightly at first then more forcefully. His head rolls to one side. I look out of the box room up and down the train. There is no one coming but it's surely just a matter of moments. The samovar is in constant demand on the journey and I can feel the train slowing as we come closer to the next station.

I open a bottle of water from the trolley and pour it over his head. His uniform is dripping wet but that is the least of my worries.

'Napoleon . . .'

He starts to mutter. His eyes open and he registers the water spillage as drops drip from his hair.

'What the devil . . .?'

'I thought we would have to stop the train, get a doctor,' I tell him, unable to keep the angry edge out of my voice. He is supposed to be keeping an eye on me, after all – not the other way round.

'Where are we?' he asks.

'I don't know, you're the *provodnik*. You work it out. I think the last stop was Tomsk.'

He looks at me through bloodshot eyes. He seems unsteady on his feet. A loud Russian lady is coming down the hallway carrying a packet of soup and a mug. She calls for help as she struggles to work the samovar. I move out into the hallway to help her, gesturing at Napoleon to stay put, but he pushes past me and slurring his words says, 'Here, fine lady, like this.'

He proceeds to throw up all over her slippers. She looks at him in disgust and then starts to wail. Passengers pop their heads out of their compartments, everyone checking to see what all the fuss is about and they see Napoleon bent over, muttering something about fish and the restaurant car, and he must speak urgently with the chef and he hopes no one has had the fish. 'You, dear lady?' He points at her and she shrinks back. 'Did you have the fish too?'

I sit in the hallway, my back to the window, curled up in a ball.

The woman is furious now and stomps off down the hallway with as much dignity as she can muster, leaving a trail of regurgitated vodka and whatever it was Napoleon had for supper, quite possibly fish, along the carriage.

'Oh no.' This from Napoleon as he watches her go.

'You had better get cleaned up, get rid of the bottle,' I say to him. He is still wobbling and swaying with the train.

'I only wanted to forget,' he says.

'Me too,' I say.

It is too late for forgetting. Within minutes the lady is back, and with her the *provodnitsa*, who sizes up the situation quickly and seizes her opportunity. When the train pulls into the station she is first off the carriage and up to the driver where they huddle in conversation. The train sits there a long while. Passengers get off and have a smoke on the platforms, stretching their legs and doing exercises.

I can hardly bear to watch as the driver and *provodnitsa* come down the platform and find Napoleon, who sits, his hands on his throbbing forehead, whimpering in the box room.

'This is unacceptable.'

The driver looks at him, stern and decided. A phone call is made from inside the station. Napoleon must gather his belongings and get off the train.

I cling to him, begging them to let him stay, but they will not hear of it.

'Either he goes or she will make a formal complaint and then we're all for it,' the *provodnitsa* says, feigning minimal concern for the wellbeing of her co-worker.

'He'll be fine,' she says. 'He'll have dried out in a few days – the next train back will pick him up.'

I look at her, surprised.

'What? You think this is the first time Napoleon's been fired?' She laughs. 'No, seriously – how sweet.'

She pats me on the head like a pet and climbs down from the train to corral all the milling passengers back on again, once more checking papers and familiar faces.

I consider going with him but what good would it do? He waves me away when I offer.

'No, Samar, you need to get to Moscow. Go and find your aunt.' He tries to smile.

I don't want to let go of his sleeve but I do. Within minutes he has packed up and gives me a hug before climbing down from the carriage. He salutes the train – unsteady on his feet – as we pull out of the station.

Chapter 31

Cy left me by the bazaar in Osh. I helped him unload his truck and then we said our farewells. He gave me a hug and a hearty pat on the back and wished me good luck for the rest of my journey.

I was to seek out a *marshrutka* to take me to the north of the country. He pointed me in the direction of the bus station and when I turned to thank him he had already disappeared into the sea of people weaving through the bazaar.

I walked along the west bank in search of a money-changer and found one between the men selling gold jewellery and a stall selling flatbreads. I felt for Ara's chain. It was still there under the scarf and I pressed it close to my skin. I still had plenty of money left and later would discreetly find a quiet corner to transfer funds from the bags to my pockets, hoping to protect myself in case of theft. Madar, I reckoned, must have been pretty angry at either Arsalan or herself to have left such riches behind.

I bought some chai and bread and sat near to the mosque, a large imposing building next to the market traders. There was an industry to the place: men, mainly Uzbek, buying and selling, chatting in the *chaikhanas*. I passed unnoticed in the bustling marketplace.

Afterwards, I ducked into a dark alleyway and took out the money I needed to change for the journey ahead.

I stopped by the first of the money-changers, who was a dour, unhelpful-looking man. I handed over the notes and he looked at me with interest.

'This is a lot of money for a boy to have.' He stood rubbing his pitted cheek.

'It's for my father,' I said, trying not to blush.

'That so, I haven't enough here to give you. Wait while the boy goes to get some extra.'

I nodded and edged nearer the bazaar, ready to run. I did not trust this man and wished now I had chosen a different place to stop. He stood looking at me for several minutes while a boy from the back of the shack went up the row to ask for more money.

'And what will your father do with all that money?' the man asked.

I shrugged. 'We are travelling, we're a large family.' I summoned up Baba and the rest of my family and there they were as if beside me in the doorway, calling for me, saying, 'Come on, hurry up.' I waved at them. The man raised an eyebrow and cast a weary look out into the market, seeing no one.

The boy returned and handed him a packet of notes wrapped in brown paper. The man slowly counted out the notes and some coins and handed them to me one by one. The boy darted off outside.

Putting the money deep in my pockets, I nodded in thanks and left as quickly as I could, heading towards the bus station as Cy had shown me.

'You'll find a *marshrutka* there that will take you north,' he had said. 'Just watch yourself.'

I kept my pace up, hurrying through the crowds passing rug sellers and meat sellers, clothes stalls and men pushing laden carts shouting, '*Bosh! Bosh!*' at everyone to get out of the way.

As I rounded the edge of the bazaar, the bus station now in sight, two boys grabbed me by the hands and swept me out of the crowd and down a dark alleyway to the side. I tried to shout but in the noise of the bazaar who could hear me?

One pulled the bag off my shoulder. The other hit me on the cheek and in the ribs. I fell to the ground as they kicked me in the stomach.

'Stop!' I cried out.

One bent down and rifled through my pockets, pulling out what money he could find. Laughing, they ran off, leaving me winded and aching on the damp earth.

Chapter 32

I sit in my compartment, worrying about Napoleon. He looked so forlorn when the train pulled away and the carriage has assumed an unhappy air since his departure. The *provodnitsa* busies herself in the carriage cleaning up after him, tut-tutting loudly to anyone who will listen. Things are no longer so jolly.

I look at what I have written in the notebooks, some of it slanted at odd angles, other paragraphs written, scratched out, rewritten. Is it the story of my family? Have I been fair to them? Is it the truth? I think about Napoleon's story, the parts he has shared with me and wonder, how do we choose? How to choose what makes sense of us to the world?

I have one notebook left. It is clear to me that the *provodnitsa* will be unlikely to bring me a new one. Whatever I have left that I want to say will have to fit on these thin lined pages. We are getting closer to the end of my journey. I switch on the reading lamp in the carriage and close the door to the compartment. The carriage is almost empty, everyone having gone to the restaurant car for supper and entertainment. Only a few people sit further up the car: two boys playing chess and a couple looking at guidebooks.

I shut the door, closing them out, and open the last notebook.

Chapter 33

The old woman found me and brought me into her home off the alleyway near the bus station. She stood pressing her hands to her chest, alarmed to find me on her doorstep in such need. I washed in a bowl in the one room that was her home, blood crusted to the side of my face, my lip swollen and cut where the boys had hit me. She helped me take off my ripped *chapan*, pulling it gently, and left me warm water to wash with before she stepped outside, leaving me alone. My body ached all over and I looked down at the bruises and cuts, washing them carefully. The boys had taken only the money I had exchanged and then only the notes, a small mercy. The remainder, unchanged, was still hidden under my clothes. I guessed they must have thought I was carrying it in the bag. I put my hand to my neck. Ara's chain was gone, broken in the struggle. I felt a tear form in my eye and I blinked it back. Each time I thought I was moving forward, that things would get better, then something would hold me back.

My hair was starting to grow longer again, the ends straggly on the collar of the *chapan* now. I brushed it to one side, surveying the damage to my face in the cracked glass on the wall above the table. It would heal and I would survive.

The woman came back in. She was holding out the necklace, snapped in two. I took it from her, mouthing,

'Thank you' – my voice almost lost to me. That night I slept there curled up on the floor, my head throbbing with pain, the old woman rocking back and forth in prayer over me. When I woke in the early morning she was sleeping on the chair by the door. I slipped past, leaving the necklace on her table.

At the station the driver gave me a strange look. I had forgotten how swollen my face must be.

'Naryn?' I asked him. He raised an eyebrow.

'I want no trouble,' he grunted warningly.

I bowed my head and got on, giving him a few of the coins that my attackers had failed to grab.

There were a couple of people on the back seats of the minivan already. We sat waiting for another hour for the *marshrutka* to fill and then we were off. I turned towards the window to avoid scaring my fellow passengers with my swollen face. The journey, long and hard going over bumpy mountain roads, was something I was so used to by now that I slept most of the way, though the minivan stopped often to let the passengers off for fresh air, to stretch, to eat or smoke or discreetly answer the call of nature by the roadside. By nightfall we were in Naryn, where I climbed down from the *marshrutka*, which stopped to the west of the bazaar, and from there I climbed onto a second one which waited to fill before it set off for Karakol on the last part of the journey to the border. The pain had worsened in my ribs and it hurt to move or cough. I wrapped the *chapan*, dirty and torn, around me and tried to close out the chatter of the other travellers, some local, some foreign – a French couple with backpacks, the girl loud and excited, enjoying the adventure. I did not care that it was night, that I was alone or in pain. All I could think of now was to reach the train, to be making my way to Moscow.

As I sat down in the minivan, this time with a shorter wait until we left for the border, I pictured Ara sitting beside me. It had been so long since I had thought of her, had spoken to her. She put her hand round my shoulders and smoothed the hair back off my cheek.

'It's okay, Samar, you will be there soon. What's with the bruises? You been fighting again? Such a tomboy,' she laughed.

I held her hand and let her sing me back to sleep as the minivan bumped its way to the border crossing where we were all told to get out. We would have to walk across.

'I'll come with you,' she said. 'You don't mind, do you, your big sister tagging along?'

It was typical Ara – not really a question, more a statement.

''Course not,' I said.

The driver gave me a strange look as I stepped down from the *marshrutka*.

I walked on, not caring. At the border the guards looked at my papers and shone a torch into my face. They did not hurry me on as they did the others from the minivan who had started to make their way to the waiting taxis on the other side.

'It's okay, Samar,' said Ara, looking right at the guard – that look she could give that would melt the sternest heart.

Ahead of me a girl turned, the French girl with her boyfriend, the adventure travellers who had shared the minivan from Naryn with me. I recognised her loud voice.

'Excuse me,' she said to the guard in lilting English. 'We're waiting for our friend.'

The men looked at her, a tall pretty girl carrying an expensive camera and an almost new rucksack.

'He's with us.' She gestured once more at me.

The men, who spoke only Kazakh and Russian, shook their heads at her, not understanding.

'W-I-T-H U-S,' she shouted at them, smiling.

'Okay, okay,' said the guard, amused. It was late at night and they had nowhere to put me and the minivan had departed now.

'Go on,' he said to me in Russian. 'It's your lucky night.'

Ara winked at me as we hurried on, the French girl holding open the door of their taxi, waiting for me.

'Thank you,' I said in English, slipping into the seat beside her. Her boyfriend sat in the front.

'That's okay, we would not leave you there.'

She winked and pressed a handful of *tenge* into my fist.

'For somewhere to stay, okay? Or a doctor?'

I realised how pitiful and broken I must have looked that she wanted to save me. A tear slid down my cheek and I wiped it away. She noticed and squeezed my hand lightly before launching into a discussion in French with her boyfriend, the gist of which I gathered was his dissent over her decision to help me. In the end she just shrugged and we drove on in silence to Almaty.

When we arrived the sun was starting to come up over the city.

I decided to stay a day or two in Almaty and took my leave of the couple, thanking them. I did not want to draw attention to myself for the remainder of the journey and it was better to let the swelling go down. I wanted to prepare, to buy new clothes, Western clothes. For two days I slept in a cheap hostel. It was quiet, the man behind the desk bored and engrossed in the television. I found a bookshop in the centre and spent hours on the floor, amazed at all the books and the fact that I could just sit there undisturbed. I looked for maps, information, anything that could help me. I found an encyclopaedia and lingered over the pages until the shopkeeper stood over me, encouraging me to leave. I reckoned I needed to get to Novosibirsk, that I could catch the Trans-Siberian train there. It would be an adventure – or this is what I wanted to believe. As I was getting closer to the end point of my journey I grew more nervous. I had the loosest of plans to look for my aunt Amira. Where would I start? What if I couldn't find her? Then I thought of her letter to Madar many years before and wondered if it was one of the ones I had taken with me, all the way from the yellow house. I thought, too, of Omar – regret over leaving Afghanistan and giving up my search for my brother stayed with me.

I was more guarded now, careful to avoid dark alleyways and suspicious-looking characters, aware that I alone was responsible for my safety. After the last border crossing Ara had given me a stern talking-to. She always had such a fierce temper. It was what I needed to hear: 'No more moping, Samar, no giving up now.'

The choice of clothes baffled me, the styles so different to home. I did not want to stick out. I watched the young girls and women on the pavements in mini-skirts and high heels, others in tight jeans and boots, short cut-off tops. It seemed incredible and somewhat terrifying. A few women wore headscarves but many didn't. I spent hours in the markets circling the clothes stalls. In the end I found some jeans, plain T-shirts and a soft zip-up jacket. I kept Omar's boots even though it was warm and they made me feel hot; I did not want to throw them away. One of the market stalls sold small black belt bags with a zip which I was able to wear under the baggy T-shirts and which made carrying my papers, the photographs, letters and what was left of the money, much easier. A small rucksack fitted a few changes of newly purchased clothes. Leaving behind Javad's old *chapan* I said goodbye to my brother too. Washed and dressed, my hair growing longer again, the swelling healed a little, I was almost Samar once more.

The train station was busy, people rushing in all directions. I decided I would travel to Astana and from there on to Novosibirsk. At the ticket office the woman barely looked at me through the glass. I had to wait an hour on the platform and then the train arrived. I had never travelled on a train before and I was intrigued by all the comings and goings in the station. It amazed me that the trains could hold all these passengers, that these tracks could take so many people across vast distances. When the train came in to the platform I watched the other passengers to see how to get on and find my carriage. I brought food and water with me from one of the stalls in front of the station and soon found my place in a compartment for four. It was a small narrow space with a tiny sink by the window and two long seats facing each other. I was next to the window and could look out at the steppes as we travelled across the country heading towards Russia. A couple and their young daughter shared the compartment with me. For a while I imagined what life would be like to be part of this family but the father leered at me when his wife and daughter went to the toilet and I decided not all families were ones you would wish to join.

After all the walking, the trucks, the minivans, to travel this way, to cover distance so quickly felt like an incredible luxury. I started to worry more about money, how long it would last, how long I would need it for. Somehow I had convinced myself that I would soon find Amira and she would welcome me in, and so I had only thought that far ahead. The thought of having nothing once more terrified me. I would have to be more careful. I slept to ignore my rumbling stomach and then walked up and down the carriage to get rid of the cramp I'd developed in my legs from sitting so long. At night the seats were turned into fold-down beds. I worried about the man in the bed below me and I stayed awake, facing into the carriage so that he could not surprise me. In the end he just slept, snoring so loudly that the people in the compartment next to us banged on the partition throughout the night. By late morning the next day we were in Astana. By now I had lost count of the miles covered, become immune to the wide landscapes, the mountains, the rivers, the grasslands.

I found myself talking constantly to Madar and Ara, to Little Arsalan and Sitara, to Javad as he was before the Taliban, to Omar who I still hoped was out there, to Baba, who I knew was gone. When they left the train in Astana, the family from my compartment hurried away from me. I realised I had been speaking out loud and they must have thought me mad.

In Astana I was fortunate. The next train to Novosibirsk was leaving later that afternoon. After that there would not be another one for four days. This time I bought the cheapest seat and immediately realised I had made a mistake – the carriage was crowded and it did not feel safe. I spent most of the journey standing in the restaurant car, looking out of the window and counting down the hours until I would be in Russia and on board the Trans-Siberian Railway at last.

I had not chosen the most straightforward of routes, I realised now, but I wanted so badly to sit in the carriages Omar had spoken of, to feel close once more to my brother, to take my family with me for this last part of the journey towards my aunt, Amira – the last possible link to all that I loved. I realised too that I was putting off getting to Moscow, scared of what would happen if I could not find her.

By the time the train pulled into Novosibirsk I had begun to doubt my whole plan. My hands shook as I stepped down from the carriage. I kept my head down and hurried along to the ticket office to buy my ticket to Moscow.

The girl at the ticket window wore bright pink lipstick and her hair was dyed blonde. I tried not to catch her eye. She took my papers, looking at them for a long time, then called a colleague, then a second man. The three of them had stood there looking at the papers for what seemed like forever – a long queue of people building behind me, all nudging and pushing, wanting to know what the hold-up was. I had grown casual, used to people not checking properly or caring. I had no plan for being stopped and questioned. Nor could I offer her more money to help me as she had involved the whole ticket office now. I didn't know whether to brazen it out, to take the questions and try to convince her or whether just to run. She picked up the telephone.

And so I ran. I did not wait to find out what would happen to me if caught with fake papers by the police.

I would have to find another way.

My Trans-Siberian journey was over before it had even started.

Part Six

'Baba, will we ever see such a thing?'
'One day, one day we will all see such a thing.'

Chapter 34

Sometimes you have to go backwards to go forward. This is what Madar used to tell us.

I see the train approaching. Its locomotive is white, red, blue, the carriages striped all three colours. It pulls in slowly to Novosibirsk. Around me stand tourists – Americans, French, a couple of tall Scandinavians with backpacks. A few local people are also getting on, heading to Omsk. I listen to their conversations. I look for someone to stand behind.

No one has seen me slip onto the platform, ducking under the barrier and crouching, waiting for the arrival of the train. I have become an expert in invisibility, in not drawing any attention. I look straight ahead and try not to catch anyone's gaze, particularly the *provodnitsa*, a girl with dark hair and ruddy cheeks, standing by the carriage door, counting passengers on and off.

I have been watching the arrival of the trains for over a week now. I know how long I will have to find a moment of inattention and slip onto the train. I try not to think about what will happen if they catch me.

The young woman is busy arguing with a fat American about his luggage allowance – he stands on the platform surrounded by expensive shiny suitcases and bags. She is lifting them one after the other and shaking her head. I take advantage and dart past her, following on the heels of the family who are just boarding. I stay close to them, observing their mannerisms, the way they talk to each other, the girl and boy older than me – seventeen, eighteen, maybe – and I think of Omar and Ara. A knot catches in my throat.

There is no time for remembering. I need to understand the workings of the train, the comings and goings of the *provodnitsa*. I need to find places I can hide unnoticed. It does not take me long to discover these are limited. Yet I have come this far, I reason.

I have read now all about the journey in the guidebooks in the shop near the station. I think of Omar talking about this train from east to west – its bridges with remarkable engineering, the landscapes it passes through, how one day we would make this journey. I think of his dreams of being an engineer, his dreams of seeing Lake Baikal and the bridge there – a feat of ingenuity. And so I know something of the route, the stopping places. I am to become an eager student of this railway.

I believe it is still possible I may find him here. I do not believe it like I did about the yellow house, but there is some small part of me that still hopes.

In a few days I will be in Moscow. There I can fade into the crowds. I will search for Amira. All I have to do is find her. And if that fails? I cannot think that far ahead. I have no plan beyond that.

Madar always used to say – hold on to your dreams. She would encourage Ara and me in particular to imagine any possible future. It did not matter that we were girls or that our education was sporadic – that we were in the end home-schooled, as she tried to laughingly call it. We were capable of great things – this she would tell us over and over. A woman can be a warrior, can run a country, can save people, can teach, be a doctor, be a famous dancer, singer, musician, an engineer, a scientist, a writer. She would ask us to dream and we would fly with her.

I sit towards the back of the carriage. This end compartment is empty. The train is not busy, perhaps only a third of the compartments holding travellers. I discover I can fit underneath one of the long seats on either side of the compartment. It is uncomfortable. My head hits against the base of the seat and my hair catches on the frame when the train jolts. My knees are bent up to avoid my feet spilling out into the carriage but here if I roll far enough back against the partition I am undiscovered. The floor is dusty and dirty. I sweep it clean as best I can using a T-shirt from my bag. This compartment is near to the bathroom, a small toilet cubicle with a tiny mirror and a cold tap that water trickles out of reluctantly. I can step out onto the end of the carriage and stand in the fresh air, taking in the passing countryside – or, as I soon discover, the not so fresh air, as it is where all the smokers congregate. However, should the *provodnitsa* approach I can hide.

It becomes almost a game. I watch her, looking for a routine, so that I can be prepared and know what to expect. I debate whether to hide the money under the seat or to continue to carry it all on me. I decide in the end not to hide it, reasoning that the compartment may fill at another station. I try to sleep. I sleep in snatches. I dream. I stretch and dance up and down on the spot. The movement of the train is soothing, encouraging somnolence. I watch, unobserved, the *provodnitsa* strike up a friendship with a Russian miner. Her ruddy cheeks blush brighter every time she passes his compartment and she stands twirling her hair around her fingers and talking to him in a low, sing-song voice. I think of Mati, something tugging at my heart. I am invisible to the *provodnitsa*, of no interest.

Smells of food waft up from the restaurant car. My stomach tightens with hunger. I debate whether or not to eat in the car. In the end I decide not to, afraid they will remark upon a young girl travelling unaccompanied, that they will ask for papers, tickets – things I cannot provide.

I will wait until the train stops – there will be sellers on the platform, I reason. I can hold out my money in exchange for cheese, bread, fruit and boiled eggs. The samovar is near the *provodnitsa* so I decide to go without hot water.

I have survived so much worse that this train feels luxurious. I am travelling in style. I think back to the walk from the camp to Kabul, of the miles travelled through the mountains, Madar and Baba guiding me all the way. Then the long hazardous journey overland to reach Russia – how both Ara and Javad too in their own ways have helped me get here, urging me on. But, still, I stay watchful.

There is no one in the compartment next to mine, and I take solace from this. In the one next to that a young couple are travelling on honeymoon. They are from Chita – this I make out from their conversations. Everything is happy between them. It is a new beginning. When we arrive at Omsk they busy themselves gathering bags and then they leave the train, hand in hand. He helps her down off the high step. I go into their compartment. They have left behind a bag of half-eaten bread, some unwanted fruit, and I gather it up. On the seat is an old paperback. I look at the cover – a lady with a fan. It is by Tolstoy, and in Russian. I pick it up too and guard it like treasure.

Only a few people join the train at this busy stop, none in my carriage. I risk sitting a while in the compartment, closing the door. I check on the *provodnitsa* – once her passengers have boarded she becomes busy chatting to the miner, sitting now in his compartment. They grow closer, their voices overlapping, their laughter dancing up the carriage. Once I am sure she is occupied, I relax and allow myself to eat the food the happy couple from Chita left behind. I savour each bite, imagining it a feast. Out of the window I watch the city while we wait on the platform as supplies are taken on board. The sky is a dark Prussian blue.

The book is well thumbed, its cover creased, the corners of its pages furled in on themselves. It is called *Anna Karenina*. I sound the words out over and over, letting them roll on my tongue. I start to read, stumbling over some of the words, but finding myself transported to a new world. I do not even notice as we pull out of the station. Instead I lose track of the journey, of the rocking of the train and disappear into this world, so that it is with horror that I hear the *provodnitsa* chatting now halfway down the carriage. I have just enough time to slip underneath the seat as she passes by, stopping to switch on the reading lamps to brighten the train as night draws in. I hold my breath, the book jammed between my knees. The smell of peeled orange lingers in the compartment and I fear she will discover me. She stands a while in the hallway, sorting through tickets and change, then carries on down to the adjoining carriage. I sigh with relief. I stay there, scrunched in on myself, waiting in case she passes by again. After a while she returns and once she is back at the top of the carriage I ease myself out, dusty and stiff, and take the book in my hands once more.

I fall in love with the characters Tolstoy has created. Reading the book it is as if Anna is sitting here next to me in the carriage, or as if I am there. Anna's struggle, caught between duty and love, her husband and Vronsky, makes me think back to Arsalan and Madar. How complicated it must be, this business of love.

It is a sign, I decide, this book; an unexpected gift, and I read through as if sifting for gold.

The *provodnitsa* is soon sorting out the compartments for the night. The travellers are encouraged to go to the restaurant car. All except for her Russian friend who lingers in the carriage. I hear her giggling and see him pull her into his compartment, his hands circling her behind. I wonder if this is love. I go to the bathroom and stretch my legs by jumping up and down in the cramped space and half-light. The swelling and bruising on my face has almost healed now. Just a shadow underneath one eye remains. I look almost normal once more.

I imagine what it must be like to travel this journey week after week – first one direction, then the next, then back again. I suppose that the *provodnitsa* finds adventure where she can, when she can. The women here shock me. They are so open, so loud. Unafraid. Unapologetic.

The ticket collector from the next carriage comes bustling past, righting the benches into beds. I hear her tut in disapproval at her colleague. Then they both break into bawdy laughter. The man laughs too. There is a clink of vodka glasses, a toast to happiness and health. The women's laughter is dark. I hide once more, waiting for the other girl to pass back down along the train but it takes a while, as she stops to help her friend turn over the remaining beds. They chat about the passengers, not in quiet, hushed tones, but loudly and without fear or concern about being overheard. The train is their territory, and all the travellers just passing through.

The tourists and travellers eventually make their way back to the carriage, smelling of cabbage and *plov* and the heat of the restaurant car. They are delighted and annoyed by turns to find the beds made up for them already, the message clear that they should retire for the night. They fall in line with the *provodnitsa*'s wishes and the carriage becomes a hush of voices and shadow play.

Someone a little further up the carriage has a radio and it plays the saddest music. The man introducing it calls it *The Firebird* by someone called Stravinsky. He tells a story of a prince and thirteen beautiful princesses. The music is eerie and enchanting by turns and I imagine all of us here, gathered round, the light flickering on the ceiling, listening to it play.

It is hard to picture my family without thinking of all that has happened, and yet they have brought me here. They stay with me, watch over me. I see them now, Javad making shadows of the bird on the partition behind Baba's head. Madar's voice is low, drawing us in. Sitara is asking Baba, 'Baba, will we ever see such a thing?'

I reach out my hand to touch them but the light flickers and they are gone. The music spirals on.

As the carriage settles down to sleep and the *provodnitsa* continues to flirt with her miner, I risk sitting a while in the car. I want to escape into another world, so I open the book once more. I am part way through the story now and eager to know more of Anna and Vronsky and their doomed love. I have carried the letters from Arsalan to my mother all this way. I wonder why it is I have held on to them, what they prove or disprove, why it should matter to me any more. They are all gone, after all. I think that it was the truth I was interested in – wanting something real when everything was shifting around me. Now it doesn't seem so important. I read about Anna and Vronsky and how their hearts lead them to do crazy things, to break away from what others think is right or proper. Is that what happened with Madar and Arsalan, or was it something different, more complicated perhaps? I realise I may never know. The only person who seemed to know something of Arsalan, to find him of interest was the elder at the compound who I never had the chance to ask. Maybe, I think, Amira will know.

The carriage is warm and I close my eyes, the movement of the train sending me to sleep. The music is still playing further down the car. The sound of gentle snoring accompanies it from the top end of the carriage. Soon the *provodnitsa* will be back, bustling about the carriage, and I climb once more under the seat. I curl my arm under my head and use the book as a pillow of sorts.

It will be two days before we reach Moscow. I say goodnight to Madar and Baba, to my brothers and sisters. It is becoming harder and harder to see them, to feel them with me on this journey. It is like I am letting go of them or they of me.

In the morning I am woken by the voices of two South Africans from Cape Town, talking about their country, the landscapes, the wildlife, comparing it to the barren rolling vistas we are passing. I listen, curious to hear about a part of the world I know of only vaguely from Najib's lessons.

'Ja, it's like Kruger.'

'No it isn't, it isn't at all.'

'Ag, it is – all that grassland, the scrubby little trees, the way the sky just stretches out over it all, flat like that.'

'I don't reckon you'd see many leopards out there.' This is the man, insistent. 'Or buffalo.'

'Well, they have leopards over by the part that's near China. Look, says so here.' This is the woman, her voice high-pitched and nasal. I hear her passing the book to him.

'Umm . . . I still reckon they're pretty different.'

'You've never been to Kruger,' she says.

'Ja, but I know about the lowveld. You don't get zebra here, or elephants.'

She says nothing.

I think of Javad, how he used to love chasing the goats and sheep on the mountains, looking after the herd with Baba Bozorg, how he loved to be outdoors – before Amin started to poison his mind.

I imagine Javad as a vet or a safari guide, taking tourists round somewhere like this place Kruger that they're talking about. Someone perhaps saying to Javad, 'I went to Siberia once and it was kind of like this.'

After a while the couple start arguing about something else and I am glad when they get off at Tyumen.

It is strange to overhear other people's lives. The train is like this all day and night – the secrets people think they hide so well, the lies they tell each other. It is so curious to me to hear the voices – Russian, English, American, German, French, South African . . . they all mix together, all so different and yet all arguing or hoping for similar things.

I imagine Omar sitting further down the train and a lump comes to my throat as I realise I do not know what he looks like now, if he has been hurt or killed, or if he has killed others. If he is alive, does he know anything of us? Perhaps someone from the compound would have told someone else of a boy called Javad looking for his brother. Another half-truth. Outside the sky is a dull heavy grey. It mirrors my mood and I feel myself slipping back into the darkness, my mind crowded with images of Ara and Sitara, of the earthquake, of Masha – all these things I wish I could undo.

It is almost 200 miles between Tyumen and Yekaterinburg. I turn to the book again, undisturbed by the *provodnitsa* who is up in the box room at the top of the carriage having her lunch break. I am reading one of the sections about Levin – he is a funny soul, never quite happy, wanting his life to mean something. I skim through these parts, hungry for more of the relationship between Anna and Vronsky. It annoys me, Levin's unhappiness. Shouldn't we be happy just to be alive? Then I know what it is that annoys me most – it is that he is right: simply being alive is not enough.

I imagine Baba sitting opposite me saying, 'Ach, Samar, always with your head in the books, always learning. We'll make a school teacher of you yet.'

That was Baba's idea of me – a teacher. And mine of him? I don't know. I knew my father and yet I didn't. I knew what I wanted to know of him, that which fitted my own ideas. And so it goes.

This thought stays with me a long while.

The people in the carriage have changed at Tyumen. Now there are a couple of Russian boys and a school teacher father in the compartment next to me – I close the door to avoid being seen. They are playing cards, *Durak*, a game Baba used to play with Arsalan in the garden of the yellow house. Their voices shout excitedly and laughter fills the carriage. I miss my brothers and sisters. I miss the stupid games we used to play, the fights and arguments we used to have, the taking of sides and righting of wrongs, the days when Javad and I would freeze each other out, each refusing to concede the other may have had a point. All this I miss, and my heart hurts in my chest. I picture Ara holding Sitara, stroking her, singing a quiet lullaby to help her sleep.

'Samar, don't you know that if you face backwards you'll get travel sick?' Madar tells me, her tone somewhere between despair and amusement. I look up, surprised, and see that she is right so I swap to the other seat.

The *provodnitsa* is taking her time over her lunch break. I wonder if her Russian miner is still with her. I peer out into the hallway. It is empty. I decide to hazard the restaurant car after all. I need to be around other people, just for a short while. Too much sitting on my own and the memories overwhelm me. I forget what is real – here and now – and what is imagined, what has gone and is no more, because in my mind it is still happening over and over and I cannot shake it from me.

The restaurant car is rowdy, a couple of large groups drinking and laughing at one end. At the other end a harassed-looking tour guide is trying to give a solemn lecture to his group of American tourists about Siberia and her past. I sit near them, looking out of the window, trying not to catch anyone's eye.

'Stalin's Gulags, anyone know how many people died in them? Anyone?' he asks the group, who shift uncomfortably in their seats, wishing for lighter conversation to accompany their lunch. He holds one arm outstretched. No one hazards a guess.

'Millions passed through them, people worked to death, dissenters shut down.' He pauses for effect. One of the women looks particularly upset and a man is rubbing her back gently. There is only silence from the group.

'That's right,' he says, 'no one knows how many . . . So you're all right!'

He chuckles at his little joke and a few join him awkwardly. The staff in the restaurant car roll their eyes. I imagine he is a regular feature on their weekly journeys. To hear it over and over, do you become hardened to it? I struggle to understand how it is that men keep making the same mistakes over and over – different countries, different times, same methods – fear and hatred at the heart of it all. In a strange way the guide's lecture heartens me as I look out at the *taiga* as the train cuts through it, the trees dense either side. At least that didn't happen to us, I say to myself. There is always someone worse off.

I haven't ordered anything and slip from the seat, passing by the raucous drinkers and the smokers in between the carriages, making my way back up carefully into my own carriage. I try to fit in, to look like I belong here on this train. People can sense fear, they can feel you unravelling, they can sense weakness.

When we arrive at Yekaterinburg station my stomach is rumbling, so I risk opening the window and reaching out to a seller to buy some food and water. The old woman smiles at me, her teeth crooked, the front few missing. A shiver runs down my spine and I try to imagine her as a young woman, thanking her and quickly pulling in the food. On board the *provodnitsa* is checking the last of the passengers joining the train. It is becoming busier. I know there are no reservations for the compartment I have hidden in but it is always possible someone will move to it, or just choose to sit in it, and so at the stops I watch her and I keep an eye on the new travellers, just in case. I do not know what I will do if she discovers me. If they took me from the train without papers, without a passport or a visa, what would happen to me? I try not to think about it and am glad of the money I have left – something to protect me. The gloom descends once more. I am so tired now, so tired of this constant moving, never knowing what I am moving towards.

'You have us, Samar.'

I look around. Ara stands in the passageway, peeking through the half-open door, smiling at me. She is right of course. They are still with me, even if I struggle, even if at times I am uncertain, and I cling to this thought to get me through. This and the distraction of *Anna Karenina* and the conversations of my fellow travellers all anchor me to the world I have grown to fear and love in equal parts.

The school teacher father sits speaking loudly in the compartment next door, attempting to educate his two sons, neither of whom seems to be paying him much attention, their shouts and squeals passing down the train as one beats the other at chess.

'Yekaterinburg was until only a few years ago a closed city,' he says.

All these secrets and walls, I think, listening to him speak, all these ways of trying to hide the truth in plain sight.

I notice the miner has got off the train here and the *provodnitsa* becomes morose and grumpy, snapping at the passengers who have just joined. I wonder if he has a family here in Yekaterinburg, if he has anyone other than the lonely *provodnitsa* who cares for him.

After Yekaterinburg the train will not stop until Perm, then Kirov, as it gets closer and closer to Moscow.

'No, look, move the castle like this. Who are you trying to protect?'

I hear the father, exasperated now, trying to show them how to play their game.

'This is all about strategy. You build a power base. You seek out your opponent's weaknesses, you aim to distract them and *bam*, when they least expect it, you corner them.' He laughs and says, 'Checkmate.'

The boys tire of the game. He tries to interest them with other ideas.

He starts to tell the story of a great warrior called Napoleon. I heard something about this man from Najib a long time ago. He was not very tall, I think. I listen with interest to the man. He has a kind, patient voice and does not deserve the unruliness of the boys. I think back to Najib and how he started to talk to himself after the earthquake and I see the dazed mad look in his eyes as he walked away from the aid workers who wanted to take him to the camp too. He had known the truth, I thought. Better to die there than suffer the camp.

'Oh, we had no love for Napoleon . . . Friedland was a terrible defeat,' I hear the father say. 'He wanted to destroy Russia, to take everything in his path. His greed was his weakness. We got our own back in the end, though. Strategy, boys. Tactics. Know your enemy, know his weaknesses.'

I hear the lid of the chess set slam shut. The boys quieten down for the evening and take to reading, glad that the game is over.

I begin to imagine a kinder and taller Napoleon (which isn't difficult given where I am starting from). My Napoleon is a different sort of leader of men, a Napoleon who can see me through the hardest of moments, who can look after me when all I want to do is stop.

Chapter 35

I slip out of the carriage leaving the book on the table and go to the bathroom, a tiny smelly cubicle with a dim and intermittent light. When I come back to the carriage I hear voices inside. I pause and then decide to enter. We are nearly at Perm, the halfway point on my journey on the Trans-Siberian Railway, getting ever closer to Moscow. I feel reckless and besides, I can't leave Tolstoy behind.

There is a young American couple sitting there, kissing. They pull apart as I come in to sit down. I am immediately sorry I have disturbed them.

'Hey,' the young man says. 'I'm Tom, this is Amy.'

He smiles, a big, wide white-toothed smile as if I haven't disturbed them at all and that they don't mind the company in the least. My book is still on the table in front of them. I reach out to take it and leave but the *provodnitsa* is walking by and so I stay, sitting down opposite them, shielding my face with the book until she passes.

'Good book?' he asks.

'Yes,' I try out my English, more uncertain than the Russian.

'What's your name?' the girl asks. She has long dark hair like Ara, tied back in a plait. She looks pretty and happy.

'I'm Samar,' I say.

'Pretty name,' Tom replies. 'Is it Russian?'

I shake my head. 'No, it's from a lot of places but not Russia.'

'Cool. What does it mean?'

His question and interest surprise me.

'I'm not sure. My mother always said it means warrior – a fighter – but my father told me it means storyteller . . .'

'Wow,' says the girl, 'like a warrior storyteller.'

She laughs, her laughter is friendly and warm.

I have not thought about that before, that it means something. She smiles at me. I smile back.

'Where are your family?' she asks.

I shrug. My throat tightens. They look at me more closely.

I hear the *provodnitsa* in the walkway once more. This time she stops outside the compartment, talking to a passenger. I panic. The strangers see the fear cross my face. In a moment the *provodnitsa* will have found me.

I have no choice. I roll under the seat. The book drops to the floor.

As the door swings wide open, Amy darts across to stand in front of the seat where I hide. She picks up *Anna Karenina* from the floor of the carriage before the *provodnitsa* has time to bend down and see me. The young couple then chat to the ruddy-faced woman for a few moments, Tom flirting with her, leading her out into the passageway to show him the view. The door closes once more. Amy bends down, her face smiling sideways at me under the seat.

'It's okay now, coast's clear!' she whispers to me.

I wriggle out and dust myself off. She gives me the book, her hand lightly touching my arm.

'It's okay,' she says. But it's not. I am shaking. I look at her, thinking of Ara.

'What does your name mean? What does Amy mean?' I ask her, trying to return to our conversation where we left off, as if it was normal to hide, to roll under seats; as if it was normal to stand there shaking, covered in dust. She pretends nothing has happened.

'Oh, it's kind of sweet, it means "beloved",' she says smiling as the door opens and Tom, the American boy, slips back into the compartment. He kisses her on the cheek.

I think of Arsalan and Madar and I wonder where my name came from, who chose it. Does a name make us who we become, in the end?

We stand there for a moment smiling at each other.

'Thank you,' I tell them, placing my hand on my heart. They have saved me.

'Safe journey, Samar,' she says and waves a small goodbye over her shoulder as Tom leads her out of the compartment, winking at me as he goes.

When they leave I lock the door and put my hands to my face, lean my elbows on the small table by the window and cry. I cry as quietly as I can manage, my shoulders shaking, everything falling apart inside me.

Chapter 36

This will be my last night on the train. Tomorrow evening we will reach Moscow.

The journey has fixed nothing. I have not found Omar. I cannot bring back my family nor can I let go of them. I do not know what I will find in Moscow, what sort of a life I can make for myself alone.

I spend the night awake watching the Urals slip past in the darkness. I hear Javad's laughter up in the mountains at my grandparents' house.

'Now you will see, now you will all see.'

I remember running, cursing them all, leaving them behind. It is all my fault. I find it impossible to shake off this thought, that somehow I triggered all that happened.

The *provodnitsa* is getting quietly drunk in the box room, angry at leaving behind her miner. She does not bother me. I lock the compartment door and try to finish my book. As the morning light streams into the carriage I am almost finished. Anna and Vronsky are coming apart. I cannot believe it, that love cannot triumph. She has gone off in a rage to find him, angry and disgusted at the world and at herself.

The train stops in Nizhny Novgorod. It will sit here on the platform a long while. The *provodnitsa* allows everyone the chance to get off and stretch their legs.

Dutifully the carriage empties until I am left sitting here alone with my thoughts.

I have tried so hard to keep pushing all that has happened out of my mind – to keep it all at a distance. I had wanted to change it, to make it someone else's story, not mine. It is not a story I ever wanted to tell. But, I realise now, it *is* mine to tell. Watching the other travellers laughing and joking on the platform, emptiness seeps into my heart. How will I ever find Amira? What madness to leave everything behind, to come here alone. My hands shake once more. I cannot make them stop.

I decide to leave the carriage. The loneliness hits me so hard that I no longer care what might happen to me. It is almost as if I am willing the *provodnitsa* to catch me. My legs are stiff and heavy and I step slowly down the high step, glancing round the platform.

On the opposite side goods trains rush by, blurring through the station at high speed as they rattle past, the horn signalling in warning: *keep back*. It is not hard to imagine standing on the platform edge, at the far end, far from the milling travellers. I could wait there – to judge the right moment. I imagine what it would feel like – what it would be like to just close everything out, to end the memories in my mind, to find peace at last.

I walk up, away from the train now and the empty carriages. The voices of Masha, of Nas and Robina, the rumble of the earth as it crashed down the mountainside covering the village, Javad's laughter, Ara's body floating face down in the grey muddy water by the camp, Abdul-Wahab's hands grabbing at me in the dark – it all weighs upon me.

At the far end of the platform it is harder to make out the voices of the other travellers. My forehead feels clammy. I cross to the very end point where the goods trains thunder out of the station, taking their cargo back out across Siberia.

I step closer to the edge. Here, shadowed by the signal boxes, no one notices me. I am invisible. If I jump I will not be missed. No one will know I have gone or that I was here.

In the distance I hear the whistling of a train approaching, the sound growing louder now so that it fills my ears. I close my eyes and lean forward. It will only be a matter of seconds. I will feel nothing. I already feel nothing. I am so tired of feeling numb. My fingers tap my leg as if checking I am still here.

'Samar!'

I turn, startled. The train thunders past me. I look around, the moment cast away from me, disappearing into the distance. I shiver in the pull of cold air that follows in the wake of the carriages hurtling by full of unknown cargo.

I walk out from behind the shadows at the end of the platform. I follow the sound of the voice.

'Samar! Come, why so sad?' I look up, surprised. Napoleon is standing there – looking much more sober than the last time I saw him. I had thought I would not see him again.

'We are survivors, you and I,' he tells me, gesturing at me to sit by him on the bench along the platform. Old newspaper flutters on the seat, news of what is happening in the world, reminding me that there is such a place, that I am not destined to spend forever going back and forth in my mind on this perpetual journey west to east and east to west.

'You know, you had me frightened there,' Napoleon says. 'Don't go giving up, you hear.' He thumps me gently on the shoulder and smiles. 'You can always start over, Samar.' He says this quietly. This time, I do not argue with him.

'Come on,' he says. 'Everyone is waiting for you.'

We walk back along the platform, crossing over to the waiting train. Some of the passengers are still milling about, clapping their hands together in the chill air and stamping their feet to keep warm.

We climb back up into the train. He gets on first, checking to make sure the *provodnitsa* doesn't catch me.

For the first time in a long while I no longer feel so numb. I start to think once more about Amira, about the possibility of finding her in Moscow. I imagine Omar out there still. I cannot give up, I realise – not on Omar, or Amira, or my family and what they would have wished for me. I cannot let all that has happened destroy me.

Napoleon is watching me. 'Begin again, Samar,' he says.

'You're not real,' I tell him.

'No, maybe not,' he says and laughs. I laugh with him. It spills out of me, a crazy laughter at the fact that I have cheated death – that I am still here.

He puts his hand on my shoulder and then he is gone. Napoleon has helped save me. I stand in the walkway looking around to thank him. But he's not here. I realise I will not see him again but the thought of losing him no longer frightens me as it did before.

This will be a new beginning.

In the compartment next to me I find some notebooks forgotten by the two boys and their father, who have left the train for good here. I pick them up. On the front cover of one, one of the boys has drawn a train, long and winding, rolling across the grasslands of the steppes. Inside are sketches from their journey: bridges, forests, deer, yurts, an unflattering picture of the *provodnitsa* that makes me laugh, drawings of chess moves, hints and clues for the boys to follow. The rest of the pages are blank. A black biro rests in the spiral of the top notebook.

I take them with me.

When I go back into my compartment Madar and Baba look up at me. So do Ara and Omar, Javad and Little Arsalan. Baby Sitara toddles in the middle between the two long seats. She holds out her little hand for me to steady her – or her me. They are all laughing. Ara will sing later. Omar and Javad are play-fighting. Little Arsalan is surreptitiously drawing a picture of the train on the back of the compartment door in red and blue crayon. Madar and Baba squeeze up to make room for me. Madar touches the seat beside her lightly.

'Here, Samar,' she says, stroking my cheek. 'We will be in Moscow soon. Amira will be expecting you, you know. I have told her you are coming, that you will find her.'

Baba nods; he is watching me. He smiles.

'Good idea,' he says, looking at the notebooks in my hand.

Madar squeezes my arm gently and tells me, 'Remember, anything is possible, Samar.'

I feel her warmth next to me and I know she is right. As I think back to the stories she shared with us – how her words would weave magic – my heart fills with love, for my family and our crazy journey, for what has been and what is to come.

I picture the yellow house, behind it the sunlight slanting over the peaks of the Hindu Kush. I see Omar's green bicycle leaning against the wall, the blossom of the almond tree overhead. I hear the voices of my family singing out all around me. I hold tight to these memories that root me to the Afghan soil. They are in me. I will carry them with me wherever I go.

I am ready for our journey to end now, to step down off the train and begin somewhere new, somewhere I no longer have to run. Somewhere safe.

Sitting down in the compartment between them all, their chatter dims as they fade and quieten and the train fills once more. The driver is eager to be off and to reach the journey's final stop soon. The *provodnitsa* is shouting at the last dawdling travellers to get on board.

Moscow is not far now. I wait for the train to pull out of the station, for the passengers to settle, for the *provodnitsa* to sweep by and then back again, leaving me at last in peace.

I wait and then I begin to write.

Author's note

We don't choose the stories we tell – they choose us and that was the case for me with this story of Samar and her family, and their journey for survival and safety.

Write, and read, not just what you already know, but what you want to know. Be curious. Step outside of what is comfortable and familiar.

Both writing and reading are acts of empathy. The writer seeks to create a particular, imagined world through understanding their characters. The generous reader surrenders for a few hours to inhabit that new world, to discover new experiences and ultimately new ways of seeing the world and themselves within it.

Growing up in Northern Ireland in the 1980s during the Troubles, my childhood self could never understand why people were so hell-bent on creating conflict. Surely we are all so much more similar than we are different, I thought. And, when I was old enough to travel on my own, I was off – keen to explore new places, learn foreign languages, open doors into worlds different to my own. That fascination for understanding the world around me has only grown over the years as I have worked with many activists, young people and writers from countries all around the world.

So, with my love of travel, the telling of this story started for me with the image of the train, the

Trans-Siberian Express, and the journey back and forth, east to west and west to east. At first I did not know it would also become a story of Afghanistan and of the ways in which conflicts change everything, but if I look back to myself as a young girl I see now why this story, and the way in which I have chosen to tell it, mattered to me.

Early first drafts saw me writing from the perspective of Azita, the mother, an enigmatic figure who I soon realised would not easily give up her secrets. I then shifted my attention to Ara, the eldest daughter – like me, also an eldest daughter, so this character's perspective I felt I understood easily. Surely Ara was the character to best tell this story. But it was a false start and almost immediately I discovered it is in writing that which is outside of your usual perspective, that the writing most comes alive. I had no idea what it was like to be the middle child of a family but I needn't have worried as Samar was quick to show me.

The novel is set through the 1960s to 1990s and so I am grateful to the many research sources I was able to draw on to help form sufficient understanding of this period of time to tell the story as I wished to. I have endeavoured in the telling of the story to be as accurate as possible where possible and any errors remaining are my own. The story is a work of fiction and any references to characters, places or events are used fictitiously throughout.

Travelling in the region gave me a sense of place and people, as did time spent with kind and generous colleagues and friends from Afghanistan, Central Asia and Russia.

Having worked over the years with young people affected by conflict in myriad different ways, I have observed that oftentimes being able to go to school, or not, was the one key thing that defined that young person's future life chances. From this came my interest in writing about a young girl and her siblings losing that route to a safe and thriving future.

During my time at PEN International I also often bore witness to stories of families split apart, sometimes forced to leave their homes and lives behind and to start over somewhere new. Many of these stories were heart-breaking to listen to. Yet what amazed me most was the capacity of these individuals to carry on – to find their way in the world despite all their loss and hardship.

This book is in part written in tribute to each of those people and for the countless others who astound us with their bravery.

And it is written for you, the reader. Thank you for coming with me on Samar's journey.

Acknowledgements

My thanks to all who have supported the writing and publishing of this story, in particular to the worldwide PEN community, which never ceases to inspire me with the constant bravery and resilience of its members around the world – remarkable individuals often writing in the most difficult of circumstances. This story is also for you and for all who believe in the power of stories to transform us.

My thanks also to the team at *Mslexia*, to Peter Florence, Winifred Robinson, Jonathan Hallewell and Julia White, who each generously helped the story on its way.

I thank my earliest of readers Catherine Cho, my agent Jonny Geller, Kate Cooper, Eva Papastratis and all the fantastic Curtis Brown team whose passion for books and support for their authors knows no bounds.

I could not ask for a more talented or dedicated publisher than Lisa Highton at Two Roads Books. She has steered this book with admirable skill and patience. My thanks also to Federico Andornino, Amber Burlinson, Mandi Jones, Miren Lopategui, Rosie Gailer, Caitriona Horne, Sara Marafini, Jesús Sotés, and to all of the wonderful team at Two Roads, John Murray Press and Hodder & Stoughton – indefatigable book gladiators, every last one.

Likewise to all of my international publishers for taking this story to readers around the world.

This story is about family and the ways in which family makes us who we are – and so to my own family. Thank you. To my parents, who gave me a home full of books to get lost in and who always encouraged me to believe that a girl can do anything she sets her mind to. To my sisters – for their friendship and encouragement.

Many friends have supported me along the way – my thanks and gratitude to you all.

And to Howard and Riley, for making me a better person and writer, with love.

About the author

Laura McVeigh grew up in Northern Ireland. She read Modern & Medieval Languages at Cambridge University.

Previously Director of PEN International, the leading worldwide writers' organisation, she has travelled widely campaigning on freedom of expression issues around the world. Laura is also a passionate advocate for girls' education having served as Director of The Global Girls Fund.

She lives in London and the Balearics with her family. *Under the Almond Tree* is her debut novel and she is currently writing her second, *The Plantation House*.

lauramcveigh.com
twitter.com/lcmcveigh